TWISTED *assist*

KATIE RAE

Please... Grandma... don't read this one.

Prologue

Tatum

Two years ago

He was gone.

For two years, I gave him everything.

I had no friends, life, or worth outside the future he and I created. We stayed up late every night, telling each other stories of how we envisioned our future. Graduate college, land our dream jobs, buy a house, and have kids.

But once graduation day came, I was reminded that despite all our plans, there was one thing he loved more than me. One thing for which he was willing to let me go, given the chance, and when that day came, it was as if we had never dreamt at all.

Our stories weren't fantasies of the future; they were fiction in a fairytale that didn't have a happily ever after. He left me, breaking up and choosing the game he coveted, hoping to live his ultimate dream.

Professional soccer.

In a desperate attempt, I pleaded with him that we could still be together. He was headed to play for League One in Lexington, but it wasn't like he would be there forever. Eventually, Miami would call him home again, returning him to play for the Inferno as their hometown hero.

"All I will be focusing on is soccer," he explained. "It's better if you aren't waiting for me."

"But what about when you come back?"

"There is nothing I want to return to Miami for."

Dammit, his words hurt. What was so bad about Miami? After all, it was where I was. Where I would always be. He had family issues, but couldn't he overcome that to come back to me?

"The only way I will return to Miami is for the Inferno or the university."

They were words I had to accept, so I held my head up and walked away from him. My brother held his arms out for me when I got home, and he cried with me almost as hard as I did.

Hunter was gone.

I had to move on.

"Leaving you just proves how weak he is," Colton tried to reassure me. "He doesn't deserve you anyway."

"I understand why he wants to leave, but why wouldn't he want to stay together?"

"Like I said," Colton huffed. "He's weak."

One month ago

He was back.

I created a new life for myself in the two years since he'd left. Instead of telling stories with him, I told them to myself about the things I wanted and needed to feel fulfilled in my life.

I worked hard at a job I loved, proving that I was capable of more than I thought I was.

But my feelings for him seemed to resurface the second he called. It was as if no time had passed, and he was calling to see how my day went.

He asked for a second chance to rekindle what he regretted about leaving. I hadn't moved on, but I wasn't sure I wanted him back either.

"The only way you will know is if you try," my brother suggested. "See where it goes. You lose nothing if it doesn't work again."

Maybe he was right.

Ultimately, I may end up with my heart in pieces again, but love was worth the risk.

"Hunt and Tay, together again," he smiled as he took my hand for the first time in two years.

"Who would have thought?"

His kiss was desperate, like he was trying to prove a point. That he never should have left in the first place. That he regretted the time apart.

We had to rebuild, and it would take time to get back to where we once were, but it was like my brother had said: if I didn't try, I would never know.

And it was time to find out if the stories we once told were destined to come true.

Chapter One

Tripp

My teammates were falling like football season, and I was still firmly planted in my summer era. I was happy for them, really. Even if they were also my only friends in Miami, I could see loneliness on the horizon, but being lonely beat the hell out of being in love.

Twisted motherfuckers.

Then again, to their credit, Rhys Peyton and Cruz Martin weren't the ones on the team who had to worry about their future. That anxiety-inducing adventure was reserved for yours truly. Tripp Maddux. The midfielder for the Miami Inferno who gets paid "entirely too much and should be cut at the end of the season."

I heard the media reports. They were hard to ignore. But what they didn't know was how aware I was. Even more so than they were. Because that was my assignment.

Every team had a fall guy, even if it was never mentioned or voiced out loud, not just in soccer but every sport. The fall guy was the one a team could blame for their season ending in flames. That guy got paid good money, but his contract was laced with so many stipulations that it was impossible to retain.

That was me—the fall guy. But I was the only one aware of it. The day I signed my contract, my agent warned me that it had a mountain of twists and turns that, with a tiny fuck up, could land me back in League One. Based on the amount of money they paid me, I'd say they were hopeful I did fuck up.

They didn't count on me being a loner. I would never have stepped outside my apartment if it hadn't been for Cruz. He was a local in Miami and thought it was his job to make me feel welcome, which he did.

We found the best clubs, the best beaches, and the best women. Cruz had always been up for a night out before his stepsister got to town. But he was officially a ticking time bomb, wanting her so badly that he couldn't even see it while everyone else could see it clear as day.

When we got to Mangos after a rough Wednesday night game, he grabbed a girl and took her to the back of the club, dead set on fucking her. Somehow, I knew he wouldn't go through with it.

Checking my watch, I clocked him being gone for two minutes so far, and when he returned, I bet myself he'd go straight home, where Lily was. If only I had more friends to make that bet with.

"Maddux?" The deep voice calling my name over the loud music made me pause. No one knew me. "Tripp?"

Setting my glass down on the table, I turned around and looked up at the guy standing beside Cruz's vacated chair. "Hunt?"

Politely, I stood up and shook his hand, then reluctantly invited him to sit with me, unsure if that was a good idea.

"Good to see ya." As he sat down, he raised a finger toward the waitress, asking for whatever I was having by doing an awkward point and then shaking his hand. Fuck, Hunter was a tool. I bet he'd put the drink on my tab, too.

I needed a bookie or something with all these winning bets I'm making.

"What've you been up to?" Not that I didn't know the answer to that question. Rhys and Cruz had a little beef with the guy, and I listened when they talked about it.

"I've been coaching the women's soccer team at the university. Assistant coaching." Hell, I knew that. Rhys Peyton's girlfriend played on that team. "It's not why I came back to Miami, but it's a start."

"I heard you took a leave of absence from the team, though?" By how pale he got, it was safe to assume he didn't want me to know that part of his story, but he had to assume that I would know. He wasn't that big of an idiot.

"Word gets around," he grimaced, and I nodded, suddenly feeling awkward about bringing it up. "Honestly, I just needed time to think. When I left League One, it was only because my alma mater told me I would get the head coaching job for the men's team. Leaving League One was hard because I hadn't gotten where I wanted to be yet. But I packed up and moved back home for the chance of a lifetime, only to get here and find out the job they had for me was assisting Colin Mestik with the women's team."

"I love women," I laughed, trying to lighten the mood, then took a sip of my drink.

"Yeah, yeah," he smirked. "But these aren't the kind of women you can touch. They'd either kill you themselves or handcuff you to the bed so the university can have their way with you. Which is good for them, but it's not what I want. Anyway, after we won the Women's Cup, I asked for some time away. Nothing serious."

"That's a rough go." I sincerely meant that. Playing with Hunter in League One, I knew how much he wanted to be a pro. When that didn't happen, and I heard he had returned to

Miami, I knew there must have been a good reason. He used to swear he would never return unless it were for soccer. Either to coach it or play it.

"It is what it is," he finally sighed as the server delivered his drink.

Holding my drink up, I nodded for him to raise his own. "To new beginnings."

Fuck, that sounded cheesy, but I wasn't feeling particularly compassionate and had to say something. Plus, I somehow knew I was in store for my own new beginning.

"Hunter Ward?" Hunter and I looked up to where Cruz had returned, standing alongside the table. Glancing back down at my watch, I laughed. Seven minutes. Way too quick to have actually fucked the girl he was with.

"You two know each other?" I asked, which was another question whose answer I already knew, but wasn't sure how to proceed socially.

"Sorta," Cruz said quietly, almost nonchalantly. "Coach Crazy? Right?"

Hunter smirked, but I could tell he was annoyed as he stood up from Cruz's seat. He didn't respond to the taunt, though, just nodded his answer.

"Hunter and I played against each other in college. Then we played with each other in Lexington League One," I explained.

"Just came to say hi," Hunter added.

"Is this a coincidence?" Cruz asked, definitely pushing Hunter's buttons on purpose. Admittedly, Hunter was hard to like, but Cruz was only being an asshole because he hadn't gotten laid in so long. His scoreless streak was nearing a whole week, which was hard for him to wrap his head around.

"It's easy to run into people when I spend every night out like this." Hunter didn't seem bothered by Cruz, and I could tell he was trying not to let him pick a fight.

"Sounds pathetic," Cruz scoffed.

Shit, that was the pot calling the kettle black, not to mention I also spent way too many nights at the bars. We had no room to judge.

"You should know," Hunter leaned over the table, slowly losing his cool.

Standing up, I pushed each of their chests and made them rethink a bar fight. Hunter could go home, Cruz would get a slap on the wrist, but I would be tossed off the team before we even made our playoff run.

Thankfully, Cruz had better things to do than drag me into whatever bullshit they had between them. He let up immediately, and I could tell he was about to leave me stranded for the night. We hadn't even been at the club for thirty minutes—and it was his damn idea.

"I gotta go," he finally looked at me. "You two have fun."

Tilting my head toward the door, I let him know I understood and that he needed to get lost. As much as it sucked that he was leaving, I would have too if I were him. "See you at practice."

"Yep," he walked out with one last glance at Hunter.

"Shit," Hunter sat back down once Cruz was gone. "What the hell is his problem?"

"He's close with Rhys Peyton, Ash Keller, and Erin Rhodes. They all think you're crazy." I admitted, giving him insight into the depth of my knowledge regarding his position.

Surprisingly, Hunter laughed and shook his head. "They're not wrong."

"So tell me then," because I was nosy and bored. "What're you going to do?"

"I have no idea. Maybe shoot for the assistant head coach of the men's team for now. They already have one, but word is he's headed out after their tournament in a few weeks."

"How'd you find that out?"

"I have my ways," Hunter shrugged with a laugh. "If that doesn't work out, maybe I'll take your job."

Was he fucking with me? We didn't even play the same position. Not that he couldn't make it work because I often jumped from midfielder to right-wing, but fuck him for even suggesting it.

Before I could ask what his deal was, he reached into his pocket and pulled out his phone, which must have been vibrating. "Just kidding man," he laughed as he answered the call.

"Yeah?"...He put a finger to his opposite ear to help him hear better... "I know, maybe tomorrow"...His eyes rolled at whatever was said... "Let me call you in a few, okay?"

He hung up and shook his head, a slight grimace on his face. "Sorry, that was my girl."

"You're seeing someone?"

"Kinda. The same girl I was seeing in college still lives here. She likes spending time on my dick, so who am I to fuck that up, right?"

In a way, I could see his point. Who would give up accessible pussy? But since it came from his mouth, I had to physically stop myself from rolling my eyes. It sounded like a line, or a way to appear more significant than he felt, and lacked truth— same ol' Hunter.

"We broke up when I left for League One. Neither of us wanted to do the long-distance thing. Then I barely got my feet back in Florida and she was calling me, asking me to come see her. It works for now. What about you? Seeing anyone?"

It seemed we were going to have an actual conversation, and if that were the case, I would need more liquor. Even if I told him about a shell I stepped on surfing the other day, scotch would make that an easier story to tell.

Calling the waitress over, I nodded to Hunter and held up my empty glass. "Drinks on me."

Chapter Two

Tatum

Once Hunter hung up the phone, I tossed mine onto my bed and fought the tears that were probably going to come pouring out of me. There was a chance I would never understand my so-called boyfriend. He was clearly out at another club, drinking and spending time with people he found more interesting than me. It should have been all I needed to finally break up with him. But we felt so unfinished.

That's why I agreed to try again.

Hunter was my college sweetheart before he left for League One, and our breakup was not easy on me. I may have found professional success in the two years that followed, but my love life was nonexistent.

When he called and told me he was returning to Miami, I tried not to care. I wanted to make him think I had finally moved on, that I was okay. But just as my mother always did when it came to my dad, I took him back, thinking that if all else failed, I would at least get the closure I needed. That, or it would finally be our chance to have everything he promised me before he left. Marriage. Kids. Forever.

It'd been a month, though, and our relationship was worse than when he left the first time. He was the assistant coach for the women's soccer team at the university and had let it turn him into a miserable human being. I knew the job took a lot of his time, especially when the head coach for his team had to leave for a personal emergency, and Hunter took over as interim head coach. Those days were the only good days we had because I could tell myself he was legitimately too busy. That we were okay.

And for a little bit, he was at ease being in charge of the team on his own.

But what was his excuse once the season ended?

"Don't dwell on it," I tried to tell myself. "Be stronger."

Flopping on my bed, I stared at the ceiling and willed my phone to ring. Hunter said he would call me in a few, so I thought that meant "very soon." But hours went by, my tears had come and gone, and he still hadn't called me back.

At the risk of being crazy, I considered marching down to the club he was probably at and asking him what the hell we were doing. If he was going to spend all his time partying and none of it with me, why were we even trying again? What kind of game was he playing with me if I was only treated like a backup plan?

The idea that I was like my mother was painful, but the facts were that I was accepting less than I deserved, and tried to tell myself it was okay. She and my dad were off and on for my entire life. Never married, because my dad never asked, but they were together until they weren't, then they'd start back up again. It was a difficult way to grow up, and my brother Colton and I paid the price.

Every time Dad moved back in, we were supposed to be happy and act like he didn't bail on us for six months at a time. Then the fighting would start again, and he would be gone, bouncing around from hotel room to hotel room, unable to spend any quality time with us.

The only constant in our lives was the fact that Mom would beg him to come home. She took him back over and over again, always hoping for a different result. Was she crazy? Yeah, she was. But was I any different? I wanted to be.

After two in the morning, I gave up on his calling and reached for my remote. As a sports public relations and marketing agent, I always turned on the sports highlights when I got in bed and let the sound of the replays lull me to sleep. Somehow, I thought the information being relayed would be absorbed into my memories and be useful one day.

Once I got the sports channel on and comfortable in bed, I closed my eyes and listened to the updates. The Atlanta Jets beat New York in football, the Atlanta Kings baseball team advanced to the World Series, and the Miami Inferno beat Austin FC in the soccer match here in Miami.

"We have to get goals at home. If we want to make the play-offs, that's all there is to it. I think we were on a good path to get some good results, but the last few weeks have been hard. A good game today. They didn't score, so it was really good. Not only for our confidence going forward but for the fans. It was electric tonight."

When I heard that voice, I leaned up to look at the screen, wanting to see who it was. Tripp Maddux, the Inferno midfielder who had come to Miami last year. Rarely had I heard him in an interview. That may have been the first time. He was known for being more reserved and quieter compared to his teammates.

Not that I knew him personally. Most of my work was kissing the asses of the Miami hockey team, trying to make them happy they signed our agency for a fan promotion. IMG, our company, didn't even work with the Inferno—yet. We were trying, though, having an agent I barely knew spend all her time pushing to land a contract. The owner of the International Marketing Group was riding us hard, and we never knew where she would put us next. So, even though I wasn't the one pushing with the Inferno, I paid attention when they were on TV.

Before Hunter got the job at the University, he was passed up by the Inferno to go pro. It made me thankful I wasn't the one pursuing them as our client. It would be awkward, but if I was asked to take over, would I really be able to, and have Hunter? After all our struggles, you'd think I would choose my career, but that little thread that tethered us together had yet to be severed. As much as I hated myself for it, I knew I was still in a place where I'd choose Hunter.

The following day, I woke up to two text messages. Neither of them were from Hunter. One was from my mom, asking me to get tickets to the football game for her and my dad, and one from my brother, warning me my mom was going to ask me for tickets to the football game.

Skipping my mom's text, I decided to call my brother while I got ready for work.

"Hey," he laughed like he knew why I was calling.

"Why does she want tickets?"

"You know Dad will leave again soon, she needs something to lure him back."

"She knows I can't just get her tickets. I work for a third party, not for the team, and I'm not covering football at the moment."

"I told her you couldn't, and to not bother you, but she

started texting you right in front of me like she didn't hear me at all."

"What were you doing there anyway?" Colton was a student at The University of Miami, the same college Hunter worked at, the one we'd both attended before. He had a full-ride scholarship and a dorm room, but you'd never know since he spent almost every night at my place or home with Mom.

"Mom lured me with the promise of a hot meal last night, then let me fall asleep on the couch like a kid. I snuck out after she fell asleep though, spent some time on the strip with friends, then went back to the dorm."

"Just like when you were a kid," I laughed, thinking of him sneaking out to party. "You know she wishes you were still home. Dad seemed to stick around longer when we were living at home."

"I'm thinking about introducing her to my English Professor. He's a good-looking guy, and maybe he could sweep her off her feet."

"Please, she's so obsessed with Dad that it's unhealthy and psychotic. She wouldn't even give your poor professor a chance."

"Well, I guess that is their problem," he sighed. "I'm headed to class, but just a heads up that I'm crashing at your place this weekend."

"No, no you're not. Hunter is coming over." At least, I thought he was.

"Hunter?" Colton scoffed. "That is all the more reason for me to show up. You two need a chaperone. Ew."

"Oh please," I tried blowing him off, not wanting him to know that Hunter hadn't touched me with a ten-foot pole since he'd returned. "I'm a big girl, little brother."

Chapter Three

Tripp

There wasn't much I remembered after I ordered that round of drinks. I wasn't even sure what my tab was, or if I paid it. Fuck, I wasn't even sure where I was.

My head was pounding, and my face was wet, but my eyes wouldn't open. It was clear that I broke the two-drink rule that Cruz had once implemented. No more than two drinks when you're out at the club, or you risk getting too fucked up to make good decisions. But he did, too, so he couldn't give me too much shit.

Oh wait, Cruz wasn't with me.

Hunter was.

My vague memory was almost sure that I had carried Cruz into his apartment because he was so drunk. His sister was there, with her see-through shirt, and he kept saying he... "No, that was last week." I finally realized, telling myself out loud so I believed it.

"What was last week?" The groan beside me was more proof that it was Hunter I had broken the rules with, and he must have been as hammered as I was.

"Cruz broke the rules," I tried telling him.

"When?"

"Last week."

"What rules?"

"We drank too much."

"Okay."

That was all we could manage before darkness took over, but when I awoke again, I finally opened my eyes. Looking around, I realized I was in my apartment, and Hunter and I were on the floor in my living room.

He was sound asleep, a soft snore being the only indication that he was alive. His arms were spread like he was waiting for a chalk outline of his body. His dark hair stood straight up, his clothes were disheveled, and he had my keys in his hand.

"Hunt?" I whispered. "Wake up."

Pulling my phone from my pocket, I noted it was almost noon and rolled over closer to Hunter. "Wake up."

"No," he mumbled in between snores.

"Hunter, what the hell happened last night?"

"We drank too much and stumbled back to your place."

Did we? That seemed too innocent and uncomplicated. My body felt like I had played a game, boxed ten rounds, and fucked a few people while standing in the sand. Everything on me ached.

"Did we have sex?"

"Not with each other," Hunter responded quietly, nearly falling back to sleep.

"No motherfucker," I kicked him, making him jolt upright. "Did we have sex with anyone?"

"Shit, I don't think so."

Hunter rubbed his face, then looked around, finally coming alive. The fact that we were both fully dressed felt like a good sign. There was too much at stake for someone like me, and I prided myself on keeping my nose clean, so there was never a reason for backlash with the team. It wasn't like me to take risks the way I had at the club with Hunter.

When I was with teammates, we watched each other's backs, but I wasn't even sure I could trust Hunter. He and I weren't exactly best friends forever. Even as teammates, I wasn't sure I could trust him. It was like he was always gunning for me, and even though he never did anything directly, I always felt an uneasy vibe around him.

I just wished I could remember.

"Sorry," Hunter started to stand up. "I remember some of last night, but I'm sure neither of us intended to wake up on your floor."

"What do you remember?"

"You kept asking for more rounds, and we talked. When the place closed, you told me you lived within walking distance, and fuck you very much for that."

"What?"

"You live like, ten blocks away," he huffed. "That was not an easy walk when you're fucking wasted."

I didn't remember walking at all, but that may have been why I was so sore. Then again, I was a damn athlete, and walking shouldn't have made me feel like I fell off my surfboard in a rogue wave.

"I'm so fucked."

"It was a good time," Hunter assured me. "Don't worry about it." He stood up and grabbed his phone, which slid from his jeans while he slept. There were a few mumbled profanities as he scrolled and then locked his phone back up and put it away.

"Everything okay?"

Standing up was hard, but I managed to do so and stood next to Hunter. He tried taming his wild brown hair, but it was a lost cause, and his face had a day's worth of uneven growth on it. There was no doubt in my mind that I was just as ugly. Even my own breath was making me gag, and my palms were moist.

"Yeah, just everything I was talking to you about last night."

I gave him a nod, but I didn't remember what we talked about. Nor did I care enough to ask him to tell me again.

"I better go," he grunted. "Thanks for last night, man. It was good to see you."

We slapped hands and bro-hugged before he backed up toward the door. All I could think was thank God he was being quick about leaving. My shower was calling my name, and the fact that we had no practice made me almost giddy. The only plan I was making was scrolling my iPad through game footage until I went back to sleep.

"Let's do it again," I lied, not wanting to be desperate enough to relive whatever happened. Hunter seemed chill enough, more so than when we were teammates, but he clearly made me act like someone I tried not to be.

"I have your number now. I'll call you."

Fuck. I gave him my number.

"Sounds good."

He opened the door and started to close it behind him before opening it again and looking at me with a sincere and meaningful gaze. "Also, thank you, man. Offering to help me will make everything so much easier. I'm glad we reconnected."

Again, I nodded but had no idea what he was talking about. All I needed him to do was leave, and once he said the last word, he shut the door and was gone.

Locking my door first, I went to my shower and turned it as hot as possible. There was also another showerhead on the other side of the shower, and once I was in, I turned that one on, too. Then I stood in the middle of the streams and let the water soothe every ache in my body.

Only when I was clean and had my teeth brushed did I pause.

Help with what?

What the fuck was I helping Hunter with? It was easy to agree when I wanted him gone, but now that my head was clearing up, I needed to know what the hell he meant.

I grabbed my phone and searched my texts and contacts but couldn't find his number. So I couldn't ask him what the hell he meant. He told me he had mine, though, and unless he called, I didn't need to worry about it.

What I knew, though, was that whatever I agreed to do was probably about soccer, and I wasn't going to like it very much.

Chapter Four

Tatum

"Fuck Tay, I'm so sorry," Hunter moaned into my ear. His lips skimmed my neck, kissing his way to my lips. It was the most affection he had given me in a while.

"I deserve better," I cried, only without the anger I initially practiced in the shower before he got to my apartment. After all, the skimming of his lips was doing something to me, making me forgive quicker than I should have. Knowing it was a ploy to calm me down still didn't make me back away from his touch, though.

When his text came in at noon, telling me he got caught up with an old friend, I started to write him back and tell him to leave me alone for good. But, like always, I hit delete instead of sending. He promised to be at my apartment after I got off work, but it was almost eight before he arrived.

The dinner I had cooked for us was cold, and I wanted to crawl into bed already. Work was hard, my heart was breaking, and my mind was twisted.

"Are you staying the night?"

"I can't," he pouted. "I'm having an early lunch with one of the advisors at the college."

"And you can't get up before lunch and go home? I mean, I have to get up at seven for work and can wake you up."

"It's across town, Tay. You know how it is."

Tears pooled in my eyes again, and I finally backed away from his hold. He looked worried, and he should have, because I was breaking right in front of him, and he was in danger of getting cut.

"Just go," I whispered, feeling a moment of strength wash over me.

"Tay," he took a step forward. "Don't do this. We're still new, and I'm still getting my wits about me trying to get where I need to be. You know that. You told me you supported that."

"We aren't new, Hunter!" I held my hands up, not wanting him to touch me while I felt so weak. "We are getting a second chance. Touching me isn't new, being intimate with me isn't new. But ever since you got back to Miami, you've barely kissed me. The one time you stayed the night, you fell asleep while I was in the shower, and you left before I even woke up. Why? What's the problem? Did you really want to try again with me?"

"Yes... Nothing!" he yelled back, getting frustrated. "I just know I fucked up before, and want to get it right this time."

"What a cop-out. You didn't fuck up, you left! And I understood why! It hurt, but you had to pursue your dreams. Now you're back and you called me, remember?"

"Because I wanted to fix us."

"There was nothing to fix. All you had to do was come back and love me the way you did when we were in college. That was the Hunter I expected to get back."

"Give me some time. It's important to me to have my life together, not only for me but for us. Just give me more time."

"Go then," I held my hand toward the door. "Go take your time."

"Fuck, don't do this."

"Maybe in a few weeks, we will have clearer heads."

He stared at me, silently begging me to change my mind, and I wanted to more than anything. But where would that get us?

"Okay," he nodded. "We can take a small break, but don't expect me to stay away from you. You and soccer are all I care about."

"I know soccer is important to you," I said more softly, taking a step forward. "So go get it, go work hard at whatever you think you need to do. If we are meant to be, we will make it in the end. But I don't think calling you my boyfriend is a good idea until you're ready to put the work into that as well."

"Are you going to wait for me?"

"I'm just going to live my life, Hunter."

"Can we still be friends? Can I treat you to dinner, and check in with you?"

"We aren't finished. That much I know for sure, but I need to remove the expectations of having you as my boyfriend. You're not ready to be someone important to anyone but yourself." He started to argue, but I held my hand up to stop him. "And that's okay. Go take care of yourself, just like I'm doing. We can meet for dinner as friends if you ever want to make that a priority."

He grabbed my hand and gently kissed my fingers before pulling me into a hug. Taking a moment to breathe him in and return his embrace, I soaked in how it felt to have his attention on me. One day, maybe soon, he would realize that soccer had done him wrong, but I hadn't, and I deserved to be his priority.

A couple of days passed, and Hunter had, surprisingly, texted me daily. There were no phone calls, and he hadn't stopped by to see me, but small texts here and there filled with sweet words. It was the minimum to keep him in my mind.

Most of his messages said how much he missed me, he couldn't wait to hold me, and he even gave me an update on what was happening at the university. In a way, I think he thought he was doing better and proving something to me, but it felt wrong. The fact that I coveted those little texts made me angry with myself.

Friday night, Colton came over, and I cried to him. He made me laugh and told me it would all be okay. But I'm not sure if he was proud of me for standing up to Hunter or if he thought I was crazy to be so needy. He was my brother, but he was also a guy, and I'm sure deep down, he thought I was asking for too much.

By Saturday, I realized I needed to celebrate being strong instead of dwelling on how weak I felt. Because despite those vulnerable feelings, I hadn't begged him to return. I was not my mother. My responses to his texts were short and cheerful, but I had been strong enough not to want more.

Nor did I expect it.

My Nikki's Beach Club membership was just for me; no one else knew I had it. If anyone knew, including Hunter, my parents, and even my brother, they would want to be invited, and that wasn't why I gave myself a membership. It was my hiding place. One that served cocktails out of an actual coconut and served lunch while I relaxed on a chaise in the sand while reading a good book under an umbrella.

"Would you like another drink?"

"No, thank you," I smiled at the waiter, dressed in a white button-up shirt and khaki shorts. His top three buttons were undone, and he didn't have shoes on. It must have been nice working with bare feet in the soft sand. My feet were aching from being in heels all week.

"Lunch will be served soon."

As he walked away, I looked around and noted the crowds filtering into the outdoor space. Good-looking men and women, people playing volleyball in the sand, and the pool splashing off to the side. There was no way I couldn't smile and take a deep breath of relaxation.

Before putting my head back in my book, I glanced ahead of me toward a man pulling his shirt off. His back was to me, but his back was incredible. Broad, muscular, with dips and definition. I would be crazy to look away. He had an old-school tribal design tattoo on his right shoulder blade. But he couldn't have been over thirty.

When he turned back to face me, I looked off quickly, trying to hide the fact that I was staring. He laughed a little, but I didn't know if it was at me or not because I refused to look. At least not until I was sure he was no longer paying any attention in my direction.

"Lunch," the waiter said happily, then set it on a small table next to my lounger. His presence with my food made me sit upright, and I practically clapped my hands together with excitement.

"Thank you," I squealed, loving the indulgence before I had even had a bite.

"Of course, anything else?"

"No, thank you." Waiting a minute, I watched as he left to be sure he didn't witness how fast I was going to shovel the food into my mouth. Most of Nikki's clientele were too refined to even use the word shovel when speaking of food. But not this girl. I just made sure to hide that part of myself so I didn't get kicked to the curb.

Dammit, I was acting like my mother after all. But at least it was about pretending to be civilized and not having anything to do with men.

Only a few bites in, I was moaning in pleasure as the cheese dip and salsa took turns hitting my tongue. There was even a little sway in my shoulders as I prepared myself for another bite. It made me forget that others were around, and it never occurred to me that someone would find me entertaining.

"I'll have what she's having," a deep, somewhat familiar voice, laced with amusement, spoke.

Freezing, I realized he was talking about me but was afraid to let him know I'd heard. But when I took a small peek and saw it was the guy with the sexy back, he saw me and smiled. There was no sense in pretending to hide anymore, so I smiled and gave him a small wave.

All the loungers had shade, but his had been pulled back, and he was angled toward mine in the direction of the late afternoon sun. His skin glistened, and his dark, dirty blonde hair was long but not quite reaching his shoulders. The locks were blowing in the wind, and he had a sexy smirk on his face. Although his eyes were covered with sunglasses, I could tell he was still looking directly at me.

"You just seem like you're having a good time," he shrugged before putting an arm behind his head to prop himself up. "So what are we eating?"

"Um, cheese dip and salsa."

"Fuck yeah," he fist-pumped the air with his free hand.

"And a piña colada," I offered, even though he didn't ask.

"Perfect."

There was a glint on the side of his head, and I realized it was an earring, gauged and big. It completed his entire surfer vibe, and my heart picked up its pace as I realized how attracted I was to him. When it came to guys, I had always been more attracted to athletes, not weekend surfers, who probably worked somewhere in the Wynwood District during the week, producing content for social media in the art district. That was a huge assumption, but the guy seemed to be pretty carefree, and for as good-looking as he was, he could have made a living posting videos online of himself exploring Miami's Art District.

Okay, that was too specific, but I followed as many influencers as possible, and my favorites were those focused on the arts. Not one single bone in my body was artistic, and it fascinated me to see what everyone was capable of. My ideas of who that guy was only made me want to know more, but I would be devastated if he told me he was a prestigious doctor and not someone I had just created in my head.

For a few minutes, we snuck glances at one another and smiled. When his drink was finally delivered, I couldn't help but giggle. The huge coconut was frilly and way too dainty for his large hands. He seemed like a red wine or bourbon drinker, but again, that was an assumption.

He was proud, though. Not caring that he looked like an Adonis and was drinking what was arguably the "girliest" drink in Miami. He went about his lunch, and I eventually finished mine. When the waiter took his plate away, he stood facing the water and stretched his shoulders. Another attendant came from nowhere with a surfboard and handed it to him.

"Ha," I accidentally mumbled too loud. But I was spot on with the surfer assumption.

"What's that?" he turned, his board being held in one arm at his waist.

"Oh um, I could tell you were a surfer. That's all."

"Am I making it too obvious?"

"You have the vibe."

We were both smiling, so despite how anxious I was about things being awkward, he went with the flow, making me feel like it was okay to say whatever was on my mind.

"It's a good vibe."

He nodded, then tilted his head a little. "What other vibes am I giving off?"

"You're not a vegan."

"Good guess." There was a lot of sarcasm in his response because of the cheese we both knew he ate, but he still found the conversation appealing. "What else?"

Maybe I had gotten a little too comfortable. It was easier to think about who he could be than to tell him what I thought. If I guessed something wrong, would he be offended? I didn't intend to find out, but my brain and mouth didn't always see eye to eye. So instead of saying something with more couth, my mouth chose, "You might be gay."

Chapter Five

Tripp

Three days after my blackout, I still wasn't sure what had happened, but I hadn't heard from Hunter again. No scandals had hit the media, and I was finally feeling like myself again. The piña colada I ordered at the beach club was the first taste of alcohol I'd had since, and the only reason I even had it was because of the woman across from me. If that drink brought her that much joy, I needed to harness that energy for myself.

Not to mention, the way her eyes glinted with humor when I raised my frilly drink made my cock twitch. So much so that after sipping half of it down, I decided to have my board brought to me so I could cool myself off in the Atlantic Ocean.

It wasn't a shock that she thought I looked like a surfer since I was born and raised in California. Surfing was my first passion before I got a college scholarship in soccer. It forced me to focus more on soccer, but I would always belong on the waves as well.

What shocked me was when she said I might be gay. It made me laugh, considering I was headed to the water to tame my dick that simply enjoyed watching her smile.

"I might be gay?" I laughed, setting my board down on my lounger, suddenly more interested in hearing her talk than riding the waves. "What brought you to that conclusion?"

Her eyes widened, probably thinking I was offended, as she tried explaining. "Your drink choice."

Getting closer to her, I licked my lips and then squatted down in front of her. "That drink seemed to make you happy, and I wanted whatever you were having."

Even though the heat had already pinked her cheeks, she turned even rosier. Dammit, I had no intention of entertaining a woman when I set out to get some lunch and catch some waves after practice. With two more games before we knew our playoff fate, it was a dumb time to get wrapped up with someone—even if it was just for a bit of fun. But that particular woman had cast a spell on me, making it impossible to walk away.

"You a surfer?"

"No," she laughed. "I can barely swim, much less balance on a board while a wave tries to kill me."

Pulling my sunglasses off my eyes and pushing them to my head, I started to try convincing her I could teach her, but her gasp made me freeze.

"Tripp Maddux?"

Dammit, I thought she knew who I was already, or didn't care. She had plenty of time to put two and two together, but since I rarely wore my earrings during a game and kept my hair pulled back with a band, maybe I was harder to recognize than I thought.

"Yeah." My response was hesitant, and I worried that whatever I was tempted to do to get her into my bed was about to be over. It should be over, Tripp. Don't get distracted.

She laughed at me, or herself. I wasn't sure which, but it eased the doubt in my chest. "What's so funny?"

"I saw you a few nights ago on TV. When you first spoke, I knew your voice sounded familiar, but I couldn't place it until I saw your eyes."

"Is this a good thing, or a bad thing?"

"Well, I just said you may be gay. For me, it's probably a bad thing."

"Maybe I am," I winked. "It's okay to make that assumption."

"You're probably not, though." Her head was shaking, and if she got any redder, I would have to call for medical help to cool her down.

"How do you know?"

"I don't know," she swallowed hard. "But one of my co-workers has been researching everything about the Miami Inferno. I work for IMG."

"Well, now things are a little unfair. You know a lot about me, and all I know about you is that you work for IMG."

Her nose scrunched up playfully, and she leaned up from her lounger. "What do you want to know?"

"The first thing I want to know is if I can sit down." I nodded toward the space on the matching lounger beside her, hoping she humored my carnal heart.

Her shrug wasn't a no, so I took the space and laid back next to her. My board was still on my chair, but the waiter grabbed my drink and brought it to me, seeing that I had changed spots. Her eyes and smile followed me as I brought the drink to my lips and sipped through the bright, curly, pink straw.

"So tell me," I asked, setting my drink down on the table. "What's your name?"

"Not sure I should tell you. What if I end up being that girl that called you gay? Among the sports community, my career would be over."

"Only if it starts a scandal. And I'm not sure my sexual preference is a good cause for a scandal. It's not like I find it offensive."

"Sometimes, any misconception can be offensive. I shouldn't have made any assumptions, considering who you are."

"That's only human nature," I laughed, trying to convince her it didn't matter what she thought. In a way, I could see how wrong assumptions, no matter what they were, could upset her career, but it wasn't like she had filed paperwork and called for a media day. "I've made a few assumptions about you. I'm curious if I'm right."

"What kind of assumptions?"

"Like, I'm assuming you get excited about food. You were dancing every time you took a bite."

"That's about as obvious as me assuming you're not a vegetarian."

"Fair enough."

She smiled and seemed to relax again finally. "What else?"

"I'm assuming you're single."

Biting her lip, she shook her head back and forth and then up and down, making her answer completely unclear. "Something like that."

"Something like that as in, it's okay that I want to fuck you, or something like that as in, it's okay that I want to fuck you, but we better not?" Because those were the only two options I had.

"We..." she trailed off, stunned by how forward I was. There had never been any sense in beating around the bush. Rarely did I fuck the same person twice, and never had I gotten too attached to any one of them. Over time, it became easier for me to be upfront, and since sex was all I had to offer in any form of human interaction, why avoid it?

Plus, the girl who moaned around a straw coming from a coconut immediately had my attention. It had been a minute since I felt so inspired to put in any effort at all.

"We what?" I urged her to keep talking with a playful smirk. "Did I take you off guard? Offend you?"

"I'm not offended, I'm intrigued. Not sure anyone has ever been that blunt with me."

"If IMG knows anything about Tripp Maddux, it's that he doesn't play the long game. Not in soccer, and especially not in his personal life. You should probably add that to the company file first thing Monday morning."

"Sounds lonely."

She hit the nail on the head and didn't even realize it. Loneliness was my main character trait. My body language told her she was right, so I didn't bother answering. I just leaned back and took a peek at the ocean.

"Something like that," I tried laughing, using her exact words to describe my own situation.

"Were you joking?" she asked with a serious tone. Was that a trick question?

My face slowly turned toward her, and I watched as her eyes bounced between mine and my lips. "Those little moans of yours were making me feel something I probably shouldn't have. No sense joking about it."

"We just met."

"Two people meeting is the only requirement for them to find pleasure. Look at us, we've enjoyed a meal together, and talking, we even share the same tastes in food and drinks. We are practically best friends."

Her mouth was slightly open, and I could tell her brain was racing a mile a minute. Turning back to the water, I decided I would be patient for her. If she needed a minute to figure out if she was in a relationship or not, or if she wanted what I had proposed, then I had time. It wasn't lost on me, though, that the time I gave her was time I'd never have given anyone else.

"I'm celebrating," she blurted, not making any sense at first. "It's only been three days, though."

"What are we celebrating?"

"My strength. Because I broke up with my boyfriend three days ago." I didn't expect her to say that, and I understood why she told me it was complicated. Three days wasn't long enough to let it go, and based on the tone of her voice, she probably wondered if the moment we were having together was another test of her strength.

"What an idiot," I mumbled, shaking my head in disgust.

"What?" Her spine straightened as she faced me a little more, clearly upset.

"Not you. Him."

"It was my idea, not his." Still defending him wasn't a good sign, and I was tempted to tell her how weak she looked. I'd never had a best friend before, so I wasn't sure what was a good thing to say.

"But he let you think it was an option," I countered instead, "and he's an idiot for that."

"As opposed to telling a woman you just met that you want to fuck her?"

"I'm sorry, was I supposed to pretend to be someone I'm not? Did you want me to make you fall in love with me first, and then leave you heartbroken when Miami sends me to another team for blinking the wrong way? That isn't how I work, but it doesn't mean I don't recognize an idiot. I knew just glancing at you what I wanted, but he had it and let it go. I'm sorry Coconut, but that's just dumb."

Her smile was soft, and my eyes followed when her tongue wet her lips. She was making it harder for me than usual, and I found it more intriguing than infuriating. I found everything about her more compelling than anyone I had ever met.

How did anyone, man or woman, resist the way she shook

her shoulders when she took a bite of food? Or the way her lips looked when they were closed around a straw? Even the way her lips quirked when she wanted to smile but didn't want to be caught was calling to me.

"Coconut?"

"You haven't given me your real name."

"Do you still want it?"

"Not really," I huffed. "We've already overshared."

Her mouth opened slightly, but she didn't respond. Reaching up, I pushed her chin to close her mouth and let my hand linger on her skin. Being attracted to someone didn't faze me, but losing control was fucking me up. She may not have thought so, but suddenly, I didn't want what I thought I did from her. It wasn't going to be enough.

Pushing some strands of her dark blonde hair back, I looked directly into her eyes and held her stare. Taking my thumb over her cheek and chin, I inched my way to her lips, testing her every reaction. She didn't back away, and from the way she started leaning toward me, I knew she was ready for me to kiss her.

If only I hadn't lost my fucking mind, I would have.

"How about," I whispered, "I help you celebrate today."

She nodded, still expecting me to kiss her, but somehow, by some power stronger than I knew I was capable of, I resisted. Coconut was celebrating, and instead of taking that away the way I wanted, I decided she deserved more.

"You feel like a bad idea, Tripp Maddux."

"I am a bad idea, Coconut. This is a bad idea. But it's a better idea than what I had planned."

"Why?"

"I don't want you to regret being weak on a day you're supposed to be celebrating your strength."

She bit her lip again and almost bit my thumb in the

process. My hand fell to avoid the contact because I was sure once her tongue touched me, my cock would be so hard I wouldn't be able to move.

"I'm gonna go hit a few waves to cool off. When I get back, tell me what you want to do next. The day is yours, Bestie."

Chapter Six

Tatum

Somehow, I started the day celebrating by myself, only to end up walking the beach with Tripp Maddux. My stomach was twisted in knots the whole time, but they were the kind of knots I never wanted to undo.

It was the same feeling I had with Hunter back in college when he would sweep me off my feet with his charm and make me almost giddy. It appeared out of nowhere with Tripp, almost like magic, but I knew it was wrong from the first twinge.

Tripp wasn't Hunter. Tripp was worse. He had been very upfront with what his intentions were, and even knowing that was all he wanted, I still felt too much, too fast. Hunter taught me that I shouldn't have let those feelings get the best of me.

However, it had been way too long since someone told me they wanted me the way Tripp had. It wasn't offensive, it was nice. Tripp found me attractive and wanted to be with me in a way that Hunter hadn't been in years. My body was practically begging for Tripp to give it what Hunter hadn't, and I was close to giving in to him right then and there. But he pulled back, changing his mind, making me both thankful and frustrated.

Our instant chemistry made it easy to lean toward him and

practically beg him to kiss me. But the little twinges and knots he was giving me wouldn't be forever, and like it or not, I was a forever kind of girl when it came to sex.

When he came back from surfing, we both had cooled off. He said he wanted to spend the day helping me celebrate, and even though that still felt too tempting, I didn't want to say goodbye to him yet. We walked the beach for hours, talking and watching everyone around us.

"So you're in sports marketing, and I'm in sports playing," Tripp nudged me with his shoulder as we walked. "Sounds like we have a lot in common."

"It would seem so," I played along, pushing him back, although he was twice my size and barely budged.

Tripp was a lot taller than I imagined him to be after seeing him on TV. My guess would be he was 6'4 compared to my 5'0 stature. His arms were twice the size of mine, and his soccer legs and thighs were as big around as my whole body.

"So tell me about this boyfriend?"

"Ex–"

"Ex-boyfriend, my bad."

"Are you fishing for more chances of having sex with me?" I teased.

"Don't be weak, Coconut," he winked. "Not today."

Laughing out loud, I nodded and took a minute to think of an answer. What could I tell him about Hunter? It wasn't exactly my topic of choice.

"He loves soccer, actually. Probably more than anything else he's ever loved. It consumes him."

"Soccer is huge in this area, more so than anywhere else I've been. It's easy to get addicted."

"Are you defending him?" I snickered, shoving him again.

"Never," he laughed, drawing the word out and flexing his arm. "I'm Team Coconut all the way."

"You better be."

"Or what?"

My smile was hurting my face, and my feet stopped moving. When I looked up at him, the sun shining behind his head nearly blinded me. His eyes were wide, full of good-natured humor, and he crossed his arms, waiting for my reply.

"Or I'll attack you."

That was laughable because of our size difference, but I flexed my arm the same way he had, not backing down. His laugh made everyone around us look our way, and he started nodding, almost taking that challenge.

"I promise I'm Team Coconut. I've never met this guy, and I already hate his guts. But," he stepped closer and leaned down to my ear. "I'd love to see you in attack mode."

There was no way he didn't notice the way my body shook—his words, his deep voice, and how serious he was all of a sudden. Tripp Maddux was making me weak whether he liked it or not, and at a rate that would have made Superman look like a snail.

When he stood back to his full height and we were again looking into each other's eyes, I reached out and touched his chest, not even considering what the contact would do to me. "You really are a bad idea."

He smiled again, a hint of something naughty in his eyes. Before I could take my hand away and regain my sanity, he lunged forward and scooped me up. Throwing me over his shoulder, he made his way into the water as I kicked and screamed.

When he was waist-deep, he sank into the water, taking me with him. My feet could touch, so I wasn't panicking, but it took me several minutes to catch my breath.

"Are you crazy?"

"No, you are, remember?"

"Tripp!" I whined and laughed at the same time. "I already told you I'm not a strong swimmer."

"I didn't take you deep, Coconut. But we both know that we need to cool off a little."

His words hit me right between the legs, in my core, when I imagined him taking me deep. Oh my God, who was I? His words alone were making me think and feel things I hadn't in so damn long.

Wading until the water was up to my shoulders, we again stared into each other's eyes. It was all I could do when it was so hard to think of words. Be strong, not weak, I reminded myself.

"I'm about to make another assumption about you," my voice was quiet compared to the sounds of the waves crashing after passing us.

"Go ahead, I can take it."

"I think you want to kiss me right now."

"I told you to be strong."

"Saying that out loud is being strong. You made me this way, Tripp Maddux. Now tell me if I'm right or not."

His soft smile was almost more endearing than if he had said the word yes. The way he was looking at me left no room for misinterpretation. Would he at least give me that?

"Again, that is a pretty easy assumption considering I already told you I wanted you."

"Wanting to fuck me and wanting to kiss me isn't the same thing."

"True."

"So am I right?"

"If you weren't celebrating a breakup, then you would be correct."

"So you're charming and noble?"

"You already know I'm not very noble. Don't make that assumption, Coconut, you'll ruin your streak."

"So just charming?"

"And good-looking," he added.

"It's great that you have such self-awareness, Maddux."

"I'm sure you're aware of what those pretty eyes and lips do to every man you're near."

No, I thought to myself. I didn't. Once upon a time, I thought I was attractive and fun to be around. But those days were long gone. Now, I always wondered what was wrong with me that made Hunter so damn elusive.

"If you're not sure," Tripp spoke softly, "Then let me show you tomorrow."

"Tomorrow?"

He closed the gap between us, barely skimming his fingers on the exposed skin of my stomach. His lips were close; his breathing was rough. Every single part of me wished he would kiss me, but instead of pressing his lips to mine, he whispered. "I'm going to kiss you tomorrow. Today, you're going to finish your celebration."

Damn, I was already forgetting about Hunter. It took me several seconds to even remember what I was celebrating in the first place. The whole idea of celebrating seemed dumb now that I had met Tripp. What was I getting out of it, other than turned on to the point of madness?

Putting my hand on Tripp's chest, I gently touched the planes of his pecs. His small groan made that knot in my stomach tighten, and my clit started pulsing without even being touched.

"I wish I had met you tomorrow," I whispered, wondering if he could even hear me.

"How about tonight, we keep celebrating. I can take you to dinner."

"Somewhere public? That seems safe if you're going to keep

pretending you didn't tell me you want me and not following through."

His laugh created a warmth across my cheek, and I moved closer to him unintentionally. "Exactly. Somewhere with a lot of eyes, just waiting to create a scandal for me."

"I'd never allow that. I'm really good at my job."

"Then it's a date."

Backing away, I slowly nodded, letting my fingers stay on his skin until I could no longer reach him. "I'm going to go home. Change. Take a cold shower."

"Me too," he smiled. "But my shower may be warm and my hand may be wrapped around my—"

"Don't," I laughed, making him throw his head back with a howling laugh.

When I managed to back out of the water completely, Tripp followed me from a distance, and I could feel his eyes on me as we walked back to the beach club. He lingered, though, not wanting to get close to me.

Back at the lounger, I packed up my things and wrote a note on a piece of paper I borrowed from a passing waiter. Then, before Tripp could trudge up the beach to meet me, I disappeared.

Chapter Seven

Tripp

Fuuuuuuck.

There was not a doubt in my mind that I should never have agreed to spend the day with Coconut. Getting up and walking away should have been my only move after I realized she was capable of making me weak.

Plenty of women could have been equally satisfying and with less complicated feelings. Then there was Coconut, a woman who danced in her seat with each bite of food and laughed at my jokes. She boldly called me out about wanting to kiss her, making me want her even more than I did before. Which was a lot.

It wasn't in my immediate plans to fall for some chick on the beach drinking a piña colada from a coconut. Being with her all day kept me from focusing on the game plan I was supposed to study. So why did I insist on sticking around? Why didn't I push her into the bathroom and push myself into her, then walk away?

When we were in the water, I could have lined my cock up to her core and eased my way into her body. No one would have known we were out there fucking, and I know she would have left barely remembering her ex's name.

But there was something else she was doing to me, and I didn't even realize it until she walked away from me and up to the lounger to get her things. Watching her hips sway in her tiny bikini, her hair wet down her back, and knowing she gave me shit when I gave it to her. Just talking to her turned me on, and that was unexpected. It knocked me off my game, almost down to my knees.

Holding the note she left for me tightly in my hand, I reread it as I walked the South Beach strip later that night.

If you loved watching me eat lunch, you'd really love seeing me swallow a hard Italian breadstick. 8:00. ;-)

She didn't say where, and I felt that it was intentional. Coconut was making me hunt her down, and I was willing to step foot in every Italian restaurant in South Beach to find her.

Thankfully, it didn't come to that. La Trattoria was known for what they called The Italian Breadstick, and they were hard, almost like a cracker. Taking that clue, I went straight there and found her standing outside.

Before she saw me, I took a minute to look at her. She wore more clothes than when we were at the beach club but looked even sexier. Her hair was the same color as mine and pulled into a high ponytail. Her white dress was strappy and tight at the top but flowed wide to her knees. Her face had very little makeup, but I could tell she got sun on the beach by the redness on her cheeks and nose.

Looking around, she finally spotted me, and her face lit up with a big smile, making me feel something in my chest I never had before. A tug I wasn't used to experiencing, and had I not been in peak physical health, I would have thought it was a heart attack.

"You found me!" She clapped as we walked toward one another.

"I know all about The Italian Breadstick, and I wouldn't have missed seeing it on your tongue for all the goals in the league."

"There you go again. Being both sexy and charming at the same time."

"But not noble, right?"

She just smiled at me as I faked a shiver at the idea of being noble. It was another moment when our eyes locked, and we couldn't look away. Not until someone had asked to get by, and we had to move out of the walking path.

There was a long wait to get into the restaurant, with people lining every wall and bench, even spilling out onto the sidewalk. But as we approached the hostess, I gave her one wink, and she seated us immediately. Coconut and I settled in and ordered water, then I leaned onto the table and smiled at her.

"Are you going to tell me your name now?"

"No," she laughed, shaking her head and making her pony-tail swing behind her.

"That seems unfair, Coconut. You know my name."

"Is Tripp your real name?"

Raising an eyebrow, I smirked and tilted my head. "Wouldn't you like to know?"

"I'm sure it's on the internet if I got curious enough."

"I'm sure I could look up IMG on the internet as well. I bet they have a list of their agents."

She gave me a fake gasp and put her hand to her chest. "You wouldn't!"

"I would," I winked. "Don't make me Google."

Before she answered me, the waiter brought our water and asked to take our orders. Coconut knew precisely what she wanted, and I asked her to order for me since I hadn't even bothered looking at the menu. Hell, I didn't even care what I ate. As long as her tongue touched the breadsticks, I was happy.

The conversation flowed while we waited for our food, which shocked me. When I suggested dinner, I figured we would spend the whole night flirting and toeing the edge of our sanity with lust-induced innuendos. But it didn't matter what she spoke about. I found each little nugget of information fascinating.

Stories about her job, being born and raised in Miami, and how she had a younger brother who would die if he knew she was having dinner with Tripp Maddux. She wasn't very open about her parents, but I ended up telling her that I was raised by a single mom after my dad had died when I was twelve.

All night, I kept asking myself why I told her details no one knew. It must have been because I knew I wouldn't see her again, so it didn't matter.

When dinner came, we dove in, taking bites while smiling and looking at each other. It was the most ridiculously simple yet amazing night. Was it a date? I didn't know. Shit, I didn't even know her name. But it felt like something.

"Here," I handed her a breadstick that had been placed in the middle of our table. "You almost forgot to wrap your lips around this."

"You're dirty," she shook her head, then took the breadstick.

"You love it," I teased her. "Do you need to get it wet first, or do you just raw dog it?"

"Depends on how I'm eating it," she joked back. "And how far I'm taking it at one time."

Dammit, Coconut was perfect.

When we were almost through with the meal, Coconut's

phone rang. She ignored it at first, but when it rang a second time, she held up one finger, and I nodded as she checked the call.

"Oh no," she moaned, her eyes going from carefree to fear instantly.

"Everything okay?"

"It's um, just..." the wince and grimace she gave me had me stirring, wanting to fix whatever I could for her. "He's calling again, shit. Let me answer this."

"Of course," I whispered, secretly hating whoever made her uncomfortable.

"Hello?" There was a moment of silence before she sighed. "I'm having dinner with a friend." The other person was talking again, but Coconut's face wasn't giving anything away. "How about I just call you tomorrow?"... "Okay then I will call you tonight, I promise."

When she finally hung up, she looked guilty and tucked her phone into her bag. "I'm so sorry. That was my ex."

"I take it he's having a hard time letting go?"

She shrugged and didn't look up at me, "It's still fresh, so like I said, it's complicated."

"Idiot," I mumbled, thinking that word deserved to be repeated.

"You are quite the charmer, Maddux." Her sarcasm was playful, trying to get our conversation back on track. "Maybe I should put that in the file at work. Warning: Tripp Maddux will charm your panties off."

"Oh damn, are your panties off?"

She laughed, throwing her napkin onto the table. "You know what I mean."

"I know that I definitely want to know if your panties are off."

It was not only true but effectively turned the conversation away from her ex and back onto the fact that I would have killed to know more details about her panties.

When we finally got up to leave the table, I held her hand in mine as I led her to the door and onto the sidewalk. Holding her hand felt scarily easy and fit my grasp perfectly. As she walked a little ahead of me, I stopped and spun her back to face me.

"Dessert?"

"I like dessert," she sighed.

"Ice cream?"

"It may melt in this warm weather."

"Wanna take the risk?"

Were we talking about ice cream? It didn't feel like it. Melting ice cream and taking risks felt like a metaphor for something way more profound than I wanted to feel. That was why I ran to an ice cream shop after she nodded that she would take the chance. As far as I was concerned, we were talking about ice cream.

Thankfully, the ice cream didn't melt, but the tension between us did. We talked, laughed more, and even shared bites of our chosen flavors. Everything seemed easy and relaxed until it was nearly midnight, and she told me she needed to get home.

Coconut allowed me to walk her to her car, and as we stood facing one another in the parking lot next to the beach, I realized I didn't want to say goodbye. Correction, I didn't want to say anything because standing face to face, our hands intertwined between us, and the wind blowing her hair around, was saying more than words.

Interrupting the peaceful moment, my phone started sounding off in my pocket. Pulling it out, I turned the alarm off and then settled it back where it was. Coconut had a questioning look on her face, so I shrugged nonchalantly.

"That was my alarm."

"Did you have it set so you could bail on me?" She winked.

"I had it set so that I knew when midnight came."

"Curfew? Or are you Cinderella?"

"It's a new day." I acted cool as if my heart wasn't beating out of my chest like a fucking rookie. "I told you I couldn't kiss you on the day you were celebrating your strength, but it's a new day."

Her mouth parted slightly, and I raised a hand to hold onto her neck. As I got closer to her, I made it clear that I was going to kiss her, and I looked for any cues that told me she didn't want that kiss as badly as I did. When I couldn't take the wait any longer, I closed my lips over hers and held onto her as tightly as I could.

A soft moan escaped, and she put her arms around my neck, practically pulling herself up on my much taller body. The kiss intensified, the moment being fucking perfect. She was the one who was Cinderella, but instead of running away from the prince at midnight, she ran into the arms of the lonely soccer player.

Unfortunately, reality sank in with the loud blaring of her ringtone. She jumped back, taken off guard, and looked sheepish as she reached into her bag to turn off the ringer. When she returned to kiss me again, the phone started ringing again, making her nearly throw the phone onto the ground.

"You need to get that," I sighed, knowing it was better if I left before things went further.

Coconut started to shake her head and argue, but I put my thumb over her lips as my hand on her neck held her still. The phone was ringing again, and I knew it was her ex. When they spoke at dinner, she was careful to keep her tone bright, and even more cautious not to mention who she was having dinner with.

"Go answer your phone, Coconut..." She started to speak, but I stopped her again. It felt like she was about to give me her name and suggest we trade numbers, but that was never my intention. Despite how much I loved talking to her and being with her, I had started the day just wanting to fuck her. Since that wasn't going to be good enough, I wasn't going to prolong the inevitable. "Maybe I will see you at the beach club again, celebrating more than just breaking it off, but celebrating moving on."

One single tear slid down her cheek, and she nodded. "I've spent years wishing he would call me at midnight. Hoping he just wanted to talk to me. Wanting him to want me as much as, well, as much as you told me you did."

"You deserve to get what you want," I winked and backed up, finally creating the space I needed to walk away. "I have a game tomorrow, so I need to head out. But Coconut? Promise me you'll get what you want, and celebrate when you get it."

She nodded as one more tear fell down her cheek. The smile on her face was sad but also a little satisfied. Maybe we needed each other that night. It may not have been what I expected, but it was more, and I would always think about that night with Coconut.

Chapter Eight

Tatum

The whole drive home, my heart was pounding as I listened to Hunter ramble on about what he did that day. He had made some moves, whatever that meant. He was vague but seemed excited, and I should have been equally enthusiastic for him.

And for me.

But the entire story felt fabricated. It all felt like he was telling me things he thought I wanted to hear. Yet, after one kiss with Tripp Maddux, I was unsure if I cared enough to call him out or worry about it.

"Hey," I interrupted him, "I'm so tired, and just pulled into my parking lot. Can I call you tomorrow?"

"Seriously?" He laughed as if I was joking.

"It's late."

"The other night when I was with my friend, you got pissed that I didn't fucking call. What do you want from me?"

He was right, except the other day, we were a couple trying to make something work. Now, we weren't. He was realizing I wasn't as weak as my mother and wouldn't be hanging on as tightly as he had hoped.

And I couldn't exactly tell him I kissed Tripp Maddux, and it felt so good that my head was spinning. Of all the people in the world, kissing Tripp would send Hunter over the edge. He hated the Inferno for not signing him and was jealous of everyone that played. He would lose his mind if he knew I'd had dinner with Tripp.

"You're right. I'm sorry, Hunt. You've been showing me how much you care about me with your sweet messages. I guess because I consider us broken up right now, things are different."

"I'm somehow going to have everything, and everyone, I want."

His words made me uncomfortable, so I wasn't even sure how to respond.

"You may not think so," he gritted out angrily. "But there aren't a lot of guys like me out there. I know I have my flaws, but I'm talented and good to the people around me."

There was still nothing to say. I was frozen as I tried to think of anything that could make us change the conversation.

"Who did you have dinner with? I know it wasn't your brother because I saw him at the university earlier."

"I told you, a friend. Someone from work." Was that a lie? Technically, yes. But I would head in on Monday and make a little file for Tripp Maddux content just to ease my guilty conscience.

"Hey," he finally sounded quieter and calmer. "Let me take you out Monday."

"Monday?"

"It's the only day I have free, Tay. Just say yes."

It wasn't like I was seeing Tripp again. We didn't exchange numbers or even my real name. Dinner with Hunter may help me remember what we were trying to work toward and be together.

"Sure, sounds fun."

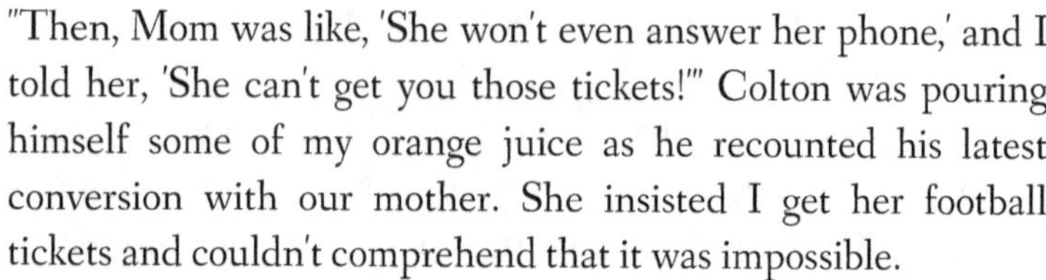

"Then, Mom was like, 'She won't even answer her phone,' and I told her, 'She can't get you those tickets!'" Colton was pouring himself some of my orange juice as he recounted his latest conversion with our mother. She insisted I get her football tickets and couldn't comprehend that it was impossible.

"So did Dad leave?"

"Not yet," Colton sighed as he took a seat on my couch with his drink. He lifted my remote and started flipping through the channels, looking for the football game I knew he wanted to watch. "What channel?"

"No clue." Returning to the book I was reading, I ignored him for a while. Talking about my parents was exhausting. I didn't want to watch football, and all I could think about was...

"Tripp Maddux, up the middle and free!" Dropping my book into my lap, I sat straight and looked at the screen. Colton had stopped at the soccer game, and the first word I heard the announcer say was the name of the man I had been thinking about nonstop.

"Shit," Colton scoffed. "The Inferno are crazy this year. If they lose the season, they're going to be in serious need of your services. Rhys Peyton and Cruz Martin both look off their game, but Tripp Maddux is taking the heat for that."

"Why?" My voice was high, and I could tell I sounded panicked. Too panicky for a casual viewer who shouldn't care what happened with the Inferno.

"For a sports marketer, you really should know more about sports. Then again, you let Hunter keep you from paying any attention to the Inferno in case it hurts his little feelings."

"Hey," I pointed at my brother. "Hunter has worked hard and deserved to be signed with an MLS team. Especially his home team."

"But they signed Tripp Maddux, and he whines every chance he gets."

"What does that have to do with them blaming Tripp for their crappy season?"

"Hey," Colton raised his hands in surrender. "I was being supportive. If they trade Tripp, maybe Hunter can try out for the team again."

"He hasn't played in almost a year. And that still doesn't answer my question."

"They're not getting rid of Rhys Peyton. No way in hell. Cruz Martin is basically a God around here since he's from Miami and a good ass player. The next highest-paid player is Tripp Maddux. If they can't get their shit together, he will be the first to go. Count on it."

"What if it's not his fault?"

"They'll find a reason to blame him. One little rumor of a scandal, and they will blame the demise of the season on it. It's just the way it works. It's the only way to protect their pride and joy."

My jaw dropped to my chest. As a marketer, I rarely saw that side of the sport. Most of my work was spent arranging promotional nights and marketing campaigns. But that didn't mean I wasn't aware that it existed. Sports teams were businesses, first and foremost.

Colton kept up with everything, so I knew he was right. He never played any sports, but I could picture him being an agent or in public relations one day.

Looking back toward the screen, the camera showed Tripp bent over, his hands on his knees as he caught his breath. The announcers were saying something about him, but I couldn't focus on the words. All I could think about was that almost twenty-four hours had passed since I sat across from him at La Trattoria. It had been less than twenty-four hours since he had kissed me.

I could still feel his warm lips on mine. My hand moved to my bottom lip, and I grazed it with my fingers as the memory came back to me. Damn him and his charm. His lips. His smile. His arms. His... just damn all of him. At least for one night, I learned what it felt like to be desired by someone other than Hunter.

"Ya know," Colton started speaking as if I wasn't next to him, silently reliving my one kiss with the guy on the TV. Something I knew I couldn't tell him, or anyone, about. "Hunter really could try out. They do the camps at the end of the year. He could join one and let the team see him play up close."

"He's gunning for the head coaching job at the university at the moment. I think. I'm sure he's too distracted for off-season camp."

"What makes him think he can get that job? Coach Probst has had it for years and has been winning. He isn't going anywhere."

"Somehow, he thinks if he gets hired as the assistant coach, he can sneak into Probst's spot when the time comes. He took his interim coaching on the women's team seriously. He has it in him."

Colton rolled his eyes at how hard I defended Hunter, but I wasn't wrong. Only a few weeks ago, Hunter had to take over the women's team while the head coach handled some personal business. He did well, took things seriously, and didn't let his inclination to be petty get the best of him. He needed the clarity to know what he wanted to do long-term.

"Well whatever he does, he gets on my nerves."

Chapter Nine

Tripp

There should have been some satisfaction watching Cruz stand in the goal like an idiot as he stared into the stands at his sister. He had a crush on her and probably even slept with her since he walked into practice yesterday with a freshly fucked face. She was wearing my jersey, though, and it was slowly killing him. Almost to the point of not even being able to concentrate.

It was hilarious.

But I couldn't laugh.

Especially when he ran off the field and left me to answer media questions. It was the second game I'd had to use my words in a row, and it wasn't my thing. It had always made me uncomfortable to have all eyes on me, and even worse when the team was struggling so badly. I mean, we won, but barely.

Against St. Louis FC, it should have been a more significant points spread. Cruz should have stuck around for his interviews. At least Rhys was there since he was the one who bailed on me the game before.

"You have a lot of pressure on you, how are you balancing that as the season all comes down to Friday's result?"

"I don't concentrate on what the bosses are doing," I lied to the reporter. "All I can do is show up and play my game."

"There are a lot of trade rumors swirling if the Inferno misses the playoffs this year. Are you prepared for that?"

"I will give 100% to whatever team I'm on. Right now, that is the Inferno, and that is all I want to talk about."

Thankfully, the questions moved on to the actual game and were things I could answer without wanting to tear someone's head off. When Rhys got to his locker, they all moved to him for questions, and I grabbed some clothes and left without even getting a shower. The quicker I got home, the quicker I could relax.

At least, that was the plan. Hunter sitting in front of my door waiting for me was not part of my plan. I actually considered backing away to hide at the beach until I was sure he was gone, but he looked up when he heard the elevator open, and I was just standing there frozen.

"Hey, good game man." He stood and stepped aside while I opened my door and followed me in.

"What can I do for you?" Maybe I was cold when I spoke, but I was fresh off the adrenaline of a game and the frustration of the media questions. If Hunter saw the game, as he apparently had, he should have known I wouldn't be in the mood for visitors.

"I need to cash in the favor you said you'd do for me."

"Right now?" My voice was loud and angry. Not only because I didn't remember telling him I'd help him but also because I was under an enormous amount of stress, and he had the nerve to pile more on for me. "What do you want?"

"Look," he held up his hands to placate me. "You know what I need and you agreed. So I didn't think asking was going to piss you off."

Instead of admitting I didn't know what I agreed to because

I didn't want him to know I didn't remember, I just asked him to repeat himself again. "What. Do. You. Want?"

"My girl," he sighed. "I'm too distracted, and she is pushing me away. Like I said the other night, she thinks I'm not into her anymore, but I'm just having a hard time balancing both."

"Have you not realized that I'm a loner? Relationship advice isn't where I shine, Hunter."

"I don't need advice, I need you to fill in for me."

"You want me to steal your girl?" Fuck, I was laughing, and it was making me feel better. Hunter was crazier than I thought he was.

"It's not stealing, it's taking my place for one dinner."

"And then what? You'd want her back? Like some toy that you're letting me borrow until you're ready to play again?"

"It's one dinner. A chance meeting with Tripp Maddux. Act interested in her, then let her tell you she has a boyfriend. Offer to buy her a meal anyway, then part ways."

"What if she doesn't want you back? What if she's interested in me back?" Fuck I didn't want Hunter's girlfriend to be interested in me. That would be the beginning of a nightmare.

"She will. She's obsessed with me."

"If she cares about you that much, why are you doing this to her?"

"We went over this the other night." Hunter started pacing and running his fingers through his hair, clearly agitated that I wasn't just saying yes and moving on. "It was your idea. I told you I kept letting her down and you said, 'Just let me know, I'll fill in and distract her.'"

I did? Fuck that didn't even sound like me, but then again, drinking as much as I did that night wasn't me either. Everything in me told me to say no and not deal with Hunter anymore, but some part of me never wanted to admit to him that I didn't remember anything about that night.

There had to be more to the story. Something he wasn't telling me that I was clearly supposed to remember. It made no sense at all why Hunter would ask a famous soccer player to casually run into his girlfriend and entertain her for the night. A happy coincidence wouldn't replace him not showing up.

"Just tell me, really quick," I sighed, "why is this helpful?"

"It'll give us something to talk about. She will tell me she met you, that I should have been there. That I missed out. I will be the one that's sad I missed the dinner, and she will gloat about it."

Everything inside of me was trying not to laugh in his face. "Shouldn't she know we already know each other? Doesn't she know we played together?"

"She may assume, once you two meet. Maybe it will be something she brings up. You can tell her, 'Yeah I know your boyfriend Hunter. He's cool.' Then that will give you another opening to keep her distracted."

Don't do it, Tripp. Tell him to get lost.

"I'll think about it."

His smile lit up, and he nodded, pumping his fist a little. "It will be just like you said it would be."

I didn't say yes.

"Tomorrow night," Hunter interrupted my thoughts. "I'm supposed to meet Tay for dinner, but now I'm gonna be at a meeting. Go in my place and casually meet her. Just be Tripp Maddux, the famous soccer player. The rest will be easy."

"What do I do if she tells me she wants me to leave? You did say that she's obsessed with you."

"She is, but it's just one night. Charm her enough to keep her happy, then say goodnight, and go home. I'll be at her place when she gets home, and I'm sure she will tell me all about it. She won't even be upset anymore that I couldn't make dinner again."

That poor girl deserved better than Hunter's shitshow, but at least it was just for a night. And agreeing to do him the favor was enough to get him to leave. If I changed my mind and didn't, it would be his bullshit to deal with, not mine.

He was one weird fucker, because I'd never want someone taking my place on a date. Why was this better than being honest with her? The only thing that made sense was that Hunter was cheating on her on top of making soccer his priority.

"You better hope I don't like her, Hunter." He was long gone, but I spoke to myself as I ran through everything in my head. "Because I don't like you enough not to tell her the truth."

The last thing I wanted to do was practice after a hard game, but when Monday rolled around, I got my ass to the stadium. Almost all day, I kept to myself and let my mind focus on the game, but when I got back to my locker and checked my phone, Hunter's text had my mind reeling. It was the address of where his girlfriend was going to be, and he was expecting me to show up.

Remember that she's mine. Just entertain her and go home.

No more favors after this.

Deal.

"Remember that guy from Mango's the other night?" I mumbled, almost to myself, but I knew Cruz was next to me at our lockers.

"Coach Crazy?" he asked, using his little pet name for Hunter.

"Hunter Ward." It wasn't so much a correction as it was a statement. A fact that I was sure of when I was so unsure of helping him out in any way. Cruz turned toward me, no doubt getting a little concerned, but I just stared into my locker.

"You okay?"

"Hunter is an old teammate of mine. He asked for my help."

"Just because I don't like him doesn't mean you can't help him."

That got a small smile out of me, and I looked up at Cruz. "This has nothing to do with how you feel about him."

Plus, I had my own reasons for not liking Hunter. Back in League One, he belittled everyone around him. He would outright say that he was the best on the team, then, instead of proving it, he'd tear down everyone else's game. I had long looked past it, but it still sat in my gut. Lingering thoughts of animosity would probably always be around inside of me somewhere.

"Well that is offensive," Cruz kept on, interrupting my thoughts, "because the only reason I don't like him is because Rhys doesn't like him. You should be a better friend to me."

"What are you? Twelve?" I laughed, letting Cruz's banter make me feel better.

"What does he want help with?"

"I don't know if I should say." Because it's stupid and dumb of me to consider it just to save face about not remembering anything. Not even Cruz knew about what happened after he left that night. No one needed to know I got that wasted.

"Is it illegal? Does he want you to shove drugs up your ass?"

"No," I laughed again. "I mean, it's a little twisted, but nothing like that."

"What are you going to do, then?"

"Guess I'm gonna steal his girl, just like he asked me to do." Because how else was I supposed to explain it to him? I'd rather get traded to Toronto than tell him I somehow came up with an idea to be a cocky famous soccer player and fill in for Hunter on a date with his girl. Cruz would probably have me committed.

"What?" Cruz's eyes were bulging out of his head. He wanted more information, but I didn't want to give him any. Not yet.

Standing up, I sighed, and as I walked away, I added, "It's complicated."

Chapter Ten

Tatum

After a long day at work, the last thing I wanted to do was go out and have dinner. But if Hunter was making the effort, I was going to see it through. It was what I asked him to do, and I didn't have an argument to save our relationship if I didn't try either.

As I sat alone at the seaside restaurant where he told me to meet him, I knew in my heart he wasn't coming. Then it was confirmed when his text came through.

Sorry, Tay. A meeting popped up, and I can't say no.

Yes, he could have. He could have told whoever called a meeting that he was headed to dinner already and couldn't make it. But he'd never choose me over soccer.

Taking one last sip of my water, I tried to devise a plan to leave and still save face with everyone around me. Humiliation wasn't something I handled well, and being stood up ranked among the highest forms of embarrassment in my book. All I could think to do was pretend I had to use the restroom and leave, never showing my face in there again.

With my head down, I took a deep breath and summoned the courage I needed to get up, but I heard a familiar voice before I did.

"Is this seat taken?"

Lifting my eyes, they locked with Tripp Maddux's, who looked just as shocked to see me as I did him.

"Coconut?"

"If you didn't know it was me, who else were you going to sit with?" For the most part, I was teasing him. "Do you go around meeting new girls every day?"

"What? No!" He pulled the chair out and sat down, looking around casually to see if we were making a scene. "I thought you were someone else."

"Who?"

"A friend of a friend, I was just going to say hi."

"Well, I was just leaving," I laughed humorlessly. "I got stood up, so I'm not staying."

Why did I tell him that? It made me look pathetic.

"By your boyfriend?"

"Yes," I lifted my chin. "My ex. Just trying to get what I want, like you told me to do."

His smile was soft and sad. "That's good—"

"Don't," I held up a hand to stop him from talking anymore. "This is just embarrassing, and I'm telling you way more than I should. I need to leave."

"Wait," he stood up just as I did and grabbed my arm. "Don't go."

"I don't want to ruin your evening as well. Do whatever you're here for."

He looked around again as if searching for someone else, then turned back to me. "There isn't anything I need to do, Coconut. Nothing is more important than making sure you're okay. Let me join you for dinner. I really want to see how you sound when you try the conch here."

Snorting a little, I shook my head in disbelief and knew I was once again falling for Tripp Maddux's charm. "I don't eat conch."

"Did you say conch or....?" Tripp waggled his eyebrows and winked, finally getting a loud and genuine laugh out of me.

"I said conch," I made sure to enunciate. "I prefer to just suck on the other thing you are thinking about."

"Oh fuck," Tripp held a hand to his heart and dramatically sat back down in the seat I had saved for Hunter. "You're dirty."

My face turned a bright shade of red, but it felt good to catch him by surprise. Sitting down again, I recomposed myself while he smiled at me. "Are we going to just stare all night?"

"Does that mean I can be your date?"

"As long as you don't make me eat conch."

"Promise, Coconut. But we aren't counting out that other thing, right?"

If there was a shade brighter than bright red, that was what I felt my cheeks were exuding. It felt like an Inferno, if you will. My heart was beating so fast, and my skin started to sweat. Being around Tripp was a cure I didn't realize I needed. Because the second he reached across the table and took my hand, I forgot Hunter existed.

At least until Tripp said something. "Sorry you got stood up."

Shrugging, I kept my hand in his as he caressed my knuckles with his thumb. "Just trying to see what's left."

"Well, I'm glad I ended up being here tonight."

"Why are you here? Are you alone?"

"I was supposed to be meeting someone, but I'd rather be here with you."

"Don't tell me you're standing someone up, too."

"Not really," he laughed. "A friend of mine just mentioned his friend would be here and before I saw them, I saw you."

Taking a glance around, I wondered who he was talking about, but he didn't seem to even bother. He had decided he was only interested in me, sitting in front of him and holding his hand the way he was mine.

"Should you at least say hi?"

"No," he snorted. "They'll be okay."

They? "Don't do to them what I had done to me, Tripp. It's not fun."

"Hey," he said softly, ensuring I looked into his eyes. "It's not like that. It was just some twisted shit my friend had going on. Not my problem. I promise."

Nodding a little, I let his words sink in, and within minutes, I was no longer worrying about anyone but Tripp and me. "I saw your game yesterday. Well, some of it."

"Ouch," Tripp blew out in exasperation. "Let me guess, you think we should have scored one hundred goals? Maybe I should have had fifty goals and fifty assists?"

He was joking, but he wasn't. "Was the media hounding you?"

"Like I was a dog," he sighed. "Everyone thinks that if we lose Friday, I'm headed back to League One, or another team. God forbid if I have some off-the-field issues to tend to, then they would oust me so fast I wouldn't be able to think straight."

"I hate that. The entire season shouldn't come down on your shoulders like that."

"That is just the nature of being everyone's third favorite. But let's not dwell on that, because it's not going to be an issue. Friday, we play Los Angeles and I have every intention of kicking their ass."

Before I could high-five him and tell him how much I loved his positivity, the waiter came up. I motioned for Tripp to order us whatever he wanted, as I had done at the Italian place. The waiter nodded as Tripp rattled off a few things, flashing his eyes my way every few words.

Tripp stopped him as the waiter was about to walk away and added, "Bring some conch, too."

"You promised!" I feigned dramatically.

"You know I'm not noble enough to keep a promise."

"I'm not eating it. No way."

"We'll see about that."

For the next hour, we spent another fantastic meal together, with more laughter and flirting.

Despite my best efforts, I caved to Tripp's charm again and tried the conch. Then, I also had to eat my words because the conch was delicious. I moaned and did a little dance when the buttered dipping sauce hit my tongue.

Tripp covered his ears and closed his eyes, mumbling what a bad idea it had been to order it. It made me want more, and I made a show of letting the butter drip on my chin.

"I think I need to know your name, Coconut. A little fate brought me in here for a second chance with you."

"A second chance to fuck me?"

"That's all I have to give," he winked.

"How come I highly doubt that?"

"Maybe because you don't really know me?"

"Maybe," I bit my lip, trying not to smile as I focused on my drink to keep from looking at him. "It's been fun, being mysterious and discreet, though."

"Tell me," he growled, leaning forward to get my attention back on him. "What name should I whisper the next time I kiss your lips?"

"Tatum O'Neil," I confessed, waving my hands like Vanna White.

Tripp's face paled, though, and his eyes widened. He sat

back in his chair, dropping his hold on my hand, and slightly shook his head.

"What?" I panicked, not sure what was happening. "Same name as an ex?"

"No," Tripp swallowed. "Just surprised me for a minute."

"Good surprise? Or bad?"

"Fuck, I don't know yet."

Chapter Eleven

Tripp

Whoever Hunter needed me to be that night disappeared the second I saw Coconut. She was the only girl I saw sitting alone and was wearing a dress like Hunter described, so I approached her thinking she was who I was meeting. But I went the rest of the night thinking, *"Fuck Hunter, Coconut is here."*

Hearing her name being the exact name Hunter texted me didn't even make sense at first. There were coincidences I wasn't blind to, like her being stood up by her ex, but I didn't connect that she was Hunter's girl.

Then it all came to me, and I realized I hadn't brushed off Hunter's request like I thought I had. I walked right to it, making it even more twisted than he did.

Coconut being Tatum made me rethink everything all over again. He told me she was his girlfriend, but Tatum referred to him as her ex. Hunter acted like an ex, but Tatum still pined for Hunter in a way I would never understand.

"What don't you know?" Tatum laughed nervously while my train of thought took a trip around crazy town and back.

"Yeah," I cleared my throat, not even making sense. But it

gave me a few more seconds to think of something. "Just sounded familiar and took me off guard."

There was no way to tell her that Hunter Ward sent me there. Especially after I spent the entire night telling her how badly I wanted her. Fucking Hunter's girl was definitely not part of the equation.

"You know another Tatum O'Neil? Or were you thinking of the actress?" Her tone was teasing, but the nerves were still there.

Reaching across the table again to take her hand, I shook my head and smiled. "No, none of that, but I'm glad I know you now."

"Give me your phone, Tripp Maddux."

Her use of my entire name made me snort as I pulled my phone from my pocket and handed it to her. She held it up to my face to unlock it and then bit her lip as she typed something in.

When she handed it back, I saw her contact added to my phone labeled Coconut. "Just in case you really do know two Tatum O'Neil's," she giggled.

"I um..." It was on the top of my tongue to tell her the truth. It would have been the smartest thing to do, but selfishly, I knew she wouldn't want to see me again. Not when I was originally there to help Hunter with his lies. "I have practice tomorrow."

"And I'm a responsible girl that gets to bed early on work nights."

"Shit," I sighed. "I actually find that sexy."

"Getting to bed earlier than my Grandma is sexy? Dang, you're in for a treat when you see what I wear to bed, then."

Her face immediately flushed at her suggestion that I would see her in bed, and I nodded and bit my lip, not making it any easier on her. It didn't matter what her relationship with Hunter was. Even without his weird request, I wouldn't have treated

Tatum any differently. Not since she was the woman I met at the Beach Club and had thought about nonstop since then.

"How about you come to my game on Friday?"

Fuck, I was overstepping. Hunter didn't ask me to actually steal his girl. It was just supposed to be once. If he found out, he would be pissed. She was supposed to go home and tell him all about meeting Tripp Maddux. But would she?

Should I care?

Up until the other night, Hunter was nothing but a shitty ex-teammate. Tatum deserved better, and even though I wasn't the relationship kind, the way Hunter apparently was, I needed more time with her, to protect her, and possibly tell her what her boyfriend was up to.

"Really?" She lit up but then almost immediately lowered her shoulders. "I mean, I want to. I just need to check my schedule."

"You mean you need to see if your ex is going to make up for standing you up tonight?"

Shaking her head, I could tell she was embarrassed, but I wouldn't let her off the hook.

"I've said before, it's a really complicated situation," she sighed.

More than you even know.

How'd it go with Tatum last night?

Fine.

Did she mention me?

She referred to you as an ex.

She was just saving face. That girl will never leave me.

Did she mention me? Because she was supposed to tell you all about it.

He never answered because his answer was no. Tatum wouldn't tell Hunter anything about our night because, as far as she was concerned, everything we said and did was not something you'd tell an ex.

I had kissed her goodnight so deeply that I was practically apologizing to her with my lips on behalf of mankind. That kiss stayed with me all night, and I ended up fucking my hand to the image of that butter dripping from the conch onto her tongue.

Tossing my phone onto my bed, I entered my closet for my running shoes. The best part about my place was the path running miles along the ocean. It made running an easy way to relieve stress.

Practice should have been enough, but when I got home, my body was still buzzing with the need to get rid of some energy. Then, that text from Hunter made it official. The sound of incoming texts from him came from where I'd tossed my phone, but I wasn't checking it or taking it with me.

Honestly, I wasn't even sure what had me so anxious. Even if Hunter found out that I was seeing Tatum again, what would he do? It was their fight to have, not mine. For me, it was a favor he asked for, so what right did he have to dictate the outcome?

When I returned from my run and let the shower wash away the rest of my anxiety, I finally read the texts he had sent me.

She will. Thanks, man.

Hopefully, that holds her over for a few weeks.

By then, we should be okay.

Fuck that guy. Tatum didn't deserve his bullshit. Hopefully, in a few weeks, she will have ridden my dick hard enough to forget Hunter even existed.

Instead of responding to Hunter, I pulled up my contacts and dialed Tatum.

"Hello?" Her sweet voice answered.

"Leaving work?"

"Tripp?" She giggled. "I just left. How did you know?"

"You told me you got off at five, so I was counting the hours all day."

"You're so full of shit," she laughed. "But I like the thought. Didn't you have practice?"

"We practiced early to avoid the heat of the day, then I went for a long run, and now I'm just making sure you know I'm thinking about you."

Her silence was deafening. It spoke so much louder than if she had said anything at all because I was doing what she had told me she wished Hunter would do. Prioritizing calling her, making a point to just talk. Damnit, was I playing games with her?

"You there?" I asked, even though I could hear her breathing and the sound of her car as she drove home.

"Yeah. I just...you surprised me. That's all."

I surprised myself.

"So I have a question."

"Should I be worried?" she giggled.

"Depends on what your boyfriend had to say after last night."

"I um..."

"Not asking for your hand in marriage, just don't want to step on any toes."

Tripp, you asshole, you were stepping on all kinds of toes knowing she was Hunter's and not backing off. But did it count since I knew her before he asked me for his favor?

"Just wondering about the game Friday."

She was quiet for a few more minutes, and I let her mull over her decision. Then, finally, she spoke so softly I wasn't even sure I heard her correctly. "Okay."

The relief and excitement I felt with that one word was foreign. I had never had someone come to my game to watch me play. I wasn't even sure how to make sure she got the tickets. It took a quick side text to Rhys to ask while she was waiting on the line.

Rhys was quick, though, and I read his directions off to her.

"I have to put your name on a list. All you have to do is give your name at the ticket booth, and they'll give you my player tickets."

"Okay," she replied with the same single word, only with a little more excitement.

"Then afterward, I want to watch you eat again."

Chapter Twelve

Tatum

It wasn't until Wednesday that I finally heard from Hunter. He had tried explaining himself, but none of it seemed important. I only reminded him we weren't together anymore and that he didn't owe me anything.

Somehow, that only pissed him off more.

A part of me wanted to tell him about meeting Tripp Maddux, but I knew I would only be trying to make him jealous, and I didn't want to go there. Whatever was happening between Tripp and me was private, and I deserved to see where it went without Hunter's interference.

Upon Tripp's request, I took a rideshare to the game. He wanted me to ride with him afterward and promised to take me home, so leaving my car at the stadium didn't make sense.

Getting into the game was easy, just like he said it would be, and I found my seat with no problems. When I sat down, though, I started to get antsy, and a bit of guilt began to sneak into my mind.

A few years ago, when Hunter wanted to play for the Inferno, I used to imagine sitting in those seats and watching him warm up. Those were the days when I used to think of us getting married and living somewhere on the beach. We would have kids and show my parents what a healthy and happy family looked like.

Yet, there I was after all the years that had passed, and I was searching Tripp Maddux out instead. He was warming up with a few teammates, and every once in a while, he would send me a slight wink or smile. From my small understanding of soccer, it was a big game for the Inferno. Win, and they made the play-offs, lose, and their season was essentially over.

Tripp spent the first few minutes of the game controlling the ball and kicking it back and forth with Rhys Peyton but never took a shot at the goal. Twelve minutes in, a player on the other team went down and had to be tended to by the medics. That was when the night ended for everyone because Cruz Martin was talking with someone a few seats down from where I was, and then he left.

Vanished.

Tripp and the rest of the team could barely wrap their minds around what was happening. The fans were utterly clue-less. The coach yelled, and another goalie entered the game within a few minutes.

The team never recovered, though.

Their loss was heavy, and the crowd booed the entire team as they walked off the field. When the final whistle blew, I was supposed to head down an elevator toward the player family exit. Tripp had given me precise directions on how to get there, but I chose to stay put until everyone around me had calmed down.

All I could think about was how Hunter lost his champi-onship game in college and didn't want to talk to anyone for a week. Tripp's plans for us were undoubtedly canceled because I couldn't imagine him feeling any differently than Hunter had that night.

There was no response and no text bubble indicating he was writing back. He was off the hook for the night, and I knew he had to have been relieved that I understood without him saying anything.

With only fifty or so people left in the stands, I finally stood up to leave, pulling a rideshare app up on my phone. Taking three steps up toward the exit tunnel, my eyes caught the soft pink jersey of Tripp coming down toward me.

A few people were snapping pictures of him, but his eyes were focused on me. It was all I could do to not drop my phone from how surprised I was, so I slid it into my back pocket and waited for him to get to me.

Then, without a word, he took my hand and led me back up the way he had come.

"What are you doing?"

"Not letting you get away," he smiled back at me.

His season was lost. They had two games left on the schedule, but it no longer mattered if they won or not. Tripp shouldn't have been smiling. He should have been angry and grumpy. What did he know that I didn't?

"What happened to Cruz Martin?" I dared to ask when we got into the elevator.

"We have no clue," Tripp shrugged, then leaned down to put his nose to mine. "The only thing I care about is making sure you don't try to sneak off."

"I wasn't sneaking. Just know how tough losing a match

can be."

"How do you know that?" The gleam in his eyes was like he already knew the answer but dared me to tell him.

"I just do," I sighed. He may have known I had issues with an ex, but he didn't have to know anything else about him.

"Okay," Tripp winked. "Well, just so you know, win or lose, all I've thought about was how much I was looking forward to spending more time with you."

The elevator opened before I could respond, and he pulled me into a small crowd lingering outside the locker room. None of them seemed bothered by Tripp being there, so I assumed it was the family area he had told me to go to in the first place.

"I have to change and shower. Promise me you won't go anywhere?"

"Promise."

"Good girl," he leaned down and kissed my cheek before running into a door a few feet away. My cheeks were heating again like they always were around Tripp, but I tried to hide it by tucking myself into a corner.

"Coach is so mad," I heard someone say in a group near me. "Cruz just left, and Tripp played like shit. Coach is ready to tear the whole team apart."

Tripp didn't play well? Sure, I was a novice when it came to soccer, but I was pretty sure the four goals the backup keeper had let through were the reason they lost. How could they blame that on Tripp?

"I'm sure they will start by trading Tripp. Coach has had a problem with him and has just been looking for a reason to get rid of him."

"What?" I accidentally said out loud, making them turn my way. It was everything my brother had predicted but seemed more matter-of-fact.

All three women, a little older than me, looked at me wide-eyed. "Are you here with Tripp?"

Did they not see us get off the elevator?

"Where did you hear all that?" I asked.

"Sorry! Tripp has never had someone at his games so I'm really sorry."

"But where did you hear that about him?" I asked again, letting the fact that I was apparently Tripp's first guest at a game go over my head for the moment.

"I'm married to Luca Simpson. Even Tripp knows he's on thin ice, I'm just really sorry you heard us talking the way you did."

Nodding slightly, I backed up against the wall I was originally leaning on and let the conversation with Mrs. Simpson end. It wasn't my place to get upset over Tripp's future, but curiosity ate away at me until Tripp finally returned from the locker room.

The ladies nodded at him awkwardly, then watched as he approached and took my hand. "Everything okay?"

Could he sense the tension?

"Of course."

"Then let's get out of here."

Holding my hand, Tripp led me across the parking lot toward an old Bronco, and I came to a complete stop when I realized it was his. Powder blue, two-door, no top, and chrome wheels. It had been restored but was still the opposite of whatever I thought he would drive.

"Another wrong assumption?" He laughed as he pushed the small of my back toward the passenger side.

"Yeah, but somehow this suits you more than I could imagine."

"This was my dad's until he died. Then it was my very first car, but I had trouble keeping her running. When I went pro, I pulled it out of my mom's garage and had it restored. Then I drove it all the way from California to Miami so I could keep her down here with me."

"Wow!" Sliding my hand across the shiny paint, I realized I was in awe. "It must be so special to you."

"She's got a brand new engine, upgrades, and a few luxuries, but she still has the same feel she did back then, and that's all I want."

"I'm surprised you don't have this thing wrapped in bubble wrap and stashed somewhere safe."

"I'd rather enjoy her."

"Does she have a name?"

"Shelly," he said quickly, then laughed at himself. "We spent a lot of days breaking shells together, riding down the beaches."

"I can picture you with a surfboard on the top, cruising across the country to play soccer for the Inferno. Not a care in the world."

"Fuck, I wish you were right about that."

Before I could ask what he meant, he opened the door and lifted me into the passenger seat. A slight squeal escaped my lips as I grabbed his shoulders to steady myself. He nudged my knees open and pushed himself closer to me, making my breathing come harder.

His lips were close to mine but not touching me. It was a tease like he wanted to see if he could break me before he put me back together. I never felt so ready for a simple kiss, not even with Hunter.

"I want to make you forget about him," Tripp whispered.

Swallowing hard, I tried not to think about the fact that he just practically read my mind. The second I thought of Hunter, something must have changed in me. Tripp must have sensed it.

"You don't have to try very hard."

"I wish I didn't have to try at all," he said before kissing my lips softly.

Chapter Thirteen

Tripp

"Where are we going?" Tatum sounded nervous, and she should have been because I was a man on a mission.

"My place."

"What?"

"I'm going to cook for you."

From the corner of my eye, I could tell she was staring at me and contemplating whether going home with me was a good idea. It was cute because she didn't have much of a choice.

"I'm not watching you moan over a meal in public tonight."

"Okay." Her voice was soft and scared, but she finally turned away and looked at where I was taking her. "You live in South Beach?"

"Not far from where I met you."

The last few miles were quiet, but I could tell she was starting to relax as the music played and the wind blew in her hair. Not until I pulled into the parking garage to my condo did she visibly tense up again.

"What assumptions are you making now?" I teased her as I climbed out of the Bronco. She jumped out on her side before I could get around to help her and was shaking her head with a smirk.

"Just wondering how many women you bring home and cook for."

"What's it matter, Coconut? You're here now."

It would have been wiser to tell the truth, that I had never cooked for a woman before, but my guard was up. It was so obvious that right before I was going to kiss her earlier, her thoughts went to Hunter. Even if she wished he didn't exist, she still thought of him, which served as my reminder of what was really going on.

When we got to the elevator, I pressed the top floor button and leaned against the wall opposite Tatum. Crossing my arms, I eyed her, almost hoping she felt uncomfortable. It wasn't like me to be callous in any way. Making a woman uncomfortable never sat right with me, but Tatum was doing the same to me, and even if she didn't realize it, I had to return the feeling.

"How long have you lived here?"

"Almost a year."

"It's nice."

"You've only seen the elevator."

She sighed and turned to face me as the doors finally opened. "I don't know what else to say, Tripp. You're making me feel a million different things, and I'm not sure which of those feelings is winning."

"Same for me," I shrugged, then pulled her out of the elevator. If I stood there and let her look at me, she would see right through me.

My apartment was the only one on the twentieth floor, so the only door made it obvious where we were going. There wasn't much to my apartment since I lived there alone and hadn't been there long. I had never felt settled in Miami, so I never invested in much. One leather couch, an armchair by the balcony door, a TV I rarely watched, and a few small tables were all I had in the living room.

"That window is the only reason I chose this place. Nothing beats waking up and seeing how the waves are acting while I have my morning coffee."

"May I?" She asked, with her hand on the door handle.

"Of course."

She made her way onto the balcony while I fixed us a drink. Thankfully, I kept a stocked kitchen and plenty of wine on hand. Despite being out almost every night, I liked to eat at home. It was just a habit I had from growing up with a single mom. She worked three jobs, and I made sure the food she bought was cooked.

"This is beautiful," she sighed as I walked up next to her along the balcony's edge. Handing her the wine, she smiled and finally seemed to be relaxing again, and I couldn't decide if that was what I wanted her to do. Not when I was still buzzing with uncertainty.

"Enjoy the view," I motioned toward the water and the moon, "I'm going to make some dinner."

"Can I help?"

"No." That one word came out way angrier than I intended. But it was better than saying, "*I need to get away from you for a minute.*"

Tatum sat down and nodded while I made my way back inside. Pausing for a minute, I flashed back to waking up on the floor next to Hunter. He had that gorgeous girl at home, willing to keep him warm, and he chose a night on my tile, barely remembering anything. There was already a lack of respect for Hunter, but knowing what I knew now, that respect was down in the basement.

The dinner I had planned was quick and corny. All I was making was my mom's coconut rice recipe. When I decided to cook for Coconut, the first thing that popped into my brain was coconut rice. Mom made hers with instant rice, meaning it took less than fifteen minutes to prepare.

She seemed content on the balcony, so I carried our two plates out and sat them on the patio table. Then I disappeared again and came back with two glasses of water. Tatum was watching me with a smile, not even touching her fork yet.

"You confuse me, Tripp."

"Likewise, Tatum."

"How so?"

"You first."

Once I was settled, she grabbed her fork and took a bite, moaning like always. My cock instantly started to pay attention, the same way it had the first moment I saw her.

"You lost a big game tonight, yet you seem okay. I don't get it," she started with her inquiry.

"It sucks, but Cruz wouldn't just leave without a good reason. Rhys has had an unusual season as well. From my perspective, even though I didn't want to believe it, we felt doomed from the start."

"What about the rest of the team? You?"

"I'm not good enough to carry the team alone."

"That isn't true!"

"How do you know?"

"Because you wouldn't be a professional athlete if you weren't good enough."

"Don't misunderstand. I'm good, and I deserve to be a pro, but I'm not Rhys Peyton good. I'm a disposable asset for the Inferno."

Her lip curled out like she wanted to argue with me but stopped herself.

"Say it." I urged her.

"I overheard some people saying you were on thin ice. What did that mean?"

The fuck? Not that it wasn't true, but who would have enough insight to even know that?

"Did your boyfriend tell you that?" I snapped.

"What? No! I heard it after the game."

Probably Luca's wife. She was standing near Tatum when I left the locker room, and she was the biggest gossip I had ever seen. But I still wouldn't put it past Hunter to bad-mouth me, either.

"Sorry," I mumbled and took another bite of my rice. "But you confuse me too."

"How? I've been nothing but honest with you."

"So here's the thing." Realizing she was no longer eating, I also pushed my plate away and stood up. Rounding the table to stand in front of her, I leaned onto the arms of the chair and got close to her lips, exactly where I liked to be. "I've wanted to fuck you since the moment I saw you. But when you told me you were celebrating being over an ex, I knew that wasn't something I was interested in being in the middle of. Then I saw you in that restaurant, and it was like I was being told I had another chance. Yet, I get the feeling that thoughts of your ex are still lingering in your gorgeous head. It makes me ask myself if I am through caring or if I need to take a step back. It's frustrating, Coconut."

From the moment I said I wanted to fuck her, her breathing had increased. Sneaking my tongue out, I gently licked her lips, teasing her as if it was her pussy. Her arms started to shake, and I knew she wanted me as badly as I wanted her. She just wasn't sure what she was going to do about it yet.

"I want to make you forget about whoever thought it was a good idea to make you their second thought. Because you've been my first thought every day since we met, and all I can think about is what it would feel like to have your mouth around me while you make those cute little moans."

"It's complicated," she whispered, her defense weakening as her lips grazed mine.

"So you've said."

"I didn't expect to meet you and feel this way," she confessed. "I thought Hunter and I had more time."

It was the first time she spoke his name, and even though I knew exactly who she was talking about, I still flinched when I heard her say it. That was just enough to make me back away and stand upright. She was still breathing hard, so I picked up her water and handed it to her, nearly pushing it up to her mouth and forcing her to drink.

After a few gulps, I pulled the glass from her hand and set it back down. Then I pulled her to her feet and kissed her hard and passionately. My hands were on her waist, then her neck, then tracing a line down her thigh. Pressing my hard cock into her, I wanted her to feel what she did to me and know that despite Hunter and whatever complications she had, it didn't change how I felt.

But that was when I pulled back and nearly pushed her back into her chair. It hit me like a truck and made my head spin. No part of me cared about Hunter when it came to fucking her. Still, there was one thing Hunter could probably give her that I wasn't sure I could. It was exactly why I needed to stop kissing her until I knew what was happening with them.

Chapter Fourteen

Tatum

"Don't stop," I begged, reaching for Tripp. He looked like he had seen a ghost, his eyes wide and contemplative all of a sudden.

"Nothing has changed. I meant what I said, fucking you is as far as I go."

"Then do it already. Stop finding a reason not to."

"If there wasn't someone else in this twisted little game we are playing, then I wouldn't have ever hesitated."

"I'm the one that has to worry about the morality of the situation, Tripp. Not you."

"That's not true," he winced, then took a few long strides to the door, leaving me alone on the balcony for a minute. I felt so conflicted because it seemed like there was a piece of the puzzle that I wasn't given.

After a minute, I followed Tripp into the apartment and found him in the kitchen, cleaning the few dishes he had messed up when he made dinner. I could only watch and wait while he worked out his hesitations.

My phone buzzed from my bag that I had tossed onto the counter, but I ignored it, already knowing who it was. Hunter had no idea where I was because after calling me on Wednesday, I hadn't heard from him again. He didn't need to know that I was in Tripp Maddux's apartment and seconds away from falling to my knees in front of him.

Whatever Tripp was warring with, all of a sudden, I wanted to take it away. He made me feel wanted and sexy, and I wanted to make him feel the same way. We all had exes, and I wasn't sure why my having one was keeping Tripp from acting on every word he spoke to me.

"I'm here," I whispered to him once my phone stopped buzzing.

"He's calling again," Tripp huffed, listening to my phone start again.

"Ignore it."

"I can't!" He threw the dish towel he was holding and ran his hands through his hair. He reached into his pocket and threw his phone onto the counter next to where I was standing. It was buzzing as well, but I didn't want to look and invade his privacy.

He stood before me, his eyes boring into mine and his fingers tapping the counter with frustration. What he was feeling was completely lost on me, but I knew it had something to do with Hunter.

"It's been two years since anyone has touched me," I confessed. "Hunter and I broke up after college, he left town, and I never thought we'd get another chance. Then he came back and wanted to try again, only it faded into nothing. He hasn't touched me since he came back into my life. Do you know how that makes me feel? To think someone wants you, loves you, then doesn't even want to be with you? I broke up with him eight days ago, Tripp. I'm not asking for a happily ever after from you, but I am asking you to do all those things you said you wanted to do to me when I was just your Coconut. Empower me. Show me I'm worth more than a frantic phone call because he can't find me on a random Friday night."

Tripp took two long strides, and I was in his arms. He was carrying me as his lips crashed into mine, and we made our way into his bedroom. We left our phones in the kitchen, and once the buzzing was no longer in our ears, it was like Hunter disappeared altogether.

My legs were around Tripp's waist, and I was pulling at his shirt, desperate to take it off, even though it was impossible with how tightly he held me. I started moving my hips, grinding on his stomach before he threw me from his arms, landing me in the center of his bed.

"You better not regret this, Coconut. Because I've been trying to be nice."

"You've been tempting me since we met and you know it."

"My honest words and my angry actions are not the same thing."

"There's no reason to be angry. We all have exes, just do what you said you wanted to do and make me forget mine."

Stepping up to the end of the bed, he pulled me by my ankles so that I was on the edge and then pushed my legs apart, making me open for him as he gazed down at me. The shorts I wore to the game and the Inferno t-shirt I bought when I got there were still covering my body. Tripp still had a tight hold on my ankles so that I couldn't move my legs, but I slowly started pulling my shirt up, exposing my stomach inch by inch.

"Don't worry," I smirked. "I'm using you, too."

His snarl told me I didn't quite hit the mark, but he didn't pull away. Letting go of my ankles, he reached behind his head, pulled his shirt off, and tossed it onto the floor. Then he popped the button on his jeans and let them hang open while his hands returned to me.

Sliding from my knees to my thighs, Tripp kneaded my skin,

making me moan. He undid my shorts and pulled them off quickly, throwing them farther than he did his shirt. My knees were bent, and the heels of my feet were on the edge of the bed, holding me up while he stared down at me.

"You better not hate me for this," he bit out.

"Please," I begged. He had to keep going, or I was going to scream.

His hands skimmed my sides, and he pushed the t-shirt over my head. My hands grasped my breasts, squeezing them as he watched me unravel.

"Why wouldn't he want to touch this? See this?" Tripp mused, almost to himself.

"Am I going to have to make you forget about him?" I teased, throwing his words back at him. He shouldn't have cared about Hunter. It shouldn't have bothered him when I was practically begging him to fuck me.

My words pushed Tripp over the edge, and he flipped me around roughly, then pulled my ass into the air. His hand came down hard on my right cheek, a sting that somehow felt like a punishment. Only with Tripp it felt good, warranted. He was having trouble with something, and I was only goading him, making him crazier.

"Again," I moaned, listening to his heavy breathing behind me. "Make it hurt."

He did, and I moaned louder, squealing from how much harder his hand came down that time. His fingers started pressing on the center of my panties that covered my pussy, and he rubbed the wetness that had gathered in the thin fabric. When he snuck a finger into my folds, I started moving against him, already wanting to come from such a simple touch.

"It's been so long," I tried reminding him. "It just feels too good being touched, Tripp. So dang good."

"You should always be touched like this," he growled. "Why hasn't he touched you like this?"

He was bringing Hunter up again, and as mad as I wanted to be, it was turning me on more to hear him so angry that someone, even if it wasn't him, hadn't been making me feel as good as I did then.

"He's scared," I guessed, unsure of Hunter's problem, but I wanted to play along with Tripp. He wanted answers, and even though I didn't have the right ones, I knew it was turning him on to hear how much Hunter had let me down and how he was the one fixing it all.

"Scared of what?"

"Not being able to make me come."

"Did he ever make you come?"

"Once," I remembered. "My eyes were closed and I was picturing someone in the corner, watching us."

"Who was in the corner?"

"No face, no name, but just the idea of someone watching us made it more erotic."

Two fingers pushed inside me, and I squealed with the sudden invasion. He rubbed my core, his fingers moving in and out of me as his other hand kneaded my stinging skin. The buildup in my body was quick, and when I started to shake, he pulled out and spanked my ass again.

"Fuck, Tripp."

He pulled me upright by the ponytail and wrapped his arms around my chest. My back was against his chest, and his mouth was kissing my neck from my ear to my shoulder.

"You taste and feel better than I imagined."

"You're making me feel more than I imagined."

"You've never been treated right, Coconut. Hunter is a fucking fool. He should have been studying every fucking way possible to make you come. He should have taken notes, recorded your moans in his phone for reference, and made it his mission to please you every goddamn night."

His hand moved down my stomach and into my panties, where he curled two fingers and moved them inside me again. His other hand was under my bra, pinching my nipples. I could feel his cock pushing against his jeans, hard and pressing into me from behind. Tempting him again, I pushed my ass back and moved, wanting to feel as much of him as possible.

"Don't make me spank you again," he growled. "I'm in the middle of learning everything I need to know to make up for all the times you didn't get what you deserved."

"I'll die if you don't fuck me, Tripp. That is all you need to know."

"Are you on anything?" He growled, pulling his fingers from my pussy and touching my lips.

Nodding, I knew I was still taking a risk with him, but I was hoping that if he trusted me, I could trust him. Until he asked, though, I hadn't even considered the repercussions of what we were doing. Protection was the last thing crossing my mind.

The sound of my panties being ripped made me gasp, and then my bra was gone just as quickly. Reaching my arm back, I held on to Tripp's neck while he rubbed his hands everywhere he could reach.

Turning my head, I urged him to kiss me, and when he did, it was a mere graze before he pulled back. "I'm done just kissing you, Coconut."

Chapter Fifteen

Tripp

When I took Tatum to my apartment, there wasn't a doubt in my mind that I wanted her in my bed, but my mind was having a hard time getting past the fact that she was the girl Hunter was pining over. Even though I'd met her before he asked me to "distract her" for a night, it still felt somewhat wrong to fuck her.

Going back and forth between not giving a shit, and wondering if I was an asshole, was making me crazy. It was fucking with me trying to decide if I needed to tell Tatum the truth. Since I hadn't planned on seeing her again, it felt wrong to ruin whatever she and Hunter had left. But then I would remember that there was no way I could let her go after one night and be satisfied.

The final straw was the fact that her phone was ringing at the same time mine was. Looking down, I saw it was Hunter, and I knew her calls were also from him. He knew she was there with me. I just wasn't sure how he figured it out. It felt like it was only a matter of time before he came pounding on my door, though, and if he did, I wanted him to hear her screaming my name from the hallway.

Tossing my phone toward Tatum, I hoped she would see that Hunter was calling me. She needed to realize why I was talking the talk but was having difficulty walking the walk. It had nothing to do with who she and I were and everything to do with Hunter. She just never looked, and I never had the guts to make her.

Which was why I kept bringing him up and asking her questions. Almost forcing her to be as fucked as I was. She wasn't, though. She just begged for more, not even caring that I kept bringing Hunter in between us.

With her completely naked, I pushed her back onto the bed and flipped her onto her back again. She was so little that it was almost unfair how much control I could have over her. Spanking her ass when she taunted me wasn't fair either, but nothing was making sense, and all I could do was whatever I felt at that moment.

She stared up at me with her legs open while I lowered my jeans and kicked them aside. I didn't wear any underwear unless I was playing a match, so I was naked quicker than she expected.

Her tongue came out and licked her lips as she stared, then her eyes widened when she saw the shiny circular barbell pierced on the underside of my cock. It was safe to say she had never seen a Prince Albert piercing, and she sat up, reaching her hand out to touch me.

"Did that hurt?"

"Like a bitch. But I had it done when I needed to feel the pain."

Pushing her back down, I climbed over and kissed her, softly running my piercing through her folds so she could feel the cool metal.

"Will it hurt me?"

"No. I won't let it."

"Tripp?"

Lifting so I could see her eyes, I waited for her to tell me whatever she needed to say.

"Would you judge me if I came right now? With just your piercing touching me? Because..."

Pressing down harder, I realized she was fucking gone, and watching her come underneath me was better than anything I could have imagined. My arms were shaking as I kept my weight off of her. Not because I was holding myself up but because I was holding myself back.

"You look beautiful when you come," I groaned, still moving my cock between the folds of her pussy. "I'm holding myself back, wanting to make sure I see you like that over and over again."

A single tear fell down her cheek, and she pushed her tits into my chest. Her hands were holding onto my biceps, her nails pressing into my skin almost painfully. When I was sure she was ready for more, I lined myself up to her core and pushed inside of her, making her scream as the metal hit nerves I was sure she had never felt.

"Feels good, doesn't it baby? Now you know why I wanted to make sure we didn't need anything between us. I wanted to make sure you got everything."

"Oh my god," she breathed as I thrust harder and harder.

Her walls were already squeezing me, and I knew she was close to coming again. Grinding myself lower, I rubbed her clit with each movement. Her head started shaking back and forth, so I lowered my head and captured her lips, keeping her still as she came.

My tongue was as deep as I could go, and my lips were ravenous as I tasted her. She fought back with her tongue, taking the energy the orgasm was giving her and forcing me to lose control.

Twitching a few times, I finally let go, my release making me pull my lips from her. Since there wasn't much in my room, my groan echoed off the walls as I spilled inside her. She wrapped her arms around my neck, almost uncomfortably, while she tried moving beneath me for more.

My cock couldn't take it, the sensation was too much, so I pulled out of her and made her stop moving with the strength of my hand on her stomach. Then I lowered down between her messy legs and stroked my tongue up, tasting the evidence of our pleasure.

Her legs started to shake again, opening even wider to accommodate my broad shoulders. When I licked her again, I closed my mouth over her clit and sucked, keeping my eyes on her to watch her reactions.

"Mmmm," I moaned, loving how we tasted together. "So good."

Her mouth fell open, and her head fell back. "Tripp," she cried. "Oh, Tripp, fuck."

I wanted to comment on her dirty mouth, but I didn't want to risk taking away the pleasure she was feeling. Once I started moving my tongue back and forth over her clit, she erupted, and I felt her practically coat my chin. It was as close to seeing a woman squirt as I had ever seen, and my cock was getting hard again.

"We are never going to be able to stop, Coconut. This is how you and I are going to have to live until we kill each other because just tasting you is making me want more."

"I can't. I'm already dead."

"The fuck you are," I growled, then sat up quickly, pushing my cock into her before she could expire. She nodded her head and started chanting, "Yes," as I fucked her harder than I did the first time. It was as if I was chasing something that I was scared would disappear if I didn't hurry. Probably because I had never come twice the way I was about to do inside Tatum's sweet pussy.

"That's my girl," I soothed her. "You can take way more than you think you can."

"You feel so good. Tripp, you feel so dang good."

"Come again," I leaned down and whispered into her ear. "Come on my cock baby. One more time, just for me."

She squeezed and screamed, the echoes of her cries carrying throughout my apartment. When I was sure she was coming, I let myself release again, growling like a fucking lion as my body felt tense and then immediately weakened.

Falling onto her petite frame, I kept moving my hips, slower and slower, until neither of us was making a sound. Tatum's hands started caressing my back, her fingertips creating goosebumps on my flesh. Somehow, I still had the urge to move my cock that was still inside of her body, but I knew I really would kill us both.

Lifting, I smiled down at her, hoping she felt as good as I did, but all I saw was confusion and a blank stare.

"Did I go too far?" Fuck, I really did lose control.

"No," she was quiet, still looking at the ceiling. "That was the best sex I have ever had in my entire life."

"Then what's wrong?"

She finally looked at me and gave me a soft smile. Her finger pointed to the crease between my brows and rubbed, trying to smooth it out.

"If you listen closely, my phone is buzzing in the other room."

"You don't have to worry about him, Tatum. I don't know what the fuck there is left between you two, but I know two things for sure. One, he doesn't care enough about you to make you a priority, and two, he doesn't know how to make you come."

She smiled and nodded, "That's true but..."

"But nothing."

She laughed, her chest shaking slightly, reminding me that I was nearly smothering her with the weight of my body. Lifting, I gently pulled out of her and then carried her in my arms to the shower.

Her body was weak, so we bathed quickly, and I helped her get dressed. I opened my mouth several times to tell her she should stay all night, but then her phone would ring again, and I decided against it.

Hunter must have called her a hundred times and called me another hundred. I had expected him to show up and bang my door down, but he never did.

But as if he knew, the calls stopped for both of us the second we got into the parking garage and back in Shelly. Tatum thought he had just given up, but every fiber of my being knew it wasn't a coincidence. Somehow, he was keeping tabs, and it made me wary of dropping her off.

"Let me walk you up," I insisted, already parking Shelly and looking around the parking lot of her apartment complex. She didn't live far, just over the bridge in Miami. Her apartment complex was older, but it seemed well-kept.

"You don't have to," she smiled.

"Just want to get you home safely, Coconut." And make sure Hunter isn't there to fuck with her.

We held hands as we walked up the stairwell to the second floor and down the open walkway to her door. She unlocked the door and turned on the light, allowing me a view of the main rooms. There was a small kitchen off the side of the living room, and a small hallway leading to what I assumed was the only bedroom.

"Do you want to come in?" She asked.

The answer was no, but I started nodding, not wanting to say goodnight yet.

Before I stepped foot into the apartment, a text sounded on my phone, and I pulled it out to read it without thinking of who it could be.

Don't go inside, motherfucker.

Chapter Sixteen

Tatum

It felt like Tripp was being protective, and I invited him in because I felt the need to be protected. The calls from Hunter all night started to scare me, and it wasn't lost on me that he could have been angrily waiting for me.

He was no longer my boyfriend, nor had he ever been violent, but after the way Tripp treated me and took care of my body, talking to Hunter was the last thing I wanted to do. A conversation with him scared me because I didn't know what to say.

"You need to sleep," Tripp stopped abruptly in the doorway after I invited him in.

"I think I know what I need, Daddy," I teased him in a way I always did, thinking it would make him laugh. But his face was blank as he stared down at his phone. "What's wrong?"

"Um," he shook his head, then slid the phone into his pocket. "I have an early meeting at the stadium tomorrow."

"Just you?" I started to panic that the lady in the waiting area was right. That conversation felt like a lifetime ago, but it all came back to me with full force. "Are they mad at you?"

"Fuck," he sighed, then wrapped me into a hug. "It's kinda cute that you are worried about me."

"You just showed me your superpower, Tripp. You can't leave me now."

It was another joke, but I could tell it made him uncomfortable for me to mention needing him. He had said from the start that sex was all he had to offer because he never did anything with permanence. Even his apartment was bare, showing he really did expect to leave Miami at any given moment. I just hoped that moment wasn't tomorrow.

"I'll call ya sometime," he squeezed me, then stepped back outside my door. He walked down the breezeway without looking back, and I watched as he took the stairs quickly. His head was on a swivel, looking around the parking lot as if the boogie man were waiting.

When he jumped into his Bronco, he looked up at me, giving me a small wave before peeling out. Then I locked myself inside and walked around to make sure I was alone, just on the off chance Hunter decided to wait for me somewhere—like my bed.

Whatever, he wouldn't be caught dead in my bed.

Once I realized he wasn't there, I felt terrible for even considering it a possibility. Hunter was a lot of things, but he wasn't a psycho. He knew we weren't together, and he knew why. There had to be a reason he had called me so much, and I felt like now that I was home, I should call him back and make sure everything was okay.

Picking my phone up to dial, I scrolled to his name and started to hit send when a knock on my door sounded loudly.

"Tay?" Hunter's voice came through the wood. "Tay, are you okay?"

Running to the door, I opened it, and he barged in, looking messy and chaotic. His hands combed through his hair, and he turned to face me as I shut the door. "What's wrong?"

"I've been trying to call you."

"I've been out," I snapped defensively. "Were you waiting for me to get home?"

"Fuck," he shook his head, trying to calm down. "No, I just have good news that I've been dying to tell you. Yeah, when you didn't answer, I got worried. Then I became more worried. Then even more... Fuck. I just drove up, regretting that I didn't try coming here earlier. Have you been home all night?"

"Um." What did I say? What was the correct answer? "No. I went to the Inferno game with a friend."

"Why didn't you at least tell me that, Tay? I wouldn't have been so worried. Or, why didn't you answer your phone, or text me, just long enough to keep my mind from thinking you were dead in a ditch somewhere?"

"Hey," I held my hands up, then walked closer to him. It took everything in me not to tell him that I didn't have to tell him where I was going. It wasn't his job to worry about me. Instead, I was attempting to settle him down, placing my hands on his chest in a calming manner. He grabbed me and held me closer than I intended to be. "I know you don't like the Inferno, Hunt, so I didn't tell you so you wouldn't get upset."

"Fuck Tay, I know sports is your job. I knew eventually you'd have to cover the Inferno."

That was the moment I should have corrected him and told him that going to the game had nothing to do with my job. But that would be when he decided to press for more information, and I was too tired to humor him.

"I was about to go to bed, Hunt. Can we talk about this tomorrow?"

"Of course," he whispered, still holding my hands against him so I couldn't back up. He leaned in closer, and I thought he might kiss me, making me cringe. "Can I at least tell you the news I've wanted to tell you all day?"

"Yeah," I smiled, seeing his mood lift and some light start shining back in his eyes. "Tell me."

"Ironically enough, it has to do with the Inferno. They invited me to their postseason camp that starts in a few weeks. If all goes well, I may end up with a spot on the roster."

My eyes widened, and my heart beat with excitement. It was all Hunter ever dreamed of, and even as his friend, I was so excited for him that I jumped into his arms. He spun me around and laughed, burying his head into my neck and laughing.

When he set me down, he held my face, and a genuine smile was exchanged between Hunter and me. For a moment, I felt guilty for not answering his call. Had I been with anyone but Tripp, I would have.

"Next year, when you have to go to an Inferno game, you can wear my jersey and cheer me on. It will be just like we always dreamt it would be."

There was no hesitation when I nodded because there was no reason why I wouldn't support Hunter if he played for the Inferno. And even though I had just spent the night being fucked ten ways to Sunday by Tripp Maddux, my heart warmed to Hunter more as he mentioned our dreams. Maybe I was wrong. Perhaps he had always been looking ahead and knew that he had to get his plans together before he could commit to me again.

"Can I stay here tonight?" He asked, with an irresistible smile on his face.

"Sure," I nodded, "But we aren't together, remember? So you need to sleep on the couch."

His excited smile fell before he pushed his cheeks back up. "I know, Tay. But everything is falling back into place."

When I woke up the following day, Hunter was already gone, and I had four missed calls and a voicemail from Tripp. It was barely seven in the morning, and I already felt like the day was off to a rocky start. The calls from Tripp worried me more than the hundred I had missed from Hunter the night before. The meaning of that wasn't lost on me. And Hunter being gone confused the hell out of me. After everything he had said the night before, I thought he might want to spend the morning together.

But I was also relieved because Hunter wasn't my first thought when I opened my eyes. My sore thighs, the stinging skin on my ass, and somewhere deep inside me all ached from being with Tripp.

The best kind of ache.

As I made some coffee, I listened to Tripp's voicemail to ensure everything was okay.

"Hey Coconut. I know it's five in the morning, I know it's Saturday, and I know I've called four times. But I haven't been able to sleep and I just needed to know if you were okay. I have practice until noon, but then I'm gonna be at our spot. Meet me there?"

The line ended, and I held my phone to my chest with a goofy smile on my face. Our spot had to mean the Beach Club, where we met. Since he didn't mention his morning meeting, I assumed he'd want to talk about it when we were together, too. So I called the Beach Club, booking a cabana for the two of us to have privacy.

A few hours later, on my way out of the door with my beach

bag, I got a text from Hunter asking me to meet him at the university. He was probably working out there since the women's team still technically employed him. That was where he'd be spending most of his days until the Inferno camp, which made me excited for him.

Despite my budding lust for Tripp and our incredible night together, I still loved Hunter. There would be a part of me that always loved Hunter and wanted him to have his dreams come true, but if I had been as in love with him as I thought I was, I probably wouldn't have fallen into Tripp's bed so quickly.

Or would I?

Was it possible to have feelings for them both?

When I got to the beach club, my phone started ringing before I could get out of the car, and I saw that it was Hunter. Since I didn't answer the night before, I did that time quickly, so he knew I wouldn't be there.

"Hello?"

"Where are you?" He sounded frustrated. It had only been fifteen minutes since he texted me, so the anger in his voice didn't feel warranted.

"Excuse me?"

"I texted you, but you didn't text me back."

"Hunter, I was driving to the beach. I just pulled into the parking lot when your call came in."

"I'm doing some workouts today," he explained, like it was apparent I had to leave the beach and run to him. "It's been a while since you saw me play. I thought you'd come watch."

"Do I have to remind you we broke up?"

"I'm just asking for some support."

"I hate that it took a breakup to get this much attention from you."

"It's the timing. That's all it is. I've been working hard for this opportunity."

"So the night you were in the club and never called me back, what? You rubbing elbows with the university advisors for that head coaching job? Or was that—"

"I was with Tripp Maddux," he cut me off, making me freeze in silence. "He's a friend of mine. How do you think I got in the camp with the Inferno?"

"Tripp Maddux?"

"Yeah Tay," he softened his tone. "I didn't want to say anything because I wasn't sure it would happen, but it did. And now that everything is righting itself, I could use the support."

"Oh my God."

"Come to the university. Come watch me play for a while."

Shaking my head, I was still too stunned to speak. He couldn't see me, so I knew I had to say something, but my chest felt like it would explode.

"You know Tripp Maddux?"

"Of course I do, we played in League One together, remember?"

No, I didn't. Despite whatever Hunter thought, I didn't pay attention to his League One career. After he left, anything to do with Hunter was too painful, and it was easier for me to live my life without checking in on him. All I knew when he returned was that he held a grudge against the team.

"I'm at the beach," I said quickly, needing to get off the phone. "We can talk later. Have fun today." His voice was still on the line, asking me to wait, but I hung up and made my way out to the cabana, leaving my phone so I didn't have to hear it ringing all day.

I still wasn't sure what it meant, that Hunter and Tripp knew each other, or whether it meant anything at all. It could have been a coincidence, but it didn't feel like that was the case. Regardless, I decided to ask Tripp about it and have him explain the connection before I jumped to any conclusions.

As I got settled in the cabana, I laughed at how crazy it was that we were all connected, but then, as I sat there waiting, my mood changed, and more thoughts ran into my head. Tripp knew Hunter, but did he know that Hunter was the same guy that called me while he was fucking me? Did he know about the ironic connection? And if not, should I tell him the truth?

Chapter Seventeen

Tripp

Tatum never messaged me back, so I was going in blind in terms of her being there. After I left her so quickly the night before, I wouldn't blame her if she didn't want to see me. But when I got that text from Hunter, I knew he was watching.

He had started calling me and Tatum at the same time, and it was obvious that he figured out we were together, but the fact that he knew I was walking into her apartment was a whole new level of disturbing. Even going as far as sending the text from an app that hid his phone number, like I wasn't going to know who the fuck it was. I wasn't caving to his demands when I left. I just wanted to try finding his sorry ass.

For an hour, I circled the parking lot and neighborhood, looking for him, but since I didn't know what he drove, it was impossible. He never answered my calls either, but I had to conclude that he was on foot and disappeared when he saw me leave.

He was being stealthy, and I couldn't even sleep thinking about him stalking Tatum the way he seemed to be doing. What lengths was he willing to go to? And was he asking me to meet up with her a part of his plan? Did he already know we'd met?

Then there was the darker part of me wondering if Tatum knew the whole time. It was easy to wash that thought away because what would she have to gain? What would anyone achieve? Plus, the entire ruse to hang out with Hunter's girl-friend was apparently my idea in the first place.

Practice had been a waste of time, and obviously, there was no meeting I had to attend. The team was defeated morally, and in the standings. For the remaining two games, the starters wouldn't even be on the field, and Cruz had taken a leave of absence. We were all worried about him, and I agreed to help keep an eye on him, but I was also selfishly distracted by my own issues.

Leaving my surfboard with the concierge, I entered the outdoor area of Nikki's, where the umbrellas and canopies were hiding everyone from the sun. Without wanting to look like a jerk, I subtly walked around and looked for Tatum before asking for my own setup and texting her to tell her I was there.

"Mr. Maddux?" The host ran up, almost out of breath, trying to get my attention. "This note was left for you."

Nodding a thank you, I took the note and smiled when I saw the same handwriting my last message was left with:

I'm in a cabana. Come find me.

The cabanas were private and way more luxurious than the standard setup. You had to reserve one beforehand, and I didn't have the forethought to do that. But I was glad Coconut had. Each cabana faced the ocean and had private curtains that fell around the other three sides of the square roof. Instead of loungers, there was a queen-sized bed with enough pillows to stock a department store. The best part was that each cabana also had its own private server, meaning we would never run out of piña coladas.

The only problem was, I didn't want to peek into each one trying to find her. The odds of me accidentally stumbling onto two people fucking was high.

"Excuse me?" I hollered back at the retreating host, who handed me the note. He had almost made his way off the beach but turned around and faced me with a big smile.

"Yes, Mr. Maddux?"

"Can you just take me to her?" He knew what I meant because he knew who wrote the note and what it said. "Please don't make me look."

He gave me a small laugh, knowing why I was hesitant, and shook his head. "She told me not to tattle. She told me twice." He held up two fingers and winked before turning around and walking into the main building.

Running a hand down my face, I groaned and looked down the beach toward the cabanas. There were only ten of them, but with my luck, Tatum would be in the last one. That was when it hit me: the tiny hint the host gave me. He held up two fingers and winked, so maybe that meant she was in the second one.

The walking path was behind the cabanas for privacy, so when I got to the second one, I stepped off the trail into the sand, making my way around the curtain wall. Thankfully, Coconut sat there with her legs crisscrossed, staring into the ocean in a daze. She barely even saw me approaching.

She jumped out of her thoughts when I knelt on the bed next to her.

"You made me find you again," I teased, running a hand up her leg.

Her straight smile wasn't full of excitement or lust; it was lost and distracted. I got up next to her and laid on my side, facing her and propping my head on my hand.

"What did he do?" I asked on instinct, feeling in my gut that Hunter had somehow fucked with her mood.

"You tell me."

"Excuse me?"

She turned to face me and tilted her head, her eyes looking angry. "Tell me what he did."

Fuck, she knew. But shouldn't I be the one that was pissed?

"Having a change of heart?" I asked bitterly, not moving from my seemingly relaxed position. My muscles had tightened, and my jaw was locked, but my eyes held hers, not giving in to whatever she wanted to fight with me about.

"He came over after you left, and stayed all night." What the fuck?

"Is that supposed to bother me? I don't care who you fuck. In fact, good for you, finally getting him to bring his dick out for you."

"We didn't...How dare you think I'd sleep with him on the same night I was with you."

"If it's his dick you want, and being with me kicked him into giving you what you want, then you're welcome."

Her hand came across my face, slapping me and forcing me to sit up and grab her wrist. Twisting around, I laid her back and hovered over the top of her. My cock was getting hard because that was the only way it knew to be when she was next to me.

She shook her arms, trying to get out of my hold, and once I was sure she knew I had the upper hand, I released her, not wanting her to feel trapped. "I knew all you wanted from me was sex. But I didn't realize it was a game to you."

"What happened last night?"

"He slept on my couch!" She hissed. "But he showed up in the first place to tell me he's been invited to the Miami Inferno postseason workouts."

"What?" Raising myself up, I almost flew to my feet but kept myself on the mattress. Before I could say anything else, the server knocked on the wooden post of the cabana, warning us she was coming in.

"Can I get you two some lunch?" A woman in tight khaki shorts and an unbuttoned, collared shirt asked. She had a tiny bathing suit top on underneath and was barefoot. The only thing that even made it look like she worked there was the fact that all the servers wore khakis.

"I'm good," I told her, hoping she left.

"Me too," Tatum whispered.

"Oh my god!" She squealed. "You're Tripp Maddux."

Nodding was all I did to confirm what she had just realized, and I hoped that was enough to make her leave.

"Can I get an autograph and maybe a picture?"

"Not right now," I tried to sound nice. "I'm spending time with my girl. Maybe as we leave."

She nodded and backed away, looking a little embarrassed. Fuck, I didn't want her feeling bad, but whatever Tatum was about to say was more important than anything else.

"I'm not your girl," Tatum snapped as soon as we were alone again.

"Would you have rather me tell her to leave because we were about to fuck?"

"Either way, it's a lie."

"Let's get back to your boyfriend. He got invited to the Inferno camp?"

"He told me you arranged it," she laughed humorlessly. "Don't act stupid."

"I did no such fucking thing. Why would I do that when I'm not even sure I'll get invited? And even if I did, wouldn't that make you happy?"

"It doesn't make me happy that you knew all along who my boyfriend was."

"He told you that?"

"He didn't have to, you just did."

"What the hell is going on, Tatum?"

"You said from day one you just wanted to fuck me and you did. I showed up today way too excited to see you, and after I got his call about knowing you, my head was all over the place. I'm not supposed to feel anything for you."

"When I met you, I didn't know who your boyfriend was, Tatum. When I saw you in that restaurant, I didn't know then, either. But when you said your name, that was when I knew. Remember that look on my face? How shocked I was?"

"Why didn't you say anything?"

"Because I was supposed to be doing Hunter a favor that night. He sent me to meet up with you so that you weren't mad at him when he didn't show up."

Her mouth fell open, and she started shaking her head. "Why would he do that? It doesn't make sense."

"It doesn't, you're right. Just like it doesn't make sense that he knew we were together last night."

"He didn't—"

"When I tossed my phone toward you, it was Hunter that was calling. Every time your phone stopped ringing, mine would start buzzing in my pocket. It went back and forth, making me crazier and crazier. You refused to look at my phone, but he wouldn't have called me and you both unless he knew."

"What are you trying to say?"

"Before I fucked you, I tried showing you, telling you, but you didn't care."

"This is so fucked up."

"Oh, Coconut, it gets even worse."

Chapter Eighteen

Tatum

Everything that Tripp was telling me was making my head spin. Before he arrived, I had worked myself up as I repeatedly thought about Tripp knowing Hunter. But if everything Tripp said was true, I had bigger problems with Hunter than I realized.

"What else?" I asked, nearly breathless.

As soon as he realized how upset I was, he softened and pulled me up into his lap. My arms wrapped around his neck, and his arms made me feel safe as they engulfed me in a hug. His head shook, and I knew whatever else he had to tell me was exactly what he promised it'd be—worse.

"He texted me last night from some messenger app as I was walking inside your apartment. He knew I was there, Tatum. He told me I better not go inside. The only reason I left was because I thought I could find him, or call him and figure out what the hell he was doing."

My body started shaking uncontrollably, the serene setting having no effect on my anxiety. The only thing that helped was that I wasn't alone. Tripp was caressing my back, whispering soothing tones into my ear, and letting me process what he had just told me.

"He called me today," I finally whispered, knowing Tripp was right. "He asked me to come to the university to watch him work out. I didn't answer the text, just came straight out here, but when I pulled into the parking lot, he called and asked me why I wasn't there."

"He knew you were at the beach, didn't he?"

"I told him, but he knew I wasn't home, that's for sure."

"Fuck," Tripp gritted out. "Has he ever been like this?"

"No. Not when we were together a few years ago. I don't know what he did when he was in League One, but he's been standoffish since we reconnected. That was why I broke up with him. I thought he was back to try again with me the way we were, but..."

"Shhh," Tripp pulled my hair, tilting my head back, and put his forehead to mine. "It's okay, Coconut. You know now and can distance yourself until he realizes you're no longer his."

"It hurts," I confessed. "Honestly, I don't understand why he asked you to meet with me that night, either. Did he know we had already met?"

"I don't know. But before I met you, he told me a little about you. I promise that isn't what any of this has been."

"Then what's it been?"

"Just me and you, meeting each other and having fun. Hunter is just a coincidence."

I didn't believe in coincidences but considered what Tripp had said. It explained why he had been so messed up the night before when he was warring with himself before we had sex.

"Okay," I nodded, my head still against his. "I know."

"You're still shaking."

"I thought today would be different. This wasn't on my

bingo card for the day. Hunter is scaring me. And I didn't get this cabana for us to argue in. I got it for us to...."

"You did good," he moaned. "No one can see us. We aren't arguing, we just had a misunderstanding. I'm no longer messed up over the morality of our situation either. Especially now that you know as much as I do. And I can make you forget Hunter, just like I told you I wanted to do."

His mouth moved to my neck, and he sucked hard on my skin, then gently bit his way to my shoulder. Running my fingers through his hair, I started rocking against him, feeling his cock already hardening.

"You deserve better than him," Tripp moaned. "And until he's out of your life for good, I want to help you not to care that he's gone."

"Please," I cried. The anxiety from hearing about Hunter was quickly turning into a need to have Tripp inside me again.

"No one can see us. But I bet you wish they could, don't you, Coconut? You want that server to come back around and watch you climbing on top of my cock?"

My moan was loud enough that anyone walking behind us could have heard and would know what was happening. Tripp was right about the server. Even though I had been upset when she came to check on us, I still wanted to claim Tripp. I considered climbing into his lap right then and there and kissing him so she knew to fuck off. All she had done was ask for an autograph, but considering he was lying next to a woman, it felt like the wrong time to fangirl. I wondered if she had done it on purpose, expecting Tripp to flirt back with her in front of me.

"Fuck that bitch," I moaned, making him smile against my skin.

"That's my girl. She may not be able to see you, but make sure she knows who belongs on this cock."

My breathing was erratic, sweat dripping out of every pore,

not only from Tripp but from the heat of the beach. "Take your shirt off."

He pulled back and pulled the plain white t-shirt over his head. His body was also coated in sweat, and I rubbed my hands over his pecs, not caring how dirty we felt. Then I reached into the waistband of his coral swim shorts and wrapped my hand around his girth.

Tripp hissed and pushed into my hand, making me feel like I had a crown on my head and ruled over his body the way he did mine. My thumb flicked his piercing, and I eyed him, wondering if it hurt.

"Slide your bathing suit over and climb on before I come in your hand."

"You make me feel crazy."

"Don't make me spank you again," he growled. "Get that perfect pussy on top of my cock or I'll make sure the whole beach hears you screaming."

Looking around, I realized my bathing suit cover did more than cover my suit. It also hid where Tripp and I were connected, making it look like I was just sitting on his lap. That made me feel more emboldened, and I lifted and pressed his tip to my clit. Rubbing his dick on me a few times, I watched as I saw what our bodies looked like against one another.

Then I lifted higher and eased down, my legs shaking from how good he felt. He let me go slow, not taking control and watching me with his sharp eyes. His tongue was licking his lips as he tried to hide a grimace from my slow pace, creating torture for him.

"That's my girl," he hissed once he was entirely inside me. From our position, it felt like he was deeper than he was the night before. It was almost uncomfortable, but at the same time, the fear of him tearing my body open was only adding to the intensity.

Rocking on his lap, I was instantly close to coming, and I had to stop moving, too scared I would crumble, and it would be over before we were both satisfied. Tripp grabbed a hold of my hips and made me start moving again, grunting as he fucked me from underneath me. His patience was wavering, and I almost cried, knowing the magic would dissipate as soon as we both shattered.

"She's watching us," Tripp whispered, then grabbed my cheeks, preventing me from looking back. "She heard you and came back, but if you look, you're going to panic."

"I'm panicking," I whined, with my eyes wide.

Tripp's eyes moved to the side of the cabana and then back to me. "Show her who owns me, Coconut. Give her something to watch. Make her think twice about coming back and asking for an autograph while I'm inside of you. The fucking disrespect."

"Can she hear you?"

"She knows I see her," Tripp spoke louder, looking toward her again. "But she's welcome to watch you ride my cock."

My clit was pulsing, and I no longer had control of my body. Moving on his cock, I moaned and ran my hands back up his chest the way I had before. Instead of grinding, I started bouncing, and Tripp was huffing as his eyes remained on me.

If the woman was still there, I no longer cared. It wasn't like I could stop even if I wanted to. Tripp lowered his hands from my neck, and instead of looking back, I held onto his shoulders for leverage and rode him harder.

"Oh fuck," he moaned, then pulled me down to kiss me. His tongue was fighting with mine, and I started squeezing his cock, unable to hold back.

"I'm coming," I moaned against his mouth, loud enough that whoever was watching could hear me.

"I feel you, baby. You're so fucking...Ahhh."

His hips started moving, but he was jerky and uncontrolled. His mouth was open against mine, and I could tell he was coming as he gasped into my mouth.

Reality sunk in when we were both nothing but noodles, and I looked back to see our voyeur. "Did she leave?"

"She was never there," Tripp growled, making me gasp from his fib. "But you wanted her to be. My little desperado loves being reckless and dangerous."

"I'm not—" I stopped talking and realized I was about to deny what he had just said but then decided I didn't want to. "Maybe I am, but I've imagined it so many times in my head that I can't help it. Call it my kink, but it gives me a little thrill."

"Don't apologize or explain yourself, Coconut. Whatever you want, you get. Remember?"

His words reminded me of the first time he said them. After he first kissed me and told me to figure things out with Hunter. That made me think about him again, and my shoulders slumped forward.

"Hey," Tripp soothed, his cock still inside of me as he wrapped me into a hug. "I'm sorry this was how the story went."

Damn, I was too. But I was also relieved.

Chapter Nineteen

Tripp

"Where's your phone?"

"I left it in my car. That was why I wrote the note for you to find me."

We had managed to disconnect our bodies and lay down next to each other, watching the waves crash onto the shore of the beach. The cabana had fans that blew directly onto us, and we were still trying to cool down.

Sighing, I almost laughed. "I thought that note was leading me to Narnia."

"I wrote it, and then was left to my thoughts for too long."

That made me laugh, not because it was funny, but because the mindfuck Hunter gave us was out of hand. What the fuck was he thinking?

The server knocked on the outside of the cabana and then poked her head around. "How are we doing? Can I get you some drinks?"

Tatum leaned over onto my chest, and my arm wrapped around her as she spoke. "Can you bring us two piña coladas?"

The server's eyes locked with mine, asking if that's what I

really wanted, so I held up two fingers and added. "In two coconuts, please. Pink straws."

"Of course," she smiled. "Any lunch?"

"Are you hungry, baby?" I squeezed Tatum, laying the affection on thick. After making Tatum think the server was watching us fuck, she was claiming me in a way that I never thought would be sexy. Yet, how she leaned in and held onto me made my dick hard again, and I wanted to feed into even more.

"How about some cheese dip?"

"Mmm, sounds perfect." Looking back to the server, I nodded. "Two orders of cheese dip as well."

"Absolutely, I'll put that order in."

She disappeared, and I started laughing again, making Tatum look up with a smile. "I couldn't help it," she confessed.

"Mmm it's sexy as fuck," I moaned.

"I practically peed on you, Tripp. You're not even mine."

"Yeah, Coconut," I sighed. "I think I am."

We were quiet so long after that I thought Tatum had fallen asleep. She was still lying on my chest, not moving, and her breathing had evened out. All I could do was lay still and think about how fast things could change and when you least expected it.

I'd have laughed if someone had told me a few weeks ago that I'd be holding someone in my arms, thinking of ways to protect them. But that was precisely what I was doing. I told myself that it wasn't my place to protect Tatum, but I felt like it was all I wanted to do.

"You're thinking hard," she whispered.

"I thought you fell asleep."

"We are both thinking hard."

"Do me a favor and check your phone when you get in your car. Maybe Hunter is tracking you that way."

She tensed up, and I hated that I made her uncomfortable

again, but before we got distracted and moved on, I needed to remind her that Hunter was crossing the line and she needed to figure out to what extent. Unless he was stalking her physically, he had to have somehow set up a way to track her phone. It was the only plausible explanation.

The mood lightened once our drinks were brought, and the rest of the day was easy. We laughed and talked, staying off the topic of Hunter and telling each other more about ourselves. Never before had I told anyone about my mom, but I found myself telling Tatum everything.

"She worked her ass off for me. When I signed with the Inferno, I took my bonus and paid off her house. It was the least I could do, and all she allowed me to do. She still works at a diner. She loves it though. All her friends are there and she likes chatting with the regulars. One day, I'll get her on a plane to come to a game, but she's not a traveler, so who knows when that will be."

"Is that why you've never had someone at a game to watch you play?"

"Yeah, it's not like I have extended family or a lot of friends."

"Me either. My parents are a mess. My mom takes my dad back, probably once a month. He isn't a terrible father, but he's a shitty husband, and my brother and I have had to learn how to separate that for the sake of our sanity."

"Yeah, that sounds complicated."

"How was your dad? Was he as complicated as mine?"

"He was a lot like me. Or I'm a lot like him. He was a good dad but didn't work. I think he had dreams of being a professional surfer, but that dream made it hard for my mom. When I think of him, I think of the Bronco and the necklace he had dangling on the rearview mirror. Beads made of driftwood, with scrolls that looked like S's carved in them. I'd be in the backseat, staring at that necklace, wondering where he got it. His name was Soli, so I assumed that's why it had the S-like scrolls. But that is almost my only memory. I was twelve when he died, old enough to have more memories, but it's just that one that has stuck with me."

"I'm so sorry." She brushed her thumb over my bottom lip, her eyes looking at me in a way I had never been looked at before. "I bet he was a good guy with big dreams. Nothing wrong with that."

"Are you like your mom?"

"I've been worried that I'd turn into her one day. That I'd never feel like I deserved more than being someone's second option. That I would become obsessed with someone, even though they weren't good for me."

"Hunter?" I asked, almost scared to hear the answer and equally afraid I would piss her off.

"Even knowing how crazy he's being, I still care about him."

That should have hurt, but it didn't. Tatum and Hunter had a history that I would probably never experience. But I did hate that Tatum knew he was following and manipulating her, and she couldn't cut those feelings off.

With the conversation returning to Hunter, I knew I had to change it again, not for her, but for me. Hate was officially the only thing I felt toward Hunter, and I didn't want that hate to dim the rest of our day.

Scooping Tatum into my arms, I ran toward the water. Just like I had the day we met, I lowered her into the water, and we went down to our knees. That day, I stopped myself from kissing her, but that was no longer an option.

My lips found hers, and my hands pulled her body into mine. The waves were calm, and it made hanging on to her easier. Nikki's was an adults-only beach club, so I knew with the stretch of beach we were on, there wouldn't be any little prying eyes.

We weren't the only couple out there in each other's arms. Spinning Tatum around, I pressed her back against my chest and put my mouth to her ear. My left hand kept her close to me while my right hand pushed into the tiny bottoms of her bathing suit.

"Look at that couple, Coconut," I whispered, loving teasing her and turning her on. "I bet that guy over there has his cock in her pussy. Just like us, they don't give a fuck who sees them or knows what they're up to."

"I...I..."

She couldn't finish her thought as I started moving my fingers back and forth over her clit. "You what? Don't want anyone to see you? It doesn't turn you on?"

"Everything about you turns me on. We could be alone in the dark and I would still come for you. You barely have to touch me, Tripp."

"I know you would," I huffed. "And later, when we are at my place, and alone in my bed, I will do just that, but right now, just look around. Enjoy how twisted this is."

In the cold water, I could feel the warmth between her legs as she started to come. Her arms came up to hold onto my neck as her body shook in pleasure.

Then she turned around and wrapped her legs around me while I pushed my shorts down. Impaling her on my cock, she moaned, but no one was close enough to hear her. Making sure she was angled toward everyone, I quickly thrust into her, chasing my own pleasure.

"Do they see us?" I asked her as she looked over my shoulder.

"Probably," she moaned. "You're making the water move and I'm bouncing up and down."

Fuck I loved when she played along.

Grunting, I started to come. It had been a long time since I had sex with the same woman more than once, and there was an appeal to knowing what each other liked. Turning her on turned me on, and I wasn't sure sex would ever feel as good with anyone else the way it did with Coconut.

She was making me just as obsessed as Hunter seemed to be.

Chapter Twenty

Tatum

As he suggested, I ended that day in Tripp's apartment, in his bed. We had ordered food to be delivered and spent the rest of the night sleeping and having sex.

Sunday was the same, but we added a few movies and a walk down the beach to break things up. Besides checking my phone and coming up empty, neither Tripp nor I brought up Hunter. We had an unspoken agreement just to do whatever the hell we wanted and leave Hunter out of it.

We didn't owe him anything, and the more time I spent with Tripp, the more I didn't even care what Hunter thought or felt. All I was doing was whatever my heart told me to do, and even though I knew Tripp was just as capable of breaking it as Hunter was, it felt safer in those moments.

Sunday evening was the first time I had returned to my apartment, and it felt like I had been gone for weeks. Luckily, I had a set of clothes in my bag to change into after the beach, but I still got home wearing dirty shorts and one of Tripp's shirts that swallowed me whole.

Knowing my brother was watching his football games on my couch again, I didn't worry about going home. He and I had texted several times over the weekend, and I told him Hunter was scaring me. It meant he would most likely be there all night, just in case I felt uneasy again about Hunter showing up.

The following week was my usual work routine sprinkled with a few texts from Tripp that made me smile. He had gone to Dallas for a game but didn't play. He also told me there was no word about Hunter being invited to the postseason camps, which added one more layer to Hunter's deceit.

By Friday, neither Tripp nor I had heard from Hunter in any context, and we both thought that maybe he had gotten the message. It had been two weeks since I met Tripp, and he had to know that we had talked and caught him in a few lies. It would have made anyone tuck their tail and run.

But I also felt terrible and was honest about it with Tripp. Caring for Hunter didn't just go away; I wanted the best for him. He was clearly spiraling for some reason, and at times, it took all the restraint I had not to call and check on him.

The following Saturday, I woke up to a pounding on my door. Trying to ignore it, I turned over in bed and covered my head with my pillow. Knowing I had no plans, there was no reason for anyone to be there, and I hoped they would leave before long.

Then I remembered Hunter had a key; if I didn't answer, he might let himself in. He never used it unless he had to, but that didn't mean he wouldn't. Scrambling out of bed, I got to the door and pulled it open, shocked to see my mom standing in the doorway.

"About time!" she threw her hands up and walked in.

"What are you doing here, Mom?"

"You don't answer my calls or my texts, and Colton said you're seeing someone besides Hunter, so I knew it was time to come check on you."

"I'm twenty-five, Mom. You don't have to check on me."

"Twenty-five or ninety-five, a mother knows when to check on her babies."

"I'm all good, just been keeping myself busy." I started making a pot of coffee as she sat down in the living room, looking perfectly put together. You'd never know that she wasn't a senator's wife or that she lived paycheck to paycheck. She ensured she was always perfectly dressed, with makeup and her hair done. When we were younger, she told me it was the only way to keep a man. It just made me sad when I realized how hard she tried and failed to keep my dad from straying.

"Your father wants to go to a football game. I've been—"

"I've told you, and Colton has told you, that I can't make that happen. I'm not working with the football team."

"Then what are you doing?" She sighed. "Maybe he will want to do that."

It felt like a trap, but I walked right in as if there were breadsticks at the end of it. "Formula One is coming to Miami, and we are prepping for that event. I've been asked to assist the hockey team with a promotion night in the coming weeks. It's been a lot of fun."

"Your father hates both of those sports," was her only response before she realized how shitty that sounded. "I'm sorry. I'm proud and happy for you, but I'm lonely and desperate for your father to come home."

Oh, so he left again?

"I love Dad, as my Dad, but I hate how he treats you. When are you going to move on from him?"

She looked at me like I had slapped her and put a hand on her chest. "I'd never! He's good to me when he's home, and that is all I need."

"You deserve better," I mumbled, knowing it was useless.

Pouring two cups of coffee, I entered the living room to join her and settled in for anything else she came to chat about. There was always more when it came to her.

"I don't like you seeing someone else." She didn't waste any time, but it took me a little off guard.

"Excuse me?"

"Hunter loves you. Why see someone else?"

"Hunter is sick!" I yelled. "He's been stalking and manipulating me."

"You should be honored and thankful. You don't know how many times I wished your dad cared enough to keep a watchful eye on everything I did."

No words in my head could adequately convey how I felt hearing her say that. She couldn't possibly mean it. My jaw was wide open, and my eyes were on the verge of popping out of my head. Meanwhile, she just mixed a little sugar in her coffee, shaking her head as if her words were gospel.

"Mom," I finally gasped, making her look at me. "You cannot possibly want me to feel manipulated and lied to by someone who claims to love me."

"I want you to realize that if you want a commitment, you better stick with the man who is willing to commit because they are few and far between."

My entire life, I'd known my mom was sick. It used to be something I thought I could catch, like a cold, but I realized it was probably worse than contagious as I got older. It was hereditary, and I would have to fight hard to ensure I didn't fall into the same self-loathing mindset that made her think it was acceptable to settle for less than she deserved.

Not just as a woman but as a human.

It was the reason I broke up with Hunter. I saw that same desperation inside myself that I saw in her, and I would have rather ended up alone than with someone like my dad.

"You know," she sighed. "You're seeing someone else, and

that probably makes it easier to think you don't need Hunter. But trust me, Tatum, that man is nothing but a rebound and a mask. He is covering up your reality with pretty words and promises, but it all goes away. Just make sure you end up with someone that keeps coming back."

"How did you hear about all this?" She seemed to know more than I even told Colton, which made me ask, "What kind of man do you want Colton to be?"

"Colton will be the kind of man that always goes back, just like his father. And Hunter stopped by the house yesterday and told me about your troubles. He loves you, Tay. Give him another chance."

Without finishing her coffee or letting me respond, she leaned over and kissed my cheek, then stood and walked out. If she had a mic, she would have felt the need to drop it with how self-assured she looked.

So much so that I almost believed her.

Chapter Twenty-One

Tripp

It was a week from hell, with two games I didn't even play, traveling to Dallas, and being pissed at Hunter. Cruz still wasn't back, so we were also taking turns checking on him. Thankfully, he didn't live far away, so even though it wasn't my turn, I found myself walking down the beachfront to his place on Saturday morning.

The season was officially over, and I had a week to relax before off-season practices started. My original plan was to fly out to California to see Mom, but I never bought the ticket. In the back of my mind, I really wanted to spend that time with Tatum, which was fucking with me a little.

Not to mention, I needed to figure out my status with the team. There had been no word on any changes to the roster, so I assumed they would watch us work out for a few weeks and make decisions then.

Knocking on Cruz's door, I tried to be patient. It had only been a week since he walked off the field, and I knew now that it had been because his stepsister was in the hospital. It was the news delivered to him right then and there, in the middle of the biggest game of our season.

Not that I blamed him. No one did. We all would have done the same thing, especially since he was so in love with her.

"Open up, Cruz," I knocked again. "This isn't about you."

He had already said everything about his situation he was going to say, but I thought maybe I could talk to him about what was going on with Hunter. It would make him see that he wasn't alone when it came to fucked up situations.

"Come on, motherfucker," I pounded, using the side of my fist to create a louder bang.

"What?" He finally opened up, looking like he had been in some kind of accident.

"Dude, have you showered?"

"She sucked my dick in that shower," he mumbled. "I can't go near it."

For fucks sake, I rolled my eyes, pointing toward his second bathroom. "You have options. It's better than looking and smelling like you've been on the streets."

"I thought this wasn't about me."

"It's not, but..." I pulled up my phone to see who was scheduled to check on Cruz later. He had been so out of it that we had started a group text. It wasn't my day, but whoever came later needed a heads-up to bring a bottle of Febreze. "Okay, Erin will be over later with something to make this place smell better."

Cruz just sighed and walked away, then tossed himself onto his couch. Taking the single chair he had, I started running my hands through my hair, trying to decide where to start when it came to my own issues.

"My mom brought food," Cruz grunted, nodding toward his kitchen. "You hungry?"

Shaking my head, I finally looked up at him and pulled the Band-Aid off quickly. "Hunter fucked me over."

He didn't look shocked, but he did sit upright, eager to hear about someone else's problems for a change.

"Remember how he asked for my, um...assistance, with his girl?"

"Yeah..."

"Well she ended up being a girl I had already met, and instead of doing what Hunter needed me to do, and just casually chatting with her, I fucked her."

"Oh shit," Cruz nearly laughed, making it worth telling him. His face hadn't looked like it had smiled in so long. I was surprised his facial muscles still worked.

"It gets worse."

"How does it get worse than fucking your friend's girl?"

"After you left the club that night, and Hunter and I were alone, I don't remember anything. He told me I agreed to help him, which was why I went through with it in the first place, but I have no idea what we said that night. I literally do not remember."

"Do you think you told him you already knew her?"

"No, I met her the Saturday afterward."

"I mean," Cruz shrugged. "Did you fuck her before you knew about Hunter?"

"No," I laughed. "I was interested, but it wasn't until after I knew who she was that I fucked her. And man, Hunter called both our phones all night. It was like he knew we were together. I even expected him to start pounding on my door."

Cruz was laughing, shaking his head, and enjoying someone else's misery almost too much. I'd have punched his teeth out if he hadn't been so desperate for a mood change.

"We checked her phone for anything that he could use to track her, but there wasn't anything. Still, I think she's done with him for good now."

"And that's good for you, right?"

"Why me?"

"Um..." Cruz shook his head and smirked. "Because you don't have to feel guilty about banging your friend's girl."

"He isn't my friend," I gritted out, angry that I let anyone think he was. "He's a twisted little fuck. He made League One feel like high school, now he's doing the same thing with Tatum. Even told Tatum that he got invited to Inferno's postseason camp. Told her that I got him in."

"He's gonna be at camp? Fuck, I bet Rhys will join you in hazing that idiot. Ya know, since we are doing the high school thing again."

Rhys had his own issues with Hunter, but he seemed to think they had found some common ground when Hunter helped him with Ash one night. They did that little nod thing that guys do, and everything was cool afterward. Well, not cool, but Rhys stopped mentioning how much he wanted to kick his ass.

"Hunter's name isn't on the lineup, or invites. I've asked a few people, and no one has even heard of him."

"So what's the plan, then? Why come tell me all this?"

"Closure?" I shrugged. "To say it out loud so you could tell me if I'm wrong."

"You're not wrong."

"Is it wrong that I think I really like this girl? I've given her more orgasms than I had goals for the entire season. It isn't like me to be that dedicated to one woman's pussy."

"Well, I can't help you there," Cruz laughed, then laid back on the couch. "I'm just as fucked as you are when it comes to having feelings for one girl."

Instead of walking back toward my apartment, I kept heading toward Lummus Park in the center of South Beach, thinking of grabbing food before jogging home. Tatum hadn't answered any of my calls yet, and I naturally started to worry, but I told myself that she wasn't mine to worry about. It would be fine. She was a big girl.

Still, I could barely finish the sandwich I ordered, and I had to sit on a bench in the park just to let my stomach settle before trying to jog home. It wasn't a jog I hadn't done before, and it usually helped me clear my head, but it felt like a feat that I wasn't sure I needed that day.

When I stood back up to stretch, my eyes caught a couple standing close to one another, his hands on her hips. It wouldn't have struck me as worth noticing, except that the guy was Hunter Ward. From behind, the girl looked like Tatum, but I refused to think that she would fall right back into his arms after all the truth she and I shared.

Hunter seemed to be smiling, too distracted to even know I was there, fifty feet away and staring him down. Turning slightly, I saw the profile of Tatum, and my stomach fell, realizing that no matter what happened between us and how fucked up Hunter was, she would always go back. Maybe he was right; she was obsessed, and while she found a little fun and reprieve in my arms, he would always be her long-term goal.

Chapter Twenty-Two

Tatum

After my mom left, I decided to call Hunter. Not speaking to him at all wasn't the best way to end our relationship. Especially when he chose to talk to my mom behind my back. Admittedly, I was back and forth with Hunter, not knowing how to feel, but the one thing I knew for sure was that he better not contact my mom again.

He agreed to meet me there since he knew I loved spending my days off at the beach. Not Nikki's. That was my safe place, and he still didn't need to know I had a membership. So we met at Lummus Park, where there were plenty of people but also pockets of privacy.

When Hunter saw me walking toward him, he smiled and pulled me into a hug, which I returned in a friendly manner. Then he led me to a bench in the shade and held my hands.

"Things have been crazy," he smiled. "But I was glad you called me."

"You lied to me," I bit out quickly, making his head jerk back. "How?"

"I've talked to Tripp Maddux. He and I were friends before you sent him into my life, and that ruined your little plan."

"What plan?"

"Don't play dumb," I snapped. "You sent him to fill in for you on our date. But you didn't know we had already met, did you?"

"He was just supposed to help me," Hunter bit back. "I thought you would like meeting him."

"Why would you rather him help you than just cancel? Why take the risk that I wouldn't find out and hate you for trying to manipulate me?"

My next question was going to be to ask him how he knew where I had been and why he texted Tripp the night he was coming inside my apartment, but that was a hand I didn't want to play yet.

"It was his idea. I told him I had been working hard to get back where I wanted to be, either head coaching or playing pro. But I also told him about you and about how hard it was to balance my personal life and soccer."

"Then why not show up that night?"

"I got a call from the university that I thought would lead somewhere, so I had to meet them for dinner instead. After you told me that you needed to break up, I knew you were feeling angry, and I didn't want to let you down again. I called in that favor from Tripp, and he agreed to just keep an eye on you and make you happy, but I promise that was all it was."

"And you didn't expect that I would sleep with him, did you?"

His jaw started to tighten, and his nostrils flared. Hearing that I had slept with him wasn't a shock, but it was pissing him off to listen to it. "You're right. I didn't expect things to go that far."

"You haven't touched me since we got back together, Hunter. Choosing to be with Tripp was an easy choice. He made me feel more in one night than you have in years." Standing up, I no longer wanted to extend the conversation. It didn't matter what else needed to be answered because I was too angry to care.

"Wait," Hunter grabbed my waist and pulled me closer to him. He had a massive smile on his face that made me uncomfortable and took me off guard. "I'm sorry."

His smile didn't match his words. The word insane popped into my head, and I was suddenly thankful we were in public. There was no reason to cause a scene, so I didn't pull away, but I knew I needed to make him understand once and for all how far he had pushed me.

"I thought our break would be good for us," I smiled back at him, knowing I looked just as insane as he did. "And it was because it allowed me the freedom to see what I needed to see. I love you Hunter, and I always will, in some way, but I'm not my mother. You may think I will be just like her and be there waiting for you at every turn, but I won't. We are done, Hunter. You've officially scared me. So no more talking to my mom, no more phone calls, no more asking me to come see you play. I want to move on."

"With Maddux?" He snapped.

"With myself, and if Tripp provides a few orgasms for me along the way, then I deserve those too."

"You—"

"Bye Hunter." I backed away and started walking quickly toward my car. Hunter was yelling something, no longer concerned about the scene we were making, but I never looked back.

When I got in my car, I called Colton to make sure he knew what happened and to ask for his help changing the locks on my front door. He agreed to meet me at home and get started, making me decide not to call Tripp right away. After I was sure Hunter couldn't help himself to my place, I would call Tripp, tell him what happened, and hope he would be up for a distraction I knew we both enjoyed.

Colton was long gone, but Tripp wasn't answering his phone. It was like we were playing a game of tag, and it was my turn to be it.

When it was finally dark, I realized I had done nothing but clean and call all day. My apartment was spick and span, but my head was a chaotic mess. Tripp didn't owe me a phone call, but it felt like he would want to know what Hunter and I talked about.

Just as I got out of the shower, I heard a pounding on my door, so I wrapped a towel around me. Peeking out of the peephole, I made sure it wasn't Hunter and was relieved to see Tripp waiting patiently. Opening the door in only a towel, I expected Tripp to be happier to see me. But he marched inside and waited for me to close the door, looking angry and out of sorts.

"Lock it," he growled.

"Are you okay?" Locking the door, I held on tight to my towel, not feeling like his visit was flirty and fun enough to be so vulnerable.

"I don't listen to anyone," he bit out. "No one can make me do anything."

"What happened?" my face must have been pale, but he softened for just a minute before his mask returned.

"Drop the towel and turn around."

"Excuse me?"

Getting closer, he leaned down to put his lips against mine

and grabbed my chin with his thumb and pointer finger. "Drop the goddamn towel, and turn the fuck around."

He didn't scare me. I felt my body react to his urgency and need. My thighs squeezed together, and my breathing started picking up. With his lips still against mine, I dropped the towel and ran a hand down his stomach before going low enough to feel how hard he was.

"You want me to fuck you?"

"Yes," I sighed, not even denying how crazy it felt at that moment to want him even though he was clearly upset about something.

"Then turn around. If I have to say it again, Coconut, I will make that ass of yours hurt so bad you won't be able to sit down for a week."

"That isn't the threat you wanted it to be," I whispered, pushing my tits into his chest. "You have no idea how fucked up my day has been, and how badly I need you right now. If you want to threaten me, then tell me you're going to leave without fucking me. Because now that you're here," I dropped to my knees and looked up at him, "I'm feeling a little crazy myself."

Chapter Twenty-Three

Tripp

No one had ever made me as angry or unhinged as Tatum O'Neil. I almost wanted to give Hunter an award for somehow being able to resist her. Then, after I presented him with that award, I wanted to jab it through his neck.

And I hadn't determined what I wanted to do with Tatum yet. At the moment, I wanted to shove my dick in her willing mouth. But I wasn't sure what was real anymore.

Making my way to Tatum's was nothing more than proving to both of them and myself that I wasn't a puppet in their little fight. If I wanted to fuck Tatum, she wouldn't say no, regardless of whether she and Hunter were together again. Everything may have been one twisted pile of bullshit, but the connection Tatum and I had when we were together wasn't something he could dictate.

When she went down to her knees, it felt not only like reassurance that I was right but submission. It was her way of showing me that Hunter hadn't gotten to her after all. She was mine.

With my hands against the wall, I hung my head and

watched as she opened my jeans and pulled my cock out. Her mouth wrapped around me, her head started bobbing, and my eyes began to roll around in the back of my head. It was the first time having her lips around me, and it seemed impossible that it could feel just as good as her tight pussy.

But it was, and she was making me weak. I needed to recapture the upper hand, and I pulled myself out, her mouth making a popping noise as I did. Her eyes lifted to mine in concern, but I was still hovering, so she stayed put.

"Open your legs and rub your pussy," I demanded.

She did, and I watched as she bounced on her hand. My cock was jutting out, still close to her mouth, but she didn't try taking me back. She knew I was in control and wouldn't open up until I told her I was ready.

And fuck, I wouldn't be ready until I knew I wouldn't break down and beg her to marry me.

"What do you want?" I demanded.

"You, Tripp."

"What do you want with me? Why was I pulled into your little game with Hunter?"

She stopped moving and looked me in my eyes, not getting up but staring a hole through my head. Grabbing my cock, she started pumping hard, but that time, instead of lust, she had a snarl on her face.

"You're not in the middle of Hunter and me. He and I were over before you and I met. You know that Tripp."

"I feel like I don't know anything anymore," I gritted out, succumbing to the feel of her hand stroking me.

"You think I have this figured out? I've never gotten on my knees for anyone, Tripp. But I want to stay here all day and get lost with you."

"Open your mouth," I groaned, knowing I was no longer going to be able to pull away. "Open up."

When she put her lips around the head of my dick, I came, slightly thrusting my hips and banging the wall above her head. "Fuck, Coconut, fuck!"

She moaned as she swallowed and stood up, pressing her lips to mine. "I'm going to finish myself off in another shower. You need to sit down and figure out what your problem is."

"You were with Hunter this morning," I yelled, not letting her walk away. "And if you want to come, that is my job. Don't fucking walk away from me."

"If you saw me with Hunter this morning, that means you are stalking me, stalking him, or already know how little room I have left for the shit you two keep bringing into my life."

"Calm down, Columbo, I jogged down there and had lunch."

"And I go to the beach every fucking Saturday."

Her eyes were fiery, and her nose was scrunched up in disdain. Somehow, she looked even more gorgeous than when dressed up for dinner or naked and begging me to fuck her. Mad Tatum was twisting me around, making me feel something I never had before, and I had to get the hell out of there.

Pushing her back against the wall, I slid my hand down her stomach. Taking two fingers, I hooked them inside her and used my thumb on her clit. As I worked her core, her tits bounced, and I put my mouth over her nipple, flicking the tight bud with my tongue.

She was already on edge, worked up from being on her knees in front of me. So it didn't take long before she started clamping around me and shaking. Tears came out of her closed eyes, and her head shook.

"You better not be picturing him behind those lids, Coconut. You better know who you're with."

"Stop!" she cried. "Stop bringing him up."

"Then stop making me question what the hell is going on."

"It's not him, you're questioning. It's you."

Backing away as if she had slapped me, I pulled my fingers from her body, a stream of her cum attaching us until it broke as I got far enough away. With my hands by my sides, I stared at her, hoping she wilted if I bored my eyes into her hard enough. But she stood her ground and smirked, shaking her head and rolling her eyes.

She was right. It was me I was questioning, but always turning it around on her, and Hunter made it easier to deal with. I felt more for her than I ever expected, and instead of embracing it, I was trying to find reasons to fight it.

With the hand that just made her cum, I reached into my back pocket and retrieved a note Hunter had left under my door. It had been folded, and handing it to her with my messy fingers felt poetic.

"What's that?"

"Another piece of a puzzle I never asked to participate in. Another reason my head is spinning with thoughts of Hunter all the fucking time. Because he's always around. Always here."

She opened the folded page and immediately dropped the paper with a gasp.

"I'm sure you can understand why I'm losing my mind, Tatum."

"Where? Who?"

"You know who," I laughed with a grunt. "It was pushed under my door."

"He was at the beach with me, when you were running, remember?"

"Don't defend him. It took me two hours to run home. He could have gotten there and then made his way back here. I bet he's outside now, waiting for me to leave."

"Then why did you risk it?"

"Because no one is going to tell me who the hell I can fuck."

"But..." she pointed at the note, that was not just a note. Along with the words, "Keep your hands to yourself," there was a picture of me on the night I drank too much at the club. A snapshot of one more thing I didn't remember doing or saying.

"Who is that with you? Is he, um...Does he have his mouth around your...?"

"My dick? I have no idea, but it sure looks like it. I have no idea who that is, I can't see his face, but I know who took the picture."

"Is this the same night you said you didn't remember agreeing to help Hunter?"

"That was where I was, and what I was wearing, so yeah, I'd assume so."

Picking the picture back up, I took another look at it, printed on computer paper with poor quality. Despite being grainy, it was clear that it was me, with my head thrown back in pleasure. Someone appeared to be sucking my dick in the corner of the dance floor. The broad shoulders indicated it was a man, with a glint of an earring in his right ear. But his face was blurry, and I didn't know if that was intentional or just the lack of quality.

"This could get you kicked off the team," Tatum cried, picking up the towel she had on earlier and wrapping it around her body. "Why are you here? You cannot possibly be so cocky that you'd risk him sending this to the team, or leaking it online."

"I don't care if the world knows where I get my pleasure from. Let him post it. What will they get rid of me for? Being with a man?"

"Being with anyone, in public, and causing a scandal for the team. That's what! Trust me, Tripp, I do this for a living and no one can market a family day at an Inferno game when their midfielder is caught doing sexual acts in public."

"That didn't stop either one of us when you were on my cock at the Beach Club."

"That was different. If anyone had seen it, it would just look like I was sitting on your lap. It would be easy to explain that we were just being a normal couple. Plus, those cabanas are supposed to be private. You're surrounded by a million people in that picture, Tripp."

"I don't mind a scandal."

"Yes you do," she called my bluff. "You don't want this to ruin your position on the team."

"Fine," I yelled, "I'm freaked the fuck out. But what am I supposed to do?"

"Leave," she begged, stepping closer to me. Kissing my lips, she zipped my jeans back up and brought her hands to my neck. "I'll fix this."

"Don't—" I started to warn her because I knew fixing it would involve her being around Hunter again, but she stopped me and kissed me again.

"Let me do my job."

"I didn't hire you."

"Doesn't matter. I know exactly what I have to do."

Chapter Twenty-Four

Tatum

Luckily, Tripp stormed out of my apartment and out of my life. It was for his own good. Maybe the picture wasn't a big deal, but he was weeks away from the Inferno deciding whether to re-sign him for next season. His name being painted across the internet for anything scandalous would destroy him.

After everything between us the last few weeks, I wanted to protect him and fix the damage. If only that didn't mean I needed to stay away from him in the meantime. Hunter was out of his mind, and if he thought Tripp and I were still seeing each other, he wouldn't hesitate to make our lives hell.

"I'm going after the Inferno," I told my boss first thing Monday morning. "Formula One and hockey are not our top priority."

"When did you decide what's important?" She snapped at me, upset about my new attitude.

"Sophia." I took a deep breath before continuing, praying I didn't lose my job. "The Inferno are about to enter their post-season workouts. Their left wing, Rhys Peyton is the best player in the world, but he lost his mind this past season. Then there is

Cruz Martin, the goalie. He disappeared twelve minutes into a game that could make or break their season, and no one has heard from him since."

"You think I don't know that?" She stood from behind her desk and walked toward me, where I stood in the middle of her office. "I have Tina on the Inferno. She will get all she needs and convince them to hire us. Don't question me again."

"I didn't question you for pursuing a contract with the Inferno, but I know something Tina doesn't, and unless I'm the one to pursue the lead, I'm not giving her any hints."

"Why? You don't get paid more for being a headhunter, Tatum."

"It's not about being paid more. But I want the job. Tina can have the hockey team."

"Show me what you got first," Sophia challenged me, just like I knew she would.

Pulling up my phone, I brought up the picture of Tripp that I had taken from the one on the paper. Then I burnt the original in my sink, not wanting anyone else to see it accidentally. My brother could stop by unexpectedly, and no doubt start to freak out. He knew I was seeing someone, but he had no idea it was Tripp Maddux.

"Here," I handed her my phone, giving her a small glimpse to persuade her. "That is Tripp Maddux."

"Who's the other guy?"

"No clue, it's too blurry, but I'm betting it's someone on his team."

That wasn't true, but it added to the scandal that Sophia now had playing out in her mind.

"Where did you get that? Is it real?"

"It's real. A friend of mine snapped the pic when he was out the other night. The club was dark and strobe lights were everywhere, so it's not a great pic, but it tells a story about the Inferno midfielder."

"And add that to the already tumultuous season their star players have had, and it will be a train wreck at that stadium before too long."

"Let me see this through. Let me take the lead."

She sighed and walked back behind her desk, picking up her phone and pressing a few buttons. Then, as she locked eyes with me, she spoke to whoever answered. "Get Tina back in the office. Tatum is taking over the Inferno contracts. Something tells me she's motivated to make sure the Inferno calls us for an assist. Let's see how she handles it."

Swallowing the lump in my throat, I realized my plan had worked. The only thing was, I may have put my job on the line. Sophia wasn't happy I had strong-armed her, so she would undoubtedly make me pay if I failed.

"Go," she waved at me once she hung up. "Leak that picture. It'll add one more layer to their need for marketing and public relations help."

"Leak it?"

"What else were you going to do with it? You have to create chaos and then tame it. It's leverage, so go use it, Miss O'Neil."

When I opened my mouth to argue, she lifted her eyebrow to stop me from speaking, so I nodded and turned around. Hopefully, before Sophia expected that picture to be leaked, I could get more information on the team. Even if it wouldn't hurt Tripp, leaking a photo wasn't my style. It never had been, and I wondered if that was why I usually got the much simpler assignments.

How often did Sophia "create chaos" in order to gain business?

I would need to eventually unpack that, but in the meantime, I went to our administrative assistant and requested a media packet for the Inferno. It would take her a couple of days to get it together, but I would have access to the stadium and the training camp once she did.

In the meantime, I had to call Hunter.

"You push me away, and then call me back, Tay. Now I'm the one that is not sure what's going on anymore."

"I want to be your friend," I reasoned, sipping the coffee I had let get cold while waiting for him to show up.

"You said not to call, text, or come by. That wasn't very friendly of you. Now what?"

"Now I am making sure you are okay."

"I sent someone I thought was a friend in your path and you both destroyed me, so no I am not okay."

Well, at least he wasn't trying to get me back with sweet words and more lies. Taking another sip of my drink, I tried to stall while I got the guts to tell him what I really needed to say.

"Tripp and I are not seeing each other, Hunter. Yeah, we hooked up a few times, but that's all it was."

He didn't know I knew about the picture because he wouldn't expect Tripp to tell me, but I had to leave him at least something to think about.

"Now, with a weird twist of fate, my boss has assigned me to create a file on the Inferno. She wants me to dig up dirt on them, and I couldn't say no."

"So you're going to start a little section on the midfielder? How Tripp Maddux fucked his friend's girl? Is that why you did it? Because you knew once you created the drama, you could be hired to fix it?"

Fuck, that almost made me flinch. He sounded just like Sophia, and the fact that it was the first thing they both thought of made me consider hooking them up so they could ruin the world together.

"No, it's just my assignment. But if we are going to be friends, I thought it'd be better to tell you."

He leaned back and smirked, looking annoyed and frustrated. Biting his lip, he glanced around at everyone walking by the coffee shop on the boardwalk. After a few seconds, he huffed again and looked at me.

"Then I guess I will see you there."

"What?" Tripp told me he didn't know anything about Hunter being there.

"Did you think because your lover boy wouldn't help me out I didn't have a way in? I tried giving Tripp the credit, but he threw it away."

Standing up, he leaned down and placed a kiss on my cheek before whispering in my ear. "See you on the field, honey. It'll be nice having you watch me practice. Like old times."

Then he was gone, and I wasn't sure how I felt. Was he really the victim in all this? Why did he always make me question everything?

Looking down at my phone, I remembered the picture he threatened Tripp with. He may not have taken that intending to blackmail anyone, but he was, and that would never be okay.

Chapter Twenty-Five

Tripp

"You shouldn't have done that!" Cruz yelled, still not feeling quite himself. His disappearing act had to be handled, though, and he had to come in for our pre-camp team meetings.

"I think I can do whatever the fuck I want," Rhys bit back at him.

Cruz ran a hand through his hair and turned around, then realizing I was standing there, he froze. Looking back at Rhys, he snarled and nodded his head. "Tell him what you can do, then. I'm not staying here, I'm going home."

"Yeah, you're not ready to be here," Rhys yelled as Cruz walked toward me. "Someone will be by to check on you later."

"Fuck off," Cruz yelled with his back to Rhys. When he got closer to me, he added in a normal tone, "Ask him what he did. Then tell Coach I said I'm not ready."

"What the—" Before I could even think of what my question was going to be, Cruz was headed down the long hall that attached our locker room to the player parking lot. I was jealous that he could confidently leave, knowing Coach wouldn't care because he was Cruz Martin.

Turning to Rhys, I lifted my arms in the air and sighed. "What the hell is going on?"

"Someone asked me for a favor and I obliged. Someone I don't like. But after he reminded me that I owed him one, I did it."

"Why is that Cruz's business?"

"I have no idea," he threw his hands in the air and sat at his locker. Cruz's locker was between mine and Rhys', so we were close enough to keep talking while we changed. "I guess it's because he creeps the girls out on the team, and Cruz is protective of Erin, but doesn't he think I considered Ash as well? I almost killed that guy once just for looking at her too long. I'm the one that invented hating him. But I couldn't exactly say no when he reminded me of—"

"Are you talking about Hunter Ward?" I stood up, the pieces connecting. "What the fuck did you do?"

"He asked for an invite to camp since he's taking time off from the women's team at the college. I asked Ash what I should do, and she didn't care. Hell, anything that keeps him away from her is a good thing. Plus, this way, I can feel him out and decide how much I hate him."

"You hate him. Cruz hates him. I hate him. Why the fuck would you invite him?"

"What the fuck does it matter to you?"

Shit, I couldn't tell him. He was our captain and would probably bench me himself if he knew what I had gotten myself wrapped up in with Hunter. Cruz knew most of it because I told him, but even he didn't know the whole story.

"You know what, never mind."

"Dude, tell me! If there is something I need to know, then tell me."

"Just not sure what he could have done that makes you feel like you owe him one."

"He called me when Ash and Erin got drunk. He kept an eye on them until I could get there. Then he didn't tell Colin that Ash and I were seeing each other. As much as I hate him, he showed me he wasn't a complete jackass. Plus, like I said, I'd rather have him here than at the college with the girls."

"Cool," I shrugged.

"Cool?" Rhys questioned. "You used to play with him in League One, right?"

"Yep."

"Is there a problem I don't know about?"

"Nope."

Rhys could tell I was lying, and I knew if I told him the truth, he would kick Hunter's ass for me, so I didn't have to. But I just couldn't risk it. Not when there was a picture of me and some random dude in a club doing indecent things. Fuck, that shame would haunt me forever. The fact that I didn't even remember letting myself get that drunk was a cherry on the wildly fucked up top.

The meetings went fast, and we did a light workout. With the season being over, we didn't hurt ourselves, but we had to keep our stamina up. It felt good to be with the team without pressure from the pending games or outside craziness messing with our flow. I was even feeling light and sound when I showered and left.

Driving down the main beach road in Shelly, I smiled at how beautiful the evening was. The only thing missing was Coconut, and it would have been perfect. But I hadn't spoken to her in days. She wouldn't return my calls, and every attempt I made at showing up at her place was thwarted when I remembered I would just end up fucking her, getting angry, and stomping out. She didn't deserve that shit.

The day I met Tatum, she was celebrating, and it felt like, from that moment, it'd been nothing but chaos for her. It was easy to blame it all on Hunter, but whether he existed between us or not, I wasn't a relationship kind of guy. She wanted something I couldn't give her, so it was better if we didn't make it harder on ourselves.

Still, I couldn't help but think about her in bed. In the shower. When I was on my board in the ocean, picturing her gasping as I drove my dick into her beneath the water. I hadn't even tried returning to Nikki's, even though I loved the waves down on that side of the beach near the inlet.

For now, I stuck to the waves right outside my front door. Not that I was actually surfing. Most of the time I spent on the board, I was thinking of her. I ended up with my dick hard and holding the board in front of me until I got back inside so I didn't risk any more public indecency pictures.

On the night before camp started, I couldn't even sleep. Knowing Hunter would be there was killing me, and I had to act like nothing happened. He got his way when I showed Tatum that picture. We were done, and I bet he was sleeping like a fucking king, knowing it worked.

When I got to the stadium, I just kept to myself and ignored him. He wasn't the only invite, and they usually had a few days of meetings to get caught up anyway.

Cruz was back and seemed better, but I didn't talk to him or Rhys either. We were done babysitting Cruz, who had clearly not told Rhys that I had issues with Hunter, and it seemed as though all I had to do was just survive.

That was all easier said than done because as soon as I took the field and started dribbling the ball toward the goal, I looked up and saw Coconut. She was standing with our head of team marketing, holding a clipboard and nodding with a big smile.

She looked up and saw me, her gaze giving nothing away. Then, just as quickly, she turned away, like she didn't know me at all. It fucked with my head because that was how it was supposed to be, yet I wanted her to run toward me and jump into my arms.

Maybe she would have if she weren't working, but she was in a tight skirt that went to her knees with a jacket and heels. Her hair was up in a twist, and she had a press tag around her neck.

Turning back to the team, I started to run back onto the field when I stopped and looked back at her. She was working. Why the fuck was she working?

Chapter Twenty-Six

Tatum

I t took everything I had to not run to Tripp, but after so many days without talking to him, I was sure he didn't even care. No matter how he felt, I was still there for him to ensure Hunter never had a chance to ruin Tripp's career. Especially when this all started because Tripp was trying to help him.

"We would like to start planning a promotion for the kids camp that starts after the new year," the woman, whose name I had already forgotten, told me. "Obviously, we have a team here, but we need an outside take for the events. We will use the main field, but also the practice fields on the outside of the stadium. Our goal is to attract kids from all over the country, not just in South Florida."

"Of course," I smiled. "What about the players? We can attract more kids if the players are involved in the marketing efforts."

"They should all be extremely helpful. There is also a team of invitees that will be working out for the next couple of weeks as well. Even if they aren't on the team, they love coming back to help, so pull them into the efforts as well."

While writing down some notes, I peeked back up to see Tripp looking at me again. He was confused, and I knew he would be. I told him I'd fix it, and he needed to trust me.

But dammit, he looked so good. He wore his number five practice jersey, and his hair was pulled back in a headband. His thighs flexed as he pulled at his shorts, and I immediately thought about all of the things those thighs and I had been through.

Being around him was going to be more challenging than I thought it would be, and then knowing Hunter was lurking somewhere made it even worse.

"It's exciting, isn't it?" The woman crooned. "The players always take a week off and then come back and get to work. After camp, the coaches and big wigs will decide who keeps going forward, and sometimes we sign new and exciting players. We are hoping to sign more locals like Cruz Martin. He attracts a ton of people to the games so they can see the hometown kid play."

"That is exciting." And I truly meant that, but it made me think of Hunter's odds of being signed. He knew the Inferno liked hometown players, so he took it to heart when they passed on him the first time. Would they look closer now that he was right in front of their eyes?

After spending two days touring the complex and meeting people, I finally got a file started on the Inferno. Sophia was pressuring me to release my picture, but after I told her we were working with bringing kids into the complex, she agreed that I could handle it confidentially as long as it secured us a long-term deal.

I sat on the sideline the day Hunter made it to the same field as Tripp. Several others around me had their own business with the team, but I was the only one with my eyes glued to the situation.

Hunter was playing in the middle of the field and didn't have much interaction with Tripp at first, but eventually, the coaches brought them together. That was when I pulled my phone up and started taking pictures.

They shook hands, but I could tell underlying hatred lingered. Hunter had gotten his way with Tripp and me not seeing each other, so I figured he'd look slightly smug. Instead, he looked intense.

The whistle blew once the guys were lined up, and Hunter kicked the ball backward towards the midfielder. That player, who I didn't recognize, kicked it to Rhys.

Tripp and Hunter had driven up the field and opened themselves for a pass. Rhys chose to kick it to Hunter, who did a fancy twist and kicked it backward towards Tripp—a perfect assist. Tripp kicked the ball into the net with his right foot, and the whistle blew again, making them line back up.

A few more plays like that and Tripp was sent to the locker rooms. From where I was sitting, he would pass right by me, and for the first time in almost a week, he would be close enough to touch or talk to me.

Hunter was still on the field, but I saw him watching Tripp walk, waiting for him to screw up. But he didn't. Tripp walked right past me without even a glance, and as much as I knew it was what I asked for, it hurt to see him so easily distant.

Staying out, I watched Hunter take a few more plays with Rhys before he was also sent off the field. Unlike Tripp, Hunter stopped and squatted beside my seat, winking at me.

"I still got it."

"Congrats," I said quietly with a straight smile. "But I'm working."

He took the hint and stood up to leave, but not before he winked at me, making me feel uneasy.

After the practice ended, I decided to return to the office and put some of my notes into my computer. As I was packing my bag, my phone buzzed with a text. Looking at the name, my heart started beating wildly.

Coach's office.

I had not answered his texts since he left my apartment the day he showed me the picture. It was for his own good because Hunter was watching, and I knew he was just waiting for a chance to pounce. I chose not to answer his text, but I did comply, curious what he needed.

The Coach's office was outside the locker room, down the hall I had to walk through to get to my car. There was a small moment when I thought I should just pass the office and keep walking, but my need to see Tripp was too much.

As I opened the door, a voice behind me made me stop.

"Where are you going?"

"Hunter?" I turned, blocking the door and smiling. "What are you doing?"

"I asked you first."

"Well, it's obvious what I am doing, I'm headed to chat with Coach Sandy."

"He's in the home locker room, I was just there."

"Then I guess I will wait, because I already told him I'd like to chat after practice."

Crossing my arms, I leaned against the wall, knowing he

would surely know I was lying if I left. All I had to do was wait for him to go, but it was never that easy with Hunter.

Crossing his arms, he leaned against the wall beside me and smiled. "I'll wait with you."

"Don't you need to shower or something?" He was still dirty and sweaty, a particular funk exuding off his body.

"Nope."

Taking a deep breath, I turned away and tried to think of some other reason I needed to leave. The only thing that came to mind was faking a phone call, but as I started digging for my phone, a door slammed near the locker room entrance, and I looked up to see Tripp walking toward us.

He paused slightly when he saw the two of us standing there, but with Hunter angled behind me, he saw the discomfort on my face and moved toward us.

"Everything okay?"

"Coming to save our girl?"

Tripp snorted and crossed his arms, leaning on the wall on my other side. "She doesn't need saving."

Unlike Hunter, Tripp had showered and changed. He was in jeans and a T-shirt, with flip-flops. His hair was slicked back from his shower, and he smelled like when we took one together at his apartment. It made those memories start coming back, and my heart picked up its pace.

"Then what are you doing here?"

"Coach asked me to meet him. Did you two get called to the principal's office as well?"

"I requested to meet with him," I answered, then turned to Hunter. "You?"

"Just waiting with my friend."

Tripp had uncrossed his arms, and I felt his light touch grazing the side of my body he was standing on. Hunter couldn't see if he looked, but it helped that his focus was on the wall ahead of us.

My body shook a little, and I played it off like I had a chill, but it only encouraged Tripp to push me further. Standing between the two of them was awkward, but Tripp was taking the opportunity to remind me who I really belonged to. Not only was I exactly where he wanted me to be, but I was falling more and more with each secret touch he gave me.

Finally, I couldn't take it anymore, so I walked away, leaving them alone to fight their little war.

Chapter Twenty-Seven

Tripp

More than anything, I hated how well Hunter and I played together when we were forced to run drills. It was like we were in League One again, and he was lining up assists for me one after the other. Until we were there on the field, I had forgotten how good he was.

Then again, one glance over toward Tatum, and I remembered how bad he was. How dirty he did her, and how he was blackmailing me to stay away from her. He may have learned to shut his mouth and play on the field, but he still wasn't my friend.

When I got to the locker room, I couldn't take it anymore and texted her. She had yet to respond to my texts, but I tried one more time, telling her to meet me in the coach's office. Coach never used his office, but she didn't know that, and neither did Hunter.

Therefore, after she walked away, we stood there like two fools, neither wanting to be the first to move. And since I had told him I was there for Coach, I really had to wait until he left first.

"You happy?"

"Why would I be happy?"

"Because she won't even look at me since you sent me that fun little threat."

"What threat?"

Huffing a laugh laced with annoyance, I lifted from the wall. "Don't fuck with me, Hunt. It's been one lie after the next with you. You got your way, so fuck off."

He also lifted off the wall, facing me and getting into my personal space. "Nothing goes my way!"

"Don't use me trying to get it. But more importantly, don't use her."

Turning around, I walked off, listening to him laugh behind me. He didn't bother responding, but his laugh made me want to turn back around and beat his ass. Lucky for him, I wasn't done with Coconut. She and I would talk, and I wasn't settling for her ignoring me. Especially when she had the nerve to look like a sexy lawyer every day while I fought for my career on the field.

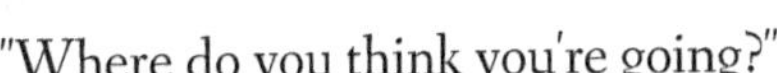

"Where do you think you're going?"

Tatum whipped around before she could open her car door. I was right behind her and pressed her against the hot metal, using my body to keep her in place.

"Why are you running?"

"I was in the middle of a dick measuring contest, was I supposed to stick around for that?"

"We needed a judge." My words were bitter, but I wasn't trying to be a jerk. I just couldn't help it. The whole week without her was spent thinking about her, and having her so close made my desperation peak at an all-time high. Lashing out was the only way I knew how to deal with my emotions. Emotions I'd spent a lifetime avoiding.

"I've already seen both of your dicks," she hissed, spitting her annoyance back in my face. "I don't have to look again to know who would win."

How come she sent fire into my veins when she fought back with me? I longed for her disparagement. It fueled me, making me want to prove her wrong. Pressing my lips to hers, I intended to show her how useless it was to fight against whatever had already happened. And she didn't try to resist.

Dropping her bag and keys to the asphalt, she wrapped her arms around my neck and tried climbing up my body. Her skirt was too tight, and her legs too little, but I helped her by picking her up and cradling her in my arms.

"He may see us," she breathed, then pressed her lips back to mine.

"I don't give a fuck."

"Don't make my job harder."

Pulling back, I kept my forehead to hers and tried to catch my breath while I made sense of what she had just said. "How will I make it harder?"

"I had to pull a lot of bullshit to get inside that stadium, Tripp. All so I could be the one that mitigated and handled anything Hunter tried doing. I'm supposed to be working on a kids camp campaign. But I'm here, and I'm keeping my eye on things."

"That's why you've been sitting in the hot seats every day?"

"Of course. I told you I'd fix it, Tripp."

"Fuck, Coconut," I set her down on her feet and held onto her neck, wishing I could devour her right there. "You didn't have to do that. I'm not worried about Hunter. If the Inferno lets me go, then fuck them. I'm good, and will play for some team, somewhere."

"But I'm in Miami," she spit out, then closed her lips quickly like she had wished she could take those words back.

"That's very selfish of you," I smiled.

"I know we aren't a thing, Tripp. Don't freak out. I just meant that—"

I cut her off with another kiss, not wanting to hear what she meant when the image I had in my head was so perfect. If she wanted me to be in Miami, then I wanted to be there, too. She made Miami feel like home, and I needed to work just as hard as she was to keep me there with her.

"Get in the car, baby. Crank it up and head straight to my place."

"I have to go to the office."

"No, you don't," I practically growled. "I have something to add to your Tripp Maddux file. Your boss will understand."

Her heart was beating so fast, I could feel her pulse where I was still holding onto her neck. Taking my thumb over her throat, I tried to ease her thoughts and assure her it was all okay. I only needed to get her alone so she could be herself and stop worrying.

"Okay," she finally nodded after thinking about what I had said. "I'll meet you there."

"Good girl," I kissed her again before letting her go. Taking a few steps backward, I picked her things up and put them in the backseat of her car. Then I turned around and hoped she really did show up. We had a lot to talk about. As long as we were anywhere Hunter was lurking, I knew she would be in a twisted mess.

And helping her unwind was a craft I had recently mastered.

Chapter Twenty-Eight

Tatum

"I'll be at the stadium the rest of the day," I told Sophia over the phone as I sat in my car in the parking garage of Tripp's apartment. My first idea was to call on the way, but I knew she would be able to tell I was driving and not where I said I would be.

"Did you leak that picture yet?"

"Not yet," I sighed. "Let me get the kids camp going before shit hits the fan."

"A kids camp is not the kind of marketing this company wants to do."

"Well that was what Tina was working on, wasn't it?"

"Why do you think I pulled her off when you showed me that picture? You have the dirt, so use it."

She hung up, and I leaned forward, pressing my forehead against my steering wheel. What had I gotten myself into? All I wanted to do was stay ahead of whatever Hunter tried to do to Tripp. Being on Sophia's bad side, not to mention her immoral side, wasn't what I wanted at all.

"Get out." Tripp said through my window with a knock on the glass.

Slowly, I turned my ignition off and unbuckled my seatbelt. When I hit the unlock button on my door, Tripp didn't wait for me to let myself out. He opened the door for me and pulled me into his arms.

"Tripp!" I squealed, taken by surprise. "Let me grab my things!"

He put me down long enough to grab my bag and phone, then scooped me back into his arms. Walking all the way across the parking garage, he acted as if I weighed nothing, not even breaking a sweat from holding me for so long.

"I can walk, you know."

"You're a flight risk."

"I am not," I laughed. "I drove myself here."

"Not taking the chance. Last time we said goodbye, I didn't see you for almost a week."

"I'm not going anywhere." Laying my head on his shoulder, I was probably revealing too much, but he was making it hard not to. I was already crossing lines I swore I wouldn't just by being there with him, but since some time had passed since Hunter's threat, I thought it was safe enough to try.

He kept me close as the elevator lifted, and I felt the tension I had been carrying slowly dissipate. It was nearing three in the afternoon, but I could have fallen asleep for days. Tripp must have sensed my waning because he took me straight to his bed and set me down gently.

Tearing at the buttons of my jacket, he slid it off, and our eyes locked. Then he pulled my skirt down, leaving me in only my white blouse and panties. His hand slid up my thigh and rested on my hip, but he didn't move to take any more of my clothes off.

"Sleep," he whispered.

"It's in the middle of the workday." I made the argument, but I didn't make a move to get up.

Sliding his shirt up slowly, he teased me with a peek of his abs. "Do I need to create a scandal so you feel justified being here?"

"Define scandal."

"We can send your boss a video of you sucking my cock."

"Or," I laughed, "let's not do that."

"Seems to be the thing these days."

I could tell by the look on his face that he was only half teasing. When he showed me that picture of him in the club, I was so angry and wanted to fix it. I didn't even take a minute to think of how he really felt about it. But it had to have been weighing on him.

"How are you feeling?" Sitting up, I reached for his hands and held them in mine. He watched my thumb move over his knuckles a few times before looking back at me.

"I'm pissed. Tatum, I don't remember that night. Clearly I was drunk and even though I put myself in that situation, I feel kind of violated."

"Kinda?"

He shrugged and then looked back down at our joined hands. Something about his vulnerable honesty had me climbing into his arms again, wrapping my legs around his waist and burying my lips against his neck.

"Maybe for guys, it's weak to feel violated in this kind of situation. But it's valid. Doesn't matter how much you drank that night, if you didn't want that to happen, it shouldn't have happened."

"But maybe I did want it to happen. I'm not the kind of guy that cares who is sucking his dick, as long as it takes away that lonely feeling I always seem to have."

"You didn't want a picture of it, though."

"Honestly, none of it would bother me if I remembered it.

But having a picture of something I have no recollection of is a mindfuck."

"I'm sorry I made you leave."

He pushed me back a little to look at me with his confused stare. "Huh?"

"When you showed me that picture, I should have asked then and there how you felt about it. But it scared me. It feels like this is my fault and I don't want your career being ruined because you fucked around with the wrong girl."

"I fucked around with the right girl."

Pushing me back onto the bed, he climbed behind me and pulled my body into his. He was so much bigger than I was, and being in his arms made me feel safe.

"Sleep baby. We can talk later."

"I haven't been sleeping well."

"Me either. Let's fix that first."

His breath was starting to slow down to small puffs behind my ear. His arms relaxed, and eventually, I could tell he had fallen asleep. Closing my eyes, it wasn't long before I was also drifting off.

When I woke up, I was alone. It was dark outside, which meant hours must have passed, but I wasn't sure how late it was. A soft tone coming from the living room sounded like Tripp was on the phone.

Giving him a few more minutes of privacy, I looked around where I dropped my bag, and grabbed my phone as well. It was only seven in the evening, and thankfully, my only missed calls were from my brother, so I called him back to see what he needed.

"Hey," he sighed, sounding upset.

"Everything okay?"

"Not really. Where are you?"

"With...someone."

"Do I even want to know?"

"Do you?"

"No."

Laughing, I gave him a minute to get over whatever he thought I was doing and explain why he had called me so many times. But he never brought it up, just sat quietly on the phone.

"Bro, what's up?"

"Have you heard from Hunter?"

"No, why? Have you?"

"God no," he laughed, sounding more worried than humored. "But I did stop by your place and found a note on your door."

"What?" That time, my voice raised, and Tripp came running into the room with his phone to his ear.

"Call you back, Mom." He hung up his phone and tossed it onto the bed as he climbed up to sit with me.

Holding a finger up, I asked him to give me a second to finish the conversation, but I didn't want him to leave.

"What did it say?"

"It said, 'Where are you?' It looks like Hunter's chicken scratch."

"He didn't call me or anything."

"Well, I set it on the counter and stole a beer from your fridge. I wanted to hang out until you got home so I knew you were okay, but I have early classes tomorrow."

"No, it's okay," I assured him. "I will be fine. I'm sure he is just trying to fuck with me."

"Are you with another guy?"

Rolling my eyes and twisting my neck, I shrugged, even though he couldn't see me. "You know I am."

"Yeah, I do."

"But Hunter isn't scaring me away from him. Not again, at least."

Tripp's eyes beaded, and his hand came to my cheek. I leaned into his touch and closed my eyes, soaking in how content he made me feel.

"I'm not a fan of Hunter," Colton reassured me, "But he's not the same. Sometimes I wonder..." He trailed off, and I gave him a minute to finish his thought, but he redirected instead. "I just want everything to be normal."

"I know," I sighed. "Me too."

"So just...I don't know."

Yeah, no one knew anything anymore.

"Look, Colt, I gotta go."

"Wait—"

Hitting the end of the call, I immediately pulled up a text to him.

I'll call you when I head home. Promise.

You better.

Once I set my phone down, Tripp grabbed my chin and forced me to look at him. "Tell me."

"Can we just do what we do best?" Lifting onto my knees, I pressed my lips to his and pushed him backward onto the bed. Crawling on top of him, I ran my hands down his shirtless torso and started grinding my pussy on his growing erection.

"Is this what we do best?"

"It's all you can give me, remember? I'll take what I can get."

"Let me give you more."

Staring down at him, I tried to determine his meaning without jumping to conclusions. When he decided to text me and then track me down in the parking lot, was it because he missed the sex or because he missed me?

No clear answer was written on his face, but I nodded anyway. It wasn't like I could get up and walk away, no matter what he thought and felt.

Chapter Twenty-Nine

Tripp

Sitting up, I grabbed Tatum under her thighs and carried her into the living room. As much as I wanted to fuck her, I wasn't kidding when I said I wanted to give her more. Or I at least wanted to try.

When I woke up with her in my arms, I knew I wouldn't let Hunter scare her away again. We both deserved to see where we were going, and what it was that was growing between us. Even though it scared the shit out of me, it scared me more to think of her ending up in his arms and not mine.

"What are you doing?"

"Trust me, Coconut. I'm going to make you come. I'll make all those worries disappear. But not until you tell me what those worries are. The living room seems safer than the bedroom for now."

Setting her down on the couch, I backed away and made us a few drinks, then placed a delivery order from La Trattoria. When I sat down with her, her legs were crisscrossed, her hair was unkempt, and her blouse was unbuttoned just enough to show me the curves of her breasts.

How the fuck was I going to resist her long enough to be someone that deserved her?

"Who was on the phone?"

"My brother. Who were you talking to?"

"My mom."

"Did you have a nice chat?"

"Her calls woke me up and I slid out of bed to see if everything was okay. She's upset because I didn't take my normal postseason vacation home to see her."

"Why didn't you go?"

"What did your brother say?"

She started fidgeting with a loose string on the end of her blouse, and I let her take her time. But the longer it took her to speak again, the more anxious I got.

"Colton went to my place, as he so often does so he can get away from campus, and he found a note on my door in Hunter's handwriting. It was asking where I was."

Shoving to my feet, I ran a hand through my hair and nearly walked out the door to find that little weasel. "What the fuck?"

"This is why I didn't want to tell you. Please, just sit back down."

"He knows you're here."

"He doesn't know anything. I had my phone reset and he hasn't been near me since. There is no way he can track me here."

"He wasn't using your phone, remember?"

"It may have been something we missed, but he hasn't been around since."

"Not until you're here again."

Making that connection, I started to demand she leave. But that was what she had done to me for my own protection, and I didn't like it any more than she would. In fact, it may push her away when I was trying hard to pull her closer.

"He doesn't know I'm here." She seemed adamant about that, facing me with her hands on her hips. "I wouldn't risk him spreading that picture around."

"Fuck that picture."

"No!" Her hands were no longer on her hips but wildly waving between us. "Just because I am here now doesn't mean anything has changed. Especially now that I have the job for my agency. All it will do is make my life harder. Let me stay close to the team and keep working just in case. Besides, the camp the Inferno does with the kids is unbelievable. I want to be a part of it, and if the focus shifts to your off field activities, my boss will forget all about the camp and that's not fair to anyone."

"Hey," I pushed my hand through her hair and held her cheek, hoping I could calm her back down. "I'm sorry, baby. I've never been this scared."

"I won't let him win."

"I'm not scared of him," I snorted. "I'm scared of you. That you will let whatever he does prevent you from getting what you truly want."

Dinner arrived, and we ate on the balcony like we did the night I made dinner for her. We were mostly quiet until she took a bite of her breadstick and shook her shoulders. Her little moan was intentional, and the spark in her eye reminded me why I was so immediately taken with her.

"Good, huh?"

"You know the way to a woman's heart."

Not really, but I knew what she meant. If I had truly known the way to a woman's heart, we probably wouldn't be in the middle of a twisted situation with her ex because I wouldn't have ever let her leave the night I first met her without her knowing she was mine. That would have meant I never would have agreed to help Hunter, and he would never be involved with what we had going on.

"I wish I had told you the night I met you that you were mine."

She froze before taking another bite, setting her fork down, and slowly finishing what was in her mouth. Her eyes bounced between mine, and I knew my words had taken her off guard. She would have to get used to it because when I said I wanted to give her more, I meant every word.

Standing up, she made her way to my side of the table, and I scooted my chair back to make room for her in my lap. When her lips landed on mine, I turned her so she was straddling me and let her feel what she did to me. It was as if my cock saw her intent before she even stood up and hardened just for her pleasure.

As she moved against me, her nails raked over my bare chest, and I moaned into her mouth. Not only should I have told her she was mine, I should have told her I was hers. I didn't realize it then, but looking back, it should have been obvious. In my entire life, I had never been so obsessed with one person.

"Don't move, Tripp."

"Where would I go?"

"You tend to pick me up and make me go wherever you want me to go, but I don't want to move." Pulling my shorts down to expose my cock, she started stroking me and telling me what she needed without saying anything.

Leaning up, I kept my eyes locked on hers while I pursed my lips and spit, coating my cock for her. She moved her hands up and down, spreading my saliva across my skin until she was ready.

Without asking, I took my thumbs to the core of her panties and ripped the lace apart, creating a hole for us to connect. "I'll buy you more."

"Or I could stop wearing panties."

"You already know how interested I am in your panty status. But when we are at the field, you have to keep that to yourself, or we won't need Hunter ruining my career, I'll do it myself when I fuck you right there in front of everyone."

"Oh the scandal," she giggled, holding my piercing against her clit before impaling herself on top of me.

We both moaned as she moved, getting situated the way she wanted. It took everything I had to hold myself together and not fill her pussy up right then. The more she moved, the closer I got, and I had to smack her ass a little to make her freeze for a minute.

"Do it again," she moaned. "Harder."

Smacking her again in the same spot, she moaned into the night breeze, and I had to grab her hips to keep her still. "You're going to make me come, Coconut."

"I want to make you come," she cried. "I want you to be as weak as I am."

Moving my hands to her blouse, I pulled it open, not giving a fuck that the buttons were flying everywhere. I'd buy her a whole new wardrobe if I had to just so I could fuck it up when it was in my way.

"Gimme your tits," I growled, lifting them so I could reach with my mouth. Sucking her nipples, I tested how hard I could push her before she begged me to stop, but she never did. Between my hand creating red marks on her ass, and my teeth elongating her nipples, I felt like I was in my own wet dream. Coconut was perfect for me, taking whatever I wanted to give her and asking for more.

Bouncing on me, her head fell back, pushing her tits into my mouth more and making me suck harder. With her pussy squeezing me, I knew she was close, so I spanked her ass again, making it where she could no longer hold off. It was a completely selfish move because it was me that needed to come, and I didn't want to go without her.

"Tripp," she breathed, repeating my name over and over.

"That's my girl," I encouraged her with a grunt, spilling inside her core so powerfully that I felt dizzy.

When we were finally spent, nothing more than a pile of exhaustion on my balcony, I pulled her hair and made her look up and into my eyes. "We don't have to tell anyone, but we don't avoid this either."

"Deal."

Chapter Thirty

Tatum

Despite Tripp's attempts to keep me in his bed all night, I pulled my blouse back together and drove home. As much as I wanted to stay with him, I needed to show up at home, just in case Hunter somehow kept tabs on me. Knowing how much I loved being home early on a work night, he would still be suspicious, but he wouldn't know for sure where I was, and that was enough for me.

Getting into my dark apartment at nearly midnight was eerie. There were no lights near the door, and had I known I would get in late, I would have left a lamp on. Instead, I shuffled across the living room, praying I didn't accidentally trip over something on my way to the couch.

Reaching for the lamp, I turned it on and sat down, immediately standing back up and screaming. Along with my screams was a male voice, trying to calm me down, but I was too hysterical to know whose it was.

"Get out!" I screamed. "I'm calling the police."

An arm wrapped around my waist and pulled me up before turning me around. Colton was staring at me, holding my shoulders with wide eyes, making soft, soothing noises.

"It's just me, Tay."

"What are you doing here?"

"I couldn't sleep in the dorms knowing someone was leaving notes on your door!"

"Why didn't you call me, or text me!"

"I wanted to, but you hung up on me when we spoke earlier, and I figured it was best to give you space and just be here if you needed me."

My chest was still heaving in fear, but I was so relieved it was my brother that I flung myself into his arms. He started rocking me in a hug, back and forth as I cried.

"Everything is a mess."

"Then why are you making it worse?"

"What?" I jerked back, looking up at him. He may have been my little brother, but he was almost as tall as Tripp, though younger and not as bulky from being an athlete.

"Don't look at me like that," he warned.

"Seeing someone else isn't making it worse on myself," I yelled. "It's making it harder for Hunter."

"Hey," he ran his hands on my arms, trying to soothe me, but as close as he and I were, my brother could never have the same effect on me as Tripp.

"Go home," I pointed toward my door. "Don't come back until you are on my side again."

"I'm always on your side. Always!"

"Then start acting like it. Instead of telling me I'm making it worse, why don't you try telling Hunter you'll beat his ass if he messes with me. Or how about just lay quietly on my couch so you know I'm safe and stop trying to do exactly what Mom and Hunter have done by trying to control me."

"You're right," he hung his head. "I guess I just didn't realize how serious you were."

"Why wouldn't I want this for myself? Why wouldn't I be serious?"

"Because of Mom," he whispered. "Fuck you've been so scared of becoming her. Almost in an obsessive way. It's all you think about."

"It's like you're still stuck on who I was a month ago," I yelled. "I'm not that girl anymore. I've become stronger, more sure of myself, more aware of what I want and need."

"How though?"

I shook my head and refused to tell him it was because of another man. How he made me feel invincible and gave me insight into myself that I hadn't had before. Being with Tripp showed me exactly what I deserved, and even if all he was in my life for was to be that lesson, I was thankful for him. Colton just wouldn't understand. He still thought the way to fix everything was to mend things with Hunter.

"I just know what I deserve, and it's not Hunter."

He nodded but didn't respond as he backed up toward the window in my living room and hung his head low between his shoulders. As upset as he was, I had nothing left in me for the day that could help ease his worries. All I could do was drop the subject and leave it for another day. Come morning, maybe we would be on the same page.

Moving into my room, I grabbed an extra pillow and threw it onto the couch to make him more comfortable. Then I shut my door and let my head hit the pillow, with only thoughts of Tripp running through my mind.

I checked in at the office the next day before driving to the stadium. There had been a lot of headway on the Inferno Soccer Camp kids campaign, and I was genuinely excited to work with the people I had been paired with.

Colton was gone when I woke up to get ready for work, but he had left a note saying he was sorry and would make sure I knew he had my back. The note reminded me of the one Hunter left on my door. I should have asked Colton for it so I could return it to Hunter if he dared to speak to me again.

So far, all he gave me was angry looks and bad vibes. On the other hand, Tripp gave me soft gazes and subtle winks. One by one, we took players off the field and asked them about the role they would want to play in the kid's camp so we had a good idea of who we could rely on.

Most of them were ready and willing to do anything we needed, especially Rhys Peyton, who I almost fangirled over because of who he was. The world's best soccer player, with a World Cup championship, and every year he was a most valuable player contender in Major League Soccer.

But somehow, I refrained from asking him for an autograph and kept the questions focused on what I needed.

"The team wants to run this camp differently than in years past, so we need to know how much time you can commit in January."

"As long as my girl doesn't mind me working, I'll be here every day."

"Would she be willing to volunteer as well?"

"Probably. With her season over, she will be jonesing to get back on the field."

"She plays soccer, right?" I'd done my homework, so I knew the answer. Having a female player in the camp would attract more girls, which would be a huge win.

"Yeah, for the University of Miami."

Again, I knew that, but it made me pause, a light bulb going off in my head. It was the first time it had dawned on me that Hunter and Rhys also had a connection.

Ash Keller. Rhys' girlfriend and Hunter's player for the women's team.

In fact, she was the girl he approached in the bar the one night he and I went out together. She and another player were drunk, and they called him Coach Crazy. I laughed and pulled him away, but he never spoke about it after that. He never told me that was Rhys Peyton's girlfriend.

So many pieces of the puzzle were falling into place right there during my interview with Rhys.

"You okay?" he asked, clearly seeing I had gotten lost in thought.

"Oh um," I started scrambling for something to say to lessen my embarrassment, but nothing came to me.

"Hey," Tripp came up, tapping Rhys on the shoulder. "About to scrimmage."

"Okay," Rhys smiled, nodding at me and forgetting how awkward I had just been. "Let's do this."

Tripp gave me a small wink as Cruz Martin walked up from behind me. Cruz looked between us, and his eyes widened. Cruz knew who I was somehow, and that small wink from Tripp was all it took for the dots to connect.

"I'm coming!" Cruz yelled toward the team. Then, before going to the goal, he stopped and stood beside me while putting his gloves on. "If he fucks with you, we will fuck him up."

He wasn't talking about Tripp; he was talking about Hunter. And if I had any doubt about that, it was made clear when he snubbed Hunter's attempt at a handshake. Looking back at me, he made sure I knew it was intentional, and my heart warmed a little. Tripp must have confided in Cruz, and he was acting the way I wished Colton had.

A scrimmage between the team and the new guys was essentially a complete game where the head coach separated them into what he felt was a competitive contest. That put Hunter, Tripp, and Cruz on the same team, with Rhys headlining the other team as the leading player.

Tripp and Hunter hadn't spoken the whole day, as far as I could tell, but once the game started, that changed as they played alongside each other. Hunter would call for a pass, and Tripp didn't hold back just because he hated Hunter. He was in the moment, and if Hunter was open, he passed it to him like the professional he was.

Tripp was heading up the field with the ball close to halftime, looking for someone to pass it to. Hunter had his arm up for the pass, but Tripp didn't appear to see him as he pushed the ball closer to the side of the field. The defender was on top of him, and he couldn't get a clean pass off, but he spun around and, without looking, kicked it with the back of his foot, trusting that Hunter was there and ready for his assist.

As if they had played together forever, Hunter had moved where he knew Tripp would pass it, taking the other team by surprise and kicking it into the goal. Both teams raised their arms at the incredible play, and the coach clapped. Hunter and Tripp, however, were eyeing each other quietly from across the field.

Rhys stopped cheering, seeming to be the only one who saw what I saw. There was pure hatred between the two players, who appeared to assist each other perfectly on the field.

"Half!" The referees there for the camp called the game for a break, and the players started making their way to the locker room for a few minutes of air conditioning. As Tripp neared the tunnel, he pulled his sweaty jersey off and tossed it over his shoulder.

My eyes couldn't help but linger, knowing how those abs

flexed when he pushed his body into mine. It was hot, and even though I had been in the shady area all day, I was practically melting in front of everyone.

"Tripp!" Rhys called, getting Tripp's attention before he could pass by me. Tripp turned around and returned to Rhys, who was standing near the field's sideline. Meanwhile, Hunter walked past me without even a glance, and I felt a twinge of relief that he didn't make that moment worse than I feared.

Both teams were off the field, but Rhys and Tripp stayed put. Rhys' hand was on Tripp's shoulder, and their heads leaned together as Rhys spoke quietly. Even though I didn't understand more than the basics of soccer, I would have loved to know what they were talking about.

But then they both turned toward me simultaneously, and my back stiffened with worry. Maybe they weren't talking about soccer after all. Rhys patted Tripp's shoulder and walked off, giving me a nod before he yelled back, "That isn't what I meant."

Then he was gone, leaving Tripp still standing there alone.

What just happened?

Tripp gave me a slight nod and then looked toward the end of the field where another tunnel existed. During the game, that was where t the field crew was, so I wondered why he was trying to get me to look that way. When he started walking toward the entrance, I casually started following him. Everyone else had already taken off for their own break, and no one was out there to see us. So, despite the risks, I took the chance and disappeared with Tripp, curious about what he had to say that was so important he couldn't wait.

Chapter Thirty-One

Tripp

"I've pieced it together," Rhys said in a low tone so no one could hear him.

"What?"

"You and Hunter are ex-teammates. Even if I hadn't known that, the way you two assist each other makes that obvious. The way you both are looking at the marketing girl tells me there is something there as well."

"So what?"

"You should have told me. Cruz obviously knew."

"I told Cruz before he went and chased Lily down. He was a pathetic mess and it didn't faze him."

"I'm the captain of the team. You should have told me," Rhys repeated.

"Tell you what? That Hunter and I are in some weird fucking love triangle? That we are both after the same girl?"

He ran a hand through his hair and looked around, realizing everyone had gone in for halftime of our scrimmage. Everyone except Tatum, who was sitting in her same seat watching Rhys with wide eyes.

"I don't know," Rhys finally sighed, "but I wouldn't have invited him."

"It's like you said, though. At least if he's here, we can keep an eye on him."

"It's the eye he has on you that has me confused."

"I'm sure he'd love nothing more than to take my place on this team."

Rhys patted my back and then started walking into the locker room. "That isn't what I meant," he yelled before disappearing into the tunnel.

With Tatum still looking at me, I nodded toward the grounds crew's corridor. I started walking ahead of her, hoping she would follow me. Not only did I want to check in with her, but I wanted to fucking touch her, kiss her.

It would make the second half of the scrimmage that much more bearable.

During the off-season, the grounds crew worked when we didn't, keeping the field clean and ready. That meant no one was in their space, making it the perfect hiding place.

Sweat was dripping down my body, and I took my shirt to my brow while I waited for Tatum to catch up. When she peeked around the corner of the tall wall and saw me standing there, I dropped my shirt to the ground and held my arms open for her.

Her smile made mine grow, and she quickly ran into my arms.

"Sorry, I'm sweaty." I kissed the top of her head as her cheek rested on my chest.

"I don't care."

"Not the first time we've been sweaty against each other."

She laughed and looked up at me, kissing my cheek, then my chin, and landing on my lips. It was just a peck, but I held her close, pushing my tongue against the seam of her lips and begging her to kiss me harder.

"What did Rhys say to you," she asked around my tongue.

"He knows I'm about to fuck you."

She got still, but I kept kissing her, leading her to the wall so I could press her against it.

"It's half time. We don't have time."

"If memory serves me correctly. It doesn't take long to make you come."

She moaned, giving in to me a little more and running her hands down my arms. When she got to my wrists, she lifted her hands again and grabbed my neck, holding me tighter to her mouth.

"Are you wearing any panties?"

"You told me not to."

Bending down to reach her thighs, I ran my hands under her skirt and lifted it to her waist, exposing her naked pussy. "Oh fuck, Coconut. You've been sitting over there with no panties on?"

"And watching you."

"You better be watching me," I teased. "I'm putting on a clinic out there, hoping you find my fancy footwork sexy."

"Everything you do is sexy."

I blushed a little, and for the first time since we had met, I could tell she saw the chink in my cocky armor. With everything we had woven between us, fighting to keep us apart, it was nice to hear the reassurance that we weren't defined by those issues. In the end, she and I were two people who met and wanted each other, just like I had told her before.

"It better be me," I snapped at her playfully.

"Are you insecure?" She teased me back the way I loved, grabbing my cock through my shorts. She always tossed the challenge I put between us back into my face, making me want her even more.

"I'm a little jealous," I admitted. "I've been making it my mission to make you forget him. But he's always around. Always a part of everything."

"He's not here now," she made a show of looking around at the empty corridor and maintenance equipment, then grabbed my chin. "And he's not the one I blindly followed behind a wall."

"Do you wish he was here?"

"Kinda," she shrugged, which almost felt like a slap in the face. How fucked up was I that I wanted her to actually slap me? Or that my biggest turn-on was bringing her ex into our intimacy? How perfect was she that she fed into that need without me having to explain myself or feel bad for it? "I wish he was watching what you do to me. How you make me feel. I wish he saw how easy it is to make me come when you know what you're doing."

Oh fuck. She wasn't just humoring me; she was better at it than I could ever be.

Pushing my shorts out of the way, I lifted her up and aligned myself to her core. Once I was inside her, I couldn't stop moving, being controlled by my need to possess her and claim her. For just a minute, I let myself envision Hunter walking around the corner of the wall and seeing us.

There wouldn't be a doubt in his mind that she belonged to me now. In fact, if he had a decent bone in his body, he would see how good I made her feel and back off. He would know he could never give her what I have been giving her, and he'd understand that any attempts at blackmail or revenge would be futile.

"I'm jealous," I admitted again, still thrusting into her as her moans got louder. "I hate he ever had you. I hate that he thinks he can take you away. And I hate that I'm still so unsure of how you feel about him."

She was chanting my name, her eyes wide open, her nose scrunching up from the pleasure she was trying to control. But it snapped right there as I watched her, and at the same time, her eyes glassed over, I felt her squeezing me as she came.

"Fuck," I whispered, then let go, loving that my cum would be running down her leg all day because she wasn't wearing anything to catch it.

Around the corner, I heard the guys coming back to the field, warming up for the other half of our scrimmage. Rhys knew where I was. I may not have told him, but he knew, and I hoped he distracted everyone from wondering.

Despite the heat, I felt a chill take over my body when I pulled away from Tatum. Her skirt fell back into place, and she straightened it while also rubbing her thighs together. I couldn't help the satisfied smirk I gave her, knowing she was trying to stop my cum from running past her skirt.

"Just to be clear," she said as she started walking toward me. "I know exactly who's fucking me when we are together. You're all I think about."

That was real. No stories, no games. I could feel it all over me as she stared into my eyes.

Taking her hand, I led her to a back door that the grounds crew used to access the back of the stadium. We walked hand in hand down the long hallway, stopping once we were next to the women's restroom.

"Clean up," I whispered, then pointed to another door. "That leads back to the main tunnel."

"Okay," she whispered. "I..."

She stopped and sighed, letting go of whatever she wanted to say. If I'd had time, I would have pressed her to say whatever she needed to say, but I knew the guys were probably waiting for me to get back to start playing again.

"I'm gonna surf after practice, but I'll call you when I get home."

She finally smiled and nodded, looking relaxed again. Kissing her cheek, I left through the door I had pointed out and crossed to the locker room.

Grabbing a fresh shirt, I went to the field and acted like nothing had happened. But Rhys was smirking, Cruz was laughing, and Hunter looked like he was ready to release that picture of me all over the internet.

But I didn't care. Fuck him.

Tatum was mine.

Chapter Thirty-Two

Tatum

When I returned to the field, I quickly grabbed my things and left for the office. There was no way I could sit there knowing my body was still pulsing from Tripp's idea of halftime. In fact, I didn't even dare look out to the field, just kept my head down and mumbled a few goodbyes.

Looking at the clock in my car, I saw that Colton should have been getting out of classes, so I called him, warning him I wouldn't be home again. He would want to come and keep an eye on me, but there was no point because I planned to pack some things to take with me and stay with Tripp all night.

We needed to spend an entire night in each other's arms. Maybe it would help ease those insecurities.

"Hey," Colton answered on the first ring.

"You still upset?"

"No," he snorted. "Are you?"

"Of course not."

"Look, I'm sorry about last night. I got there and the note, and everything else. Mom has been in my head, wanting me to make sure you don't throw your life away."

"She wants me to be with Hunter, but he's already out of my head, Colton." Unless Tripp made up stories about him. Stories that turned me on and teased me about him watching me. Getting jealous and wishing he could do what Tripp did.

My very own cuckold.

"I get it," he sighed, pouring proverbial ice water on my head, remembering who I was talking to and that I wasn't in my own porn fantasy with Tripp. "You know how she is though. So persistent that I'll do anything to get her off my back."

"You didn't tell her about the note, did you?"

"God no," he laughed. "She'd think that was romantic."

"Exactly."

"You want me to come stay over tonight?"

"No. I'm okay. Hunter didn't pay me any attention today. He's probably figuring out I'm okay without him."

"I'm only a phone call away. But I bet that Inferno midfielder is on stand-by as well."

My cheeks pinked, and I swooned a little, thinking of how Tripp would come to me in a heartbeat if he thought I needed him. It may have been silly to expect so much so soon, but Tripp was just itching for a reason to kick Hunter's ass. One call, one text, and he'd be at my front door.

After hanging up with Colton, I entered the office and headed to my desk. The pictures I had taken needed to be sorted into ones I could let Sophia see and ones I took for myself. The ones for myself were mostly Tripp and Hunter.

It was so obvious that they played together before. They fed off one another, and I couldn't help but think that if I hadn't been between them, they'd make a good duo on the pitch. The front three would be unstoppable with those two vibing and Rhys Peyton being Rhys Peyton.

The coach and whoever made the decisions probably thought the same thing. It had been since college that I'd seen

Hunter play, but clearly, he still had it. And with Tripp being his midfielder in League One, how did he not get signed?

"Hey, you're here," Tina smiled as she walked past my desk. It was the first time I'd seen her in the office since I stole her job, and I was worried her visit wasn't going to be full of pleasantries.

"Hey!" My voice was as high and perky as I could get it, hoping that if she was pissed at me, she'd have a harder time saying it to my happy face.

"Congrats on taking over the Inferno contract. They've been a tough one to land."

"Yeah." I shrugged. "No big deal. Just pushing my foot into the door."

"It had to have been more than that. I'd been trying for a month to squeeze them."

That was true. But I must have had a unique charm because even without them knowing about the pending Tripp Maddux scandal, they welcomed me right into the mix. They agreed to sign with IMG in no time and immediately put me on their kids' camp initiative.

"The luck of the draw," I mumbled, my head spinning with those tiny questions. How did I land the Inferno contract so quickly? "You must have primed them for me."

"Which is why I can't figure out why Sophia took me off the job."

"Look," I stood up, wanting to clear the air. "I'm sorry if I—"

"No," she smiled. "Sophia has her reasons and she's the head of this company for a reason. I trust her and don't need an explanation."

All I could do was nod and sit back down. Sophia had her reasons, but it wasn't a card I actually wanted to play. Even if it cost me my job, I didn't want to expose Tripp's negligence and indecency at the club that night.

With Tina walking away, I pulled my camera out and connected it to my computer. Images filled my screen, and I immediately got to work, putting some in the files for Sophia and some in a private file for me.

It took hours to sort through them all, and the office had cleared out by the time I looked up. The time in the corner of my screen said six p.m., and my tummy rumbling told me it was time for dinner.

Shutting everything down, I made my way back out to my car, yawning and dragging my feet. The heels I had on clicked across the pavement, echoing into the empty parking garage. I was never the last one out of the office, and the eerie feeling that washed over me made me start walking a little faster.

It wasn't quite dark, but it was dark enough inside the parking garage that anyone could have been hiding anywhere.

"Dammit," I scolded myself, letting the notes from Hunter get inside my head. He was crazier than he used to be but not crazy enough to hurt me. Was he?

Pulling out my keys, I unlocked my car and hurried in, locking the doors quickly. Breathing a sigh of relief, I cranked the engine and started to back out of the parking space. But an alarm in my car started blaring, and I looked to the dash to see what was wrong.

"Low tire?"

In my haste to get in my car, I didn't look at my tires, but the dash told me my right front tire had 3 PSI. That wouldn't get me anywhere.

Making sure no one was around, I climbed from my car and noticed that the right front tire was slashed. Not a nail or screw but an intentional slash that made driving anywhere a bigger risk than standing alone in that parking garage.

Without hesitating any further, I ran toward the stairs and down to the main floor, exiting onto the busy sidewalk. All the people around me made me feel safer, but it didn't last long. A feeling washed over me like I was being watched, and I knew Hunter was trying to creep me out.

"It's working!" I cried a little too loud, making everyone stop walking and look at me.

The crazy part was, had I not known it was Hunter, I'd have called him first for help. Together or not, he lived close by and would have been the first one to come and help me.

That wasn't what I wanted to do, though. Not anymore. It may have been presumptuous, but I knew Tripp would help me. In fact, I didn't want to wait. I wanted to run to him and tell him what was going on.

My phone was in my bag, which was in my car, so I couldn't call him without going back up there, and that wasn't happening. So I pulled the cash I kept in my bra and waved down a taxi. It had been so long since I took a cab anywhere that I wasn't even sure what the cost would be, but I'd deal with that when I got where I was going.

"South Beach," I told the driver quickly. "Nikki's."

Chapter Thirty-Three

Tripp

It had been months since Rhys and I surfed together. He wasn't quite as into it as I was, and with him being nine years older, he usually found better things to do. But when I told him in the locker room that I was heading to the waves, he practically begged me to let him tag along. Not that I let Rhys do anything; Rhys did what he wanted. Which was why when I waved him off, he came anyway.

He didn't have a membership to the Nikki's, but again, he was Rhys Peyton. He walked up, and they practically rolled out a red carpet for him. It kind of made me sick how they treated him like a king when I knew for a fact he could burp the alphabet.

"This is how I like to surf," he sighed with contentment.

We were laying on our boards past the break, looking into the dimming sky. The sun was behind us, setting in the west, making the water look dark and ominous.

"When are you going to tell me why you're here?"

"I can't like surfing?"

"You like being with Ash more."

"Can't argue with that. But she's studying, and I've kinda been a shitty captain this year. I wanna make up for it."

That was true. Before he met Ash, he was spiraling. Rhys had been acting like the opposite of the person he was known to be—fighting everyone and barely giving a shit about the team. With his life back together, he was taking more of an interest, and that meant he was seeing everything. Even the stuff I didn't want him to see.

"Sorry I invited Hunter."

"You have more issues with him than I do."

"Somehow I doubt that." So perceptive.

"I just got myself mixed up with him and his ex. Now she's someone I won't let go, and he's out for revenge."

"Well barring some crazy scandal, your job is safe." My wince was all it took for him to sit up and straddle his board. "Tell me now so I can stop whatever it is."

"I'm not your problem. Captain or not, my personal life isn't something you need to worry about." Because I'm not sure he'd understand that I got black-out drunk and let a stranger suck my dick.

"Okay then, do me a favor."

"What?"

"Keep an eye on his eyes. Pay attention to where he's focusing his attention."

Before I could tell him I was doing exactly that, I heard my name being called over the waves. Rhys was already sitting up and saw her first.

"What the...?"

Flipping on my board, I saw Tatum pushing herself past the break in the waves, fully clothed and waving her arms. The distance and the wind made it hard to hear her, but the closer she got to me, the better I could hear the strain in her voice.

"Tripp!"

"Fuck she's not a good swimmer." Paddling my board back in, with Rhys right behind me, I got to her just as the water started getting above her head.

"Tatum!" Jumping off the board, I knew I could reach the bottom, and I scooped her into my arms, her legs immediately wrapping around my waist. She started crying into my neck, and I looked at Rhys, who had grabbed my board and was watching us.

"I had to take a cab and I didn't have enough to pay so I—"

"Slow down."

Rhys started making his way out of the water as he yelled, "I got the cabbie."

Tatum was crying inconsolably, and instead of walking her to the shore, I got to the shallow water and knelt down.

"Tell me what's wrong!"

"I only had $20 on me because I keep it just in case but the cab was $30 and he's out there—"

"Rhys is taking care of the cab. It's okay. Why are you taking a cab?"

"My phone is in my car and I was too scared to go back."

"Scared?"

"He sliced my tires, Tripp." She took a few deep breaths, trying to get control of her emotions, and then pulled back to look into my eyes. "I ran from the parking garage and came straight here. I knew you'd be here, and I didn't know what else to do."

"You did good, baby. You came straight to me."

My words were trying to soothe her, but my body wanted to kill him. Hunter went too far. He was supposed to target me, not her. Not anymore.

Scooping her into my arms, I walked her onto the beach where most everyone else had left for the evening. Rhys came running back to us just as I set her on my board. Her arms wouldn't let me go, but I needed to look into her eyes and assure her she was okay.

"You're staying with me tonight. Tomorrow, I'm beating his ass."

"Fuck, I'll handle it," Rhys sighed, running his hands through his hair.

Standing up, I pushed his shoulders, making him stumble and look at me like I had lost my mind. "I'm handling him."

Expecting Rhys to argue with me, I readied myself to practice what I would do to Hunter on Rhys. But Rhys just nodded and squatted back down. "I'm so sorry," he told Tatum. "But Tripp has back up if he needs it."

Tatum nodded and sniffed, understanding what Rhys meant as well. When he stood back up, he squared his shoulders and shook his head with a snarl. "I knew that guy was a piece of shit."

He grabbed his board off the sand and looked up toward the few lingering people under the umbrellas, even though the sun had completely faded. Then he looked back to Tatum and to me, nodding before disappearing. It was apparent he was having to tell himself to stand down.

Hunter may have pissed him off in the past because of his girl, Ash. Cruz may have wanted to kill him because of his friend Erin. But they had to leave him for me. Hunter was mine to handle, and even though I wasn't sure what to do, I trusted they would have my back if I needed it. But would leave me to handle him in the meantime.

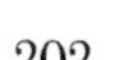

When Tatum and I got to my place, I ran her a bath and settled her into the warm bubbles. She wanted me to stay with her, but I had a few calls to make first.

"Just relax, I'll bring some water and snacks back with me, and we can spend all night in there if you want."

Her smile was hesitant, but she gave me a quick nod.

My body was still salty and sandy, but I washed my hands and put my phone to my ear while grabbing cut-up fruit from my fridge.

"Yo Tripp," my friend Aiden answered. "Everything okay with Shelly?"

Aiden had worked on my Bronco since she had been in Miami with me. When it came to cars, he was my guy, but it wasn't Shelly who needed his services.

"Shelly is purring like a kitten." Even though my Bronco was okay, saying those words felt like a lie. I was trying too hard to sound casual when I really just wanted to scream. "Can I get a favor?"

"Of course, what's going on?"

"My girl has a flat." I rambled off where Tatum's car was and what it looked like, asking if he could get to it as soon as possible.

"Tonight?"

"I'll pay you triple. She will sleep better tonight knowing her car is out of the lot. Then can you deliver it to my place? Drop the keys in my box?."

"All new tires? And delivery?"

"Yeah, man. Give it new shoes and bring it over. I'll feel better knowing she's safe again."

"Fuck," he sighed. "I'll have to explain this last minute job to my wife, but I'm sure she will find something to do with your incentive."

"Thanks man."

Hanging up with Aiden, I finished making the food, arranging the fruit on a paper plate. I hoped that Tatum was feeling better, but when I pushed the door open to the bathroom, I dropped the plate and bottles of water, rushing to her once again.

Chapter Thirty-Four

Tatum

My head was leaning back on the bathtub, and I tried to relax, but all I kept thinking about was how far we had come to get to that point. How deep Hunter had to fall to become who he was.

Eventually, I balled myself up and started crying again. Tripp came back and dropped everything he was carrying, jumping into the bath with me, fully clothed, and pulling me into his lap. I didn't want Hunter, but what Tripp had done was what I wished Hunter would have always done.

Put me first.

Anger and confusion with myself were consuming me, and I cried into Tripp's shoulders, scared that if he knew the truth, he would run away. Little nuggets of Hunter's words were trickling back into my head, filling the spaces that had been left vulnerable each time we spoke.

"Coconut, baby. You're safe."

It wasn't about not being safe. Maybe I was naive, but I knew in my heart that Hunter would never hurt me. Not physically. Taking his anger out on my car sucked, but it didn't make me fear for myself. It made me scared for him, even for Tripp.

What would they do to each other to get what they wanted? And why did I feel like I was in the middle of a game I wasn't even playing?

"Hey," he said again, lifting my chin and forcing me to look into his eyes. "You're safe."

"I know," I admitted. "But…"

Trying to turn my head, he stopped me and kissed my lips. He gave a small peck before pulling back and putting his forehead against mine. "But what?"

"Are you really going to hurt him?"

Tripp pulled back like I had slapped him, and tears came down my cheeks, knowing it wasn't what he wanted to hear from me. "He can't keep getting away with the threats."

"But what about the picture?"

"You're more important to me than what anyone thinks."

My tears were more aggressive, flowing rapidly, and my chest felt like it could cave in from the pain. "I still care, Tripp. I don't want either of you to ruin your lives. I'm scared for me, but I'm scared for you too… and him."

The way he licked his lips and flared his nostrils showed me he was slightly annoyed with my words, but he didn't push me away the way I expected him to.

"I know. You think I don't know? Dammit Coconut, I think he is a twisted dick, but he's still more likely to get down on one knee for you."

"You think I want that from him? After all this?"

"I'm just saying I know you haven't stopped caring about him."

"I wish I didn't, Tripp. I swear I wish I didn't."

"You ran to me. Not him. That's all that is important."

"I know you told me you're a risk, but you feel safe to me."

He didn't respond, just kept his eyes on me. Our lips were getting closer and closer; his breathing matched mine, and how his hand ran down my side and dipped below the water made me tremble. "Please don't hurt him. He needs soccer because he isn't getting me. He isn't getting anything else."

"I'll see what I can do," he whispered, swallowing hard before adding. "But only for you."

Now that I had told him what was hurting me so much, I closed our gap and pressed my lips to his. He held me tight, pushing his pelvis up slightly so I could feel how hard he was. Then he pulled away and stood up, making me slide into the water as he stepped out of the bath.

"What...?" I trailed off when I saw him start the shower. It was glass and right in front of the bathtub, so as he stepped in, I leaned back and watched him.

He took his shirt and shorts off and leaned forward, placing his hands on the glass in front of him and looking down at me. The water was spraying onto his back, and I could see his cock bouncing as he rolled his shoulders in the force of the water.

"Don't look at me like that," he demanded. "Let me get the salt and sand off my body and I will take you to bed."

Still, with streaks of tears drying on my face, I pushed my hand to my own core and started spreading my lower lips open for him. The bubbles had long since disappeared, and his eyes could see through the clear water as I tempted us both.

"I'm sorry for how I feel," I whimpered, meaning the words but also loving the pleasure of my own hand.

"Don't," he slapped the glass. "Don't be sorry."

He didn't say not to touch myself, so I slid one finger inside of me and pushed up, hoping my fingers were strong enough to hit my G-spot. Leaning up to get a better angle, I tried over and over, using two fingers and pumping in and out of my channel.

"You wish it was my dick, don't you?"

"I like you watching me try. Looking down on me and knowing damn well you could do better."

He lifted his face into the water and then brought it back down with drips falling from his eyelashes. "What do you want me to do?"

"Just watch."

He grabbed his cock and started to pump himself, using his free hand to clear the steam that had built up on the glass. "Fuck, you loved being watched."

Wiping away the rest of my tears, I knew we had officially moved on to what we did best together. Talking, laughing, and spending time together were special for us, but it felt like my body was using Tripp to compensate for lost time. All the nights I was left wanting, needing, and never feeling satisfied were in the past. Tripp was making sure I had enough memories to always take the edge off when I needed to.

"Promise me," I moaned.

"You know I'll do anything for you."

"Promise you will come on that glass, then take me to bed and make me scream."

"Fuck!" he yelled, moving his hips erratically with the rhythm of his hand and watching my fingers move back and forth on my clit. "Promise, baby. Fuck I promise."

With his words so hoarse and strained, and his fist holding his cock just right, I let myself go, coming on my hand and keeping my tits above the water so they peeked up for him as I shook.

"That's it, Coconut, I can see your cum mixing with the water. Look up at me, now!"

My eyes popped, and I watched his cum paint the glass between us, just like I asked. He grunted with each release, and his head fell back, his mouth slightly open.

It made me unable to stop. I was so immediately turned on again that I started rubbing myself harder and faster, chasing my next high before the feeling suddenly faded.

"Tripp!" I breathed in what sounded a little possessed to my own ears. He had finished coming and watching me as he took his finger through the mess he made on the glass.

"That's it, come for me again. Make my cock hard again."

With four feet and a thick pane of glass between us, I had one of the most erotic moments of my life. But my body was spent, my arm aching from the tense movements, and it felt like I needed to clean between my legs.

Tripp was soaping his body, then rinsed quickly. Then he brought a rag out of the shower and placed it between my legs. "You have no idea how perfect you are."

"You make me feel like I can do anything."

"Good," he smiled. "Because I want to make all your fantasies come true."

Exhaustion was taking over, but Tripp scooped me into his arms and dried me off. Then, just as he promised, he took me to his bed. Instead of the crazy sex we always seemed to have, he gently pushed himself inside me and made love to me in a way I had never experienced.

Slowly, he brought my body back to the edge and kissed my lips, neck, and chest. He pinned my arms above my head with one arm and used the other to caress every part of my skin he could reach. Despite feeling like I had never had time to get over Hunter, I found myself falling more and more for Tripp. Even knowing it was a mistake, I couldn't help myself, and I prayed that when it all ended, I would once again be strong enough not to wait and beg for Tripp to be someone he wasn't.

Chapter Thirty-Five

Tripp

Tatum slept soundly in my arms, but I stayed awake all night, thinking of what to do about Hunter. When I told Rhys I'd handle it, I seriously considered getting on the field with him the next day and making it impossible for him to ever kick a soccer ball again.

One kick to his ACL, and he wouldn't even be able to walk for a fucking year. Much less slice Tatum's tires open. But she confessed what I already knew. Somewhere inside of her, she still cared about him. It wasn't enough to make me worry about losing her, but it was enough to make me rethink hurting him.

I didn't know what I could offer Tatum when all was said and done, but I knew I wanted more time to figure that out. Risking her running from me wasn't an option.

By morning, I still had no idea what I should do, but I had run out of time to worry about it when we got called in for a random piss test. It was protocol to surprise us four times a year so that if we took any performance enhancers, we had no heads up on getting it out of our system. It caught us in the act, but I never had to worry about it because I never touched anything the league outlawed.

But then I had a thought. Were the guys invited to training camp getting tested as well? Would Hunter pass something like that? He was clearly not acting like he once did, and it had crossed my mind that he may have been using performance-enhancing drugs that altered his temperament while trying to pursue his career again.

In fact, I was willing to bet anything that was what was happening, and there was a chance if he got called in for a piss test, he wouldn't even show up. It made me happily ease out of bed and leave Tatum a note explaining where I went. Instead of confessing to her that Hunter may not show up or pass, I saved that conversation for later, when we were once again alone and safe in our little bubble.

Meanwhile, I got to the stadium and joined the guys already forming a line outside the training offices. While we waited, we were all handed bottles of water. We chatted about how much we hated the morning surprise piss tests just because they insisted on it being at the crack of dawn.

As I suspected, some of the guys from the invite squad were there, meaning they were also being asked to take the drug test. And Hunter was nowhere to be found.

"What happens if you guys don't show?" I asked one of the new guys, trying to sound casual.

"Automatic cut," he shrugged, then turned around for his turn.

Looking back down the line behind me, I saw Cruz looking like he wished he was still asleep, and Rhys nodded at me as if to say good morning but also that he was thinking about me. He knew I had some decisions to make when it came to Hunter. Even though he didn't know everything, he didn't have to understand how much I needed to be the one who handled him. But if Hunter helped me out and didn't show up, that would make confronting him off the field and away from my career that much easier.

My turn came, and I went into the office. They had to watch us take our piss, but I had done it so many times that it didn't even phase me anymore. It wasn't like I had to show them my dick, but they had to make sure I wasn't changing my piss out for someone else's. Then it crossed my mind that Hunter may think he could pull that shit too, so before I left, I told the trainer in charge to keep an eye out if he showed up.

Not that I expected him to.

Which made it a huge surprise when I left the office and saw him standing at the end of the line. His eyes narrowed at me, and he snarled a little before turning around and ignoring me. When I looked back, Rhys was still watching me and was waiting to see what I did, but I shook my head at him. Not here, not now.

Rhys nodded back, then turned around to talk to Luca. It would have been easy to grab Hunter by his hair and force him to the parking lot, but I refrained and stuck with my plan to see if he failed his piss test first.

After the morning surprise drug testing, almost everyone waited for practice to begin in the locker room. The invitees were in the visitor's locker room but still had access to ours, so again, I sat and waited to see Hunter walk in like the smug-ass bastard he was.

But he never came, and I smiled, thinking he was caught swapping his piss out for someone else's. The results usually took hours, so it was unlikely he had already been popped, but I told Cruz and Rhys my thoughts on his mood swings, and they both agreed it was likely what would happen.

"Then that's it?" Rhys asked.

"Is that where it would end for you?" Cruz added.

"No."

Cruz mumbled something in Spanish and leaned back against the side of his locker, crossing his legs and arms. At the same time, he watched everyone moving about the locker room. He didn't have to speak English for us to know what he meant.

"And here I thought he was just misunderstood," Rhys huffed.

"I mean, I did too. This all started because I gave him a chance. It got worse when he asked me for a favor. And now it's an all-out war. It's like he's going through the lineup and seeing who he could fuck over to get in with the team."

"I think it stops with you, though." Rhys stood up and stretched, then started walking toward the center of the locker room, where breakfast foods were spread out for us. "It's not us he wants, it's you."

Rhys was too far away to hear my response, but I turned to Cruz, who was still watching and listening. "He wants to be me, and that shit stops today."

"Tread carefully," he sighed. "But know we got your back."

"Holy shit!" Luca was breaking through the group of guys standing near the food tables and marching toward me, holding a piece of paper.

Sitting up straight, I tilted my head until he got closer, then grabbed the paper he was holding out for me to take. When I flipped it over, Cruz was over my shoulder looking as well, and I could feel his breath on my neck as he huffed out his disbelief.

There on the paper was another printed picture of me. In the corner of the club, my head was tilted, and I was holding onto someone's hair. Someone that looked like they were bobbing on my cock. It wasn't the same picture as before, but it was the same person, which made me feel a little bit better for some reason. At least if everyone was going to see me being promiscuous, it was with the same fucking person.

Rhys grabbed the paper from my hand and then looked down at me in shock. "The midfielder is searching for a scandal," he read the printed headline over the picture out loud. "What the fuck?"

"Dammit," I stood up, everyone turning their attention my way. My first instinct was to defend myself and tell them I could do whatever I wanted, but I knew they deserved the truth—that I didn't remember that shit at all and that Hunter took the damn pic.

"At least we know why he was late to the piss test," Cruz grunted. "Making sure while we were distracted he could get it pinned to the board."

"Fuck him!" I yelled, pushing through my team toward the hallway leading to the other locker room.

No one stopped me, and no one followed me. It was time to settle the score and confront him once and for all. But before I could barrel in there and tear Hunter apart with my fists, Coach called my name.

He was coming from the direction of the training offices, and the head trainer was walking with him. If the picture was pinned to the board in the locker room, I had hoped he hadn't seen it yet, but from the look on his face, I knew he had.

"Maddux," he grumbled when he got closer. "Head home. You're suspended from the team."

"Coach! I was set up, I can explain. I had no idea that—"

"Your piss says otherwise. Positive for any illegal drug is automatic suspension. Head home. We will contact you about protocol from here."

"What?" That couldn't be right because I never took a drug in my life. Not even when I was a kid.

"It was faint," the trainer explained. "Meaning it wasn't recent. But we can still see it, Tripp. So you need to head out."

What was happening?

The visitor's locker room door opened as I stood there stunned, but when I saw Hunter walk out, I leaped toward him. His face was full of anger as I grabbed his neck and pushed him against the wall. Pulling my arm back, I took a shot to his jaw, landing a hard punch as he tried to fight back.

Arms were wrapped around me, and I was dragged away from Hunter as I yelled. "Now leave her alone. Keep taking all you want from me, but leave her the fuck alone."

"Hey, hey, hey," Coach said in my ear as he pulled me back. Both locker rooms were emptied, and there was a crowd watching us. Hunter just looked toward me and spit, missing but sending a clear message.

"Get off me!" I yelled, tugging my arms out from the tight hold Coach had on me. If I tried to get to Hunter again, I wouldn't make it before being held, so I shoved past my team and into the locker room. Grabbing my keys, I raced for the exit and hopped into my old Bronco just as Tatum showed up for the day.

My phone immediately started ringing, and I answered because I knew it was her.

"Where are you going?"

"Put it this way, I just figured out why I can't remember anything about the night Hunter and I went out, and it just ruined my career. That motherfucker won before I even knew there was a fight."

Chapter Thirty-Six

Tatum

Waking up in Tripp's bed made me smile. He had left a note explaining his random drug test and that my car was in the parking garage. My keys were next to the note, and I gripped them, realizing he had the tire fixed and my car brought to me at some point in the night.

With a little extra time, I got home, changed for the workday, and then went to the stadium just in time to see Tripp speeding away. Thankfully, he answered my call, but he wasn't making any sense, so instead of going into the stadium, I followed him, tracking his every turn until he was in the parking garage of his apartment. The day was overcast, with rain on the horizon, but instead of going inside, he walked out toward the beach.

Taking my shoes off and leaving my phone in my car, I started walking toward the waves behind him in the sand. It had been less than twenty-four hours since my last trek across the sand, frantic and trying to get to him. My dress wasn't as tight as the day before, so it flew up in the wind as I ran.

"Tripp!" I yelled, knowing he could hear me, but he didn't

turn around. He did stop walking, though, and flexed his hands at his sides.

Slowing down, I walked the remaining ten feet between us and touched his back. It was still early in the day, and the wind without the sun was cool since it was late in the year.

"What happened?" I asked, then pressed my head to the middle of his back.

"He drugged me."

My head came up, and I rounded the front of him, looking up into his grim eyes. "What?"

"I failed my drug test and it all clicked into place. That night I agreed to help him with you, the night that picture was taken, the night I don't fucking remember...he drugged me."

Tripp wasn't looking at me, but he brought one of his hands to my head and pulled me into his embrace. He was so much bigger than me, and it made consoling him hard, especially on the uneven sand.

I held him the best I could for a while as he rested his chin on my head. But as the rain got closer and the lightning in the distance strengthened, I knew we needed to get inside.

"Take me home."

He snorted and shook his head, letting his hands drop from around me. "You need to get back to work. Maybe this is your chance to do damage control, get on your boss' good side for having dirt that needs your hand in managing."

"No."

"There's another picture as well. He pinned it to the fucking team announcement board and Luca found it. Different picture but same thing."

My gasp made him finally look down at me. His eyes were like fire, and I felt I could melt with that look if I stood still too long. Behind him, I could see lightning, and it snapped me into action, making me push his chest a little.

"I don't care what happened today, Tripp. Take me home. We can figure out how to deal with it after we both calm down."

It took him another few minutes, but then he turned around and walked toward his building. Following behind, I watched the tension in his body pulse with every movement. Just like he had done with me, I was going to make him forget. Make him feel. Then, after our heads were clear and our bodies were free from the tension, I was going to help him figure out what to do next.

Before we could get inside, the rain started, and Tripp stopped, letting it soak into his clothes, hair, and skin. My work clothes were officially ruined, but it felt therapeutic to let the mix of wind and rain seize my pulse.

When Tripp started walking again, I did as well, and we got into the elevator, thoroughly drenched and barely touching one another. We both knew that once we made contact, we were bound to go up in flames, so we kept our distance, even in the small lift.

The doors opened, and Tripp walked out first, leading the way and making me follow him. It felt like a test because he was usually more of a gentleman. But I was going to pass whatever he put me through. He needed me to show him I would be there.

"The fuck?"

Against his back, I didn't immediately see what made him yell. All I could see was a balled-up piece of trash on the floor that wouldn't warrant his reaction. But when I looked around his body, I gasped, realizing that a tiny bit of trash was the least of his worries.

"Before you start hitting me again," Hunter yelled. "Why don't you start by telling me what the fuck your problem is."

Tripp didn't bother telling Hunter shit, just pushed him

into the wall next to his door and wrapped his hand around his neck.

"Tripp! Wait!" I yelled, making eye contact with Hunter for a second. "Go inside first."

Using his free hand, he unlocked his door, pushed it open, and forced Hunter inside.

"What the fuck?" Hunter yelled as Tripp pushed him hard enough that he nearly fell to the ground.

"I just don't understand why," Tripp yelled. "Why did you—?"

"You ruined my life," Hunter yelled, getting in Tripp's face. "I'm the one that should be asking why."

"You ruined your own life!"

They were face to face, their labored breathing making it almost unbearable to talk. It was quiet for a minute while they stared one another down.

Their sizes were similar, and I had no doubt that if fists started flying, the whole apartment would be turned to rubble. It felt like I had to do something, but I didn't know what. I walked slowly toward them and put a hand on each of their shoulders, counting on neither of them risking hurting me if I was there.

Looking up at Hunter, I started recounting everything that had happened since I met Tripp. The calls, the notes, the anger, the tires, and even the manipulation. It made me want to move Tripp out of the way and punch Hunter myself.

But when he finally looked at me, I saw a glimmer in his eye that made me wonder how I ever loved him. It was the first time in a while I had been so close to him, paying enough attention to see everything I never saw before.

Small details.

"Tripp?" I moaned, touching his bicep and running my fingers down his skin. Then I pushed my body between them and faced Tripp, making him lose focus on Hunter and look down at me instead. His hard stare instantly softened, and my heart squeezed a little more, telling me everything that happened was always supposed to lead to Tripp.

"Coconut?" It was a question spoken so softly that I felt Hunter tense behind me.

"We came up here to calm down. Let's calm down. He isn't worth it."

"He…" Tripp never finished his thought, just turned his head as unspoken words passed between us. His breathing was heavier, and I knew he wanted to hurt Hunter with more than fists or words.

"Calm me down," I whispered.

Vague and scared, I hoped Tripp could see what I was asking in my eyes. That if ever there was a chance to hit Hunter where it really hurt, it was then and there.

When Tripp's eyes returned to Hunter, they steeled again, and his nose scrunched in distaste. It was clear that Tripp was still oblivious to what I saw so clearly now. How could I have ever missed it?

When I turned to face Hunter, Tripp wrapped a possessive arm around my waist. Hunter knew I saw him, and I could see the fear in his eyes as I opened my mouth to expose him.

"It's never been about me, has it?"

"Stop Tay," Hunter snapped.

"Did you ever love me at all?"

"You know I did!"

"But not since you came home, right? Things changed?"

"Tay," he warned again. I kept waiting for him to run, flee the apartment, and save himself, but he stood still, also knowing that he had to be there to defend himself.

"Was I always a pawn in this game?"

"Fucking hell," Hunter hissed as Tripp tensed up, creating a tighter hold on my waist.

Taking my hand to Hunter's cheek, I gently wrapped my fingers around his ear and then pressed my thumb to his ear lobe. It was small, but there was a faint hole where he had an earring before.

Bringing it to Tripp's attention made him gasp, and the pieces fell into place. "It was you."

Chapter Thirty-Seven

Tripp

"**M**e?" Hunter snapped. "What was me?"

Reaching over Tatum, I grabbed Hunter's shirt and pulled him as close to my face as possible. Tatum's hands went up to Hunter's chest to keep him from crushing her, but she didn't get upset. She knew I had just realized what I needed to see all along.

"You didn't take the picture," I snarled at him, "You were in the picture."

His face paled, and his mouth parted. "What?"

"Did I taste good? Did I scratch the back of your throat?"

I could practically see his heart beating from the vein in his neck as he swallowed.

"Honestly, baby," I continued to taunt him. "If you wanted to suck my cock, all you had to do was ask."

He started shaking his head, but I could see the truth in his eyes. The only thing I didn't know was why he did it. To ruin me? To set me up? Or because...?

"Wait—" he tried to defend himself before I interrupted him.

"You didn't count on me not giving a fuck, did you?" Laughing, I pushed him away from Tatum and me, making him fall back on my couch. "Coconut?"

"Yeah?" She never looked at me but kept her eyes on Hunter as I spoke into her ear from behind.

My body was thriving off the bitter hatred in the room. Somehow, I was turned on just knowing how miserable he must have been. "No one sucks my cock better than you do. Hunter wasn't good enough to even remember."

She turned around and glanced up into my eyes, looking possessive, like when she thought the server was watching us on the beach. It wasn't just me that was balancing all my emotions. She was checked out in a way I'd never seen before.

Taking a finger down her cheek, I quietly begged her to calm me down. To keep me from spiraling.

Placing a soft kiss on my finger, she nodded, giving me the strength to turn my attention back to Hunter.

"Why?" I asked him.

All he did was shake his head as he focused on Tatum, seeing her practically submit to me in a way that probably made him uncomfortable. She listened to everything he said, but her eyes stayed on me, letting me know she cared more about my reaction.

"Why set me up with Tatum? Why risk losing her?"

"She wasn't mine," he finally said. "I knew I had lost her before I sent you."

"Why?" I asked with more anger. "How?"

"You met her at the beach, and she was no longer the same."

"How did you know I met her at the beach?"

With a gasp, Tatum fell to her knees, unable to respond to Hunter or deal with her anger as she kept listening to us. All she could do was keep her back to him, soothingly running her hand up and down my legs. Hunter kept his eyes on her, tilting his head and running his own questions through his mind.

Through Hunter's shorts, I could see his cock hardening, watching her on her knees, and he shifted, trying to hide it, before wincing and turning his head.

"Look at me," I demanded. "Tell me the truth."

"The truth is," Hunter stood up, "I wish Tay would fucking look at me. Wish she wouldn't be on her knees like you are some God, and she's not allowed to even speak."

Tatum stood quickly, turned around, and slapped Hunter across the face. "All I have been trying to do is control myself. Following me, stalking me, blackmailing Tripp, slicing my tires..." She took a breath and then raised her arms in the air. "Do I need to go on?"

"What the fuck are you talking about?"

"Drugging Tripp, leaving letters on my door. You still want me to go on?"

"I never did that shit!" Hunter yelled, making me step forward and grab Tatum back in case he blew his shit on her. "I followed you to the beach and watched you meet Tripp, and I asked Tripp to hang out with you because I knew you two had met. I thought it would be a way to keep him close. But I never drugged anyone."

"Then how come I just failed a piss test and the only night I don't remember a fucking thing is the night you and I were out together?"

"Dude, I have no idea."

"Do you remember sucking my dick?"

"I remember trying," he sighed. "I remember everything. But I had no idea you didn't. At least not at first."

He was still hard as he grabbed himself through his shorts and groaned in frustration. Tatum was looking between us before she returned to me and buried her head into my chest. She was taking deep breaths, once again trying to calm herself down before her head popped back up, and she faced him again.

"Who took the picture?"

"What fucking picture?"

Tatum pulled her phone out and showed Hunter, who stepped back and sat back on the couch in panic. No one was that good of an actor, and in that one moment, I chose to believe him. He had no idea who took that picture, and he had no idea who was blackmailing me.

"I will admit I used Tay to try to get closer to you, and I will admit I told a few lies. But I never left any notes, and I sure as fuck didn't slice any tires."

"I loved you," Tatum finally said softly.

"You were never going to love me the way you love him," Hunter sighed in defeat.

We both stilled when he said that word because it was something we both avoided. Love wasn't the name of the game. It only made the outcome of what we had between us that much harder.

Hunter looked up at me and shrugged. "I only showed up today because I thought you two had me kicked off the camp squad. You weren't the only one with traces of something in your piss, but I immediately thought it was one of you."

"Why would I do that?"

"I just assumed that you finally figured it out. That I came back to Miami for you, not Tay."

My heart started racing as Tatum began crying. Pulling her into my arms, I soothed her, letting her know in small whispers that it was all okay.

"I'm sorry, Tay. I know using you to get to Tripp was wrong, leading you on, making you think I was someone I wasn't. That night at the club, I thought Tripp wanted me too." He moved his eyes to mine before he kept talking. "When we woke up and you asked if we had sex, my heart almost exploded, because I wasn't sure what to make of it. Or how you felt. All I knew was that you didn't remember."

"Fucking hell," I groaned.

"How did you know where I was, though?" She cried. "We checked my phone."

"It wasn't you I was tracking, it was Tripp. That night at the club, when he left his phone on the table to piss, I turned his location on and paired it with mine. Fuck, it went too far but I wanted to know where I could accidentally run into him again."

"The beach," I sighed. "When Tatum and I met, you were hoping I was alone."

"Yeah. And I was fucking livid that you were with Tay. It was like losing both of you in one chance meeting."

"You never had me," I bit out, fucking angry while almost feeling sorry for him.

"And I apparently never had you," Tatum told him. "There was nothing to lose."

"Exactly," he threw his hands in the air and ran them through his hair. "Nothing to lose. But I reacted and told a few lies. Then I had to let it go and called in a favor with Rhys Peyton, thinking I could at least try for my career. The job as the head coach at the university sure as fuck wasn't happening. I was losing everything."

"But you didn't stop!"

"I haven't done anything but react to your wrath since the night I slept on your couch. Nothing."

"By stalking us and telling me not to go into her apartment?"

"Excuse me?"

Pulling my phone out, I showed him the text he sent me in the app, and he turned white just like he did when he saw that picture.

"Fuck, I didn't send that. I swear. The only time I followed either of you was when I went to the beach, thinking Tripp would be alone. But whoever sent that is probably the same person that drugged us, and the same person leaving notes and slicing tires. I crossed a few lines, but I didn't do that shit."

Chapter Thirty-Eight

Tatum

I believed everything Hunter said for some reason, but that only left me wondering who else was involved.

"You called a million times. Both of us. You knew we were together," I fought back with him.

"I assumed, but wasn't sure. I had called Rhys and gotten into camp that day and you weren't answering your phone. I'll admit that the idea of you two being together that night made me sick, but I didn't do anything about it. Just called. I really did get worried about you."

"Made you sick? Because of me? Or because of him?"

Hunter picked a pillow up from the couch and threw it, his anger finally overflowing. "Him, Tay. I told you, after that night at the club, I thought maybe we stood a fucking chance. I didn't force myself on him; he let it happen. I knew he was drunk, but I had no idea we were drugged. I thought he would remember. And I'm sorry. I've said it before, and I will say it again. I'm fucking sorry for using you, and I will do anything to make it up to you."

Embarrassment was taking over my whole body. Red skin, shaky nerves, and a rapid heartbeat. I felt like a pathetic mess, hearing that my boyfriend never even wanted me. That he was using me.

Hunter got hard just watching me kneel in front of Tripp, but it wasn't because of me. It was because he wished it was him, kneeling for Tripp, ready to give him what he needed.

It may have been my own brand of twisted when it came to our fucked up situation, but I wanted to take my power back. "Seems you and I have a lot in common. We both have been on our knees for Tripp. We've both chosen him over each other."

"He chose you," Hunter tried placating me, seeing I was shaking with ire.

"He didn't just choose me. He's owned me. He's given me everything that you never could. You may not be responsible for all the twisted shit we've been facing, but you are guilty of wasting years of my life. Making me feel like I was the problem when it was you all along."

Before he could speak again, I turned back to face Tripp and shrugged. He could see the defeat in my eyes, the thrashing of my heart. Fuck, I was hurt.

Raising a hand for me, I placed mine in his, and he pulled me into his arms. "It's okay, baby. I'll make it better."

His lips skimmed my neck, and I moaned, tears threatening to fall.

Behind me, I could hear Hunter starting to move, clearly feeling like he was no longer welcome. But Tripp pulled away and held his hand up. "Stop."

"What now?" Hunter sighed.

Tripp didn't answer him. He looked down at me and caressed my cheek with his pointer finger. "Can he stay?"

My jaw dropped open as I realized what Tripp was getting at. My only response was a quick nod. With just the idea of Hunter staying, I could feel my strength seeping back into my pores.

"Stay," Tripp gritted out at Hunter. "Sit down."

"What the fuck?" Hunter asked, confused.

My chest was heaving with nerves. I couldn't believe what Tripp was suggesting or that I was immediately on board. Maybe I didn't think Hunter would actually stick around. But when I turned to face him, whatever he saw in my eyes made him submit, and he sat down in the chair by the window.

Tripp guided me to the couch, and we sat together, making it seem as though we were just there to have a friendly conversation.

"Did you know..." Tripp asked Hunter as he leaned back in a relaxed position. "My girl here used to have to close her eyes and picture someone watching you two fuck, just so she could get off?"

"You son of a—"

"Don't finish that sentence," Tripp warned. "Take your shirt off."

"What?"

Tripp started to pull the elastic down on his shorts, exposing his already hard cock for Hunter. He stroked himself a few times while Hunter's eyes kept track of Tripp's every move.

"Take your shirt off," Tripp said again, slower but with less patience.

Hunter looked up at me, and I nodded, letting him know we were serious. "Do it."

Just when I thought he would finally run, he surprised me and reached behind his neck, pulling his shirt over his head.

Hunter wasn't as big as Tripp, but he was an athlete with a body that used to make my mouth water. Even though I was on the edge of hating him, I could still acknowledge what his body did to me.

"You like that?" Tripp asked me, groaning a little as he continued to stroke himself.

"I'd like it more if he was doing to himself what you were doing."

Hunter's eyes widened again, but I could tell he was hard and too turned on not to see where we were going with our little game.

After thinking it through, he lowered the elastic on his shorts and started fisting himself. "Are you trying to make a fool of me?" he asked. "Because in case you forgot, I have nothing to lose."

"Not a fool," Tripp answered. "But you and I are giving Coconut her power back. Power that you took from her. All those times you two were fucking and she had to envision someone else watching her just to get off. You made her feel like something was wrong with her, when in reality, it was all you. So now she wants you to watch her, Hunter, and she's being nice letting you fuck yourself in return."

"Use me," Hunter gritted out as he continued to fuck his hand. "If this is what helps you forgive me, then I'll do whatever you want me to do."

"This isn't about forgiveness," I laughed.

"Then what's it about? Tripp at your mercy, me at his?"

"You don't get to touch either one of us, it's your job to watch."

"I don't have to touch either one of you to be at your mercy."

"You're gonna make me come," Tripp hissed. "Keep talking like that and I won't be able to stop myself."

Hunter's eyes were on Tripp, but Tripp's were on me. Feeling emboldened by the boundaries being set, I started to unbutton my blouse, which was still wet from the rain. Tripp took his hand off himself and helped me, sliding the silky fabric off my shoulders.

"Stand up," he whispered, then slid off the couch and onto his knees. When I did, he ran his hands up my tight skirt, looking into my eyes. "You remember when I bunched your skirt up and fucked you at the stadium?"

Biting my lip, I nodded, knowing he wasn't reminding me as much as he was telling Hunter.

"How about when we were in the cabana? The server was watching."

"Not the way I wished she had been. Not the way he's watching now." My head nodded toward Hunter, but I didn't look up at him. Tripp had me in a trance, and I couldn't look away from him if I tried.

Undoing my skirt, he let it slide down, and I stepped out of it, being left in my bra, panties, and heels. Hunter moaned a little from his chair, but he didn't move, and I didn't give his noise any attention.

That moment, between the three of us, was more than just being twisted and dirty; it was leaving no room for misinterpretation. My heart, body, and soul belonged to Tripp from the moment I met him. Hunter knew, but somehow, we left him thinking there was still a chance.

"Maybe," Tripp teased as he kissed the apex of my thighs, "Maybe Hunter was watching that day. He said he was working out at the university, but maybe he was watching us in the cabana."

Hunter grunted, wanting to deny what Tripp was saying but choosing to stay silent.

"Nah," I chuckled. "If he had seen us together that day, he would have already known he could never have you."

"I've been jealous," Tripp whispered, still on his knees. "Knowing he's had you before, had seen you before, felt you before."

"I am too," I admitted, finally giving Hunter a short glance, making sure he understood another layer of what was happening. "He had you first."

Sucking in a breath simultaneously, it was like Tripp and Hunter had just realized what I knew when I saw that picture. Even if I didn't know then that it was Hunter, I was jealous that someone wrapped their mouth around Tripp, and I had to see it. Now that I knew it was Hunter, it meant that he had Tripp before me. I was jealous of Hunter in a way that wouldn't even make sense if I spoke it out loud.

"Are you wet, baby? Do you need me?"

"I'm always wet for you, Tripp. Since the day I met you."

Reaching up, he snapped my bra off and then helped me step out of my heels. Lifting my right leg, he placed my foot on his shoulder, exposing me to Hunter as he ran a finger through my wet folds.

"My perfect girl," Tripp moaned, then pushed a finger inside me. Grabbing onto Tripp's hair was the only thing that helped me keep my balance, and I yanked, making him wince from the pain. "You want to hurt me?"

From the corner of my eye, I saw Hunter start moving more, resituating himself. His fist was moving up and down, his eyes on Tripp and me, and his hips were gradually jerking.

With Tripp pumping his fingers inside of me, he leaned to lick at my clit with a gentle taste. Just enough to make my eyes water but not enough to make me come. Jerking his hair again, I tried to tell him how frustrated I was, but he kept teasing me over and over.

"How many times do you want to come?" Tripp asked, making Hunter laugh with incredulity.

"Twice," I moaned.

"Four times," Tripp countered.

"Three!" I cried, knowing he would kill me with four.

Pressing his tongue harder to my clit and curling his fingers inside of me, I started shaking, an orgasm just about to make me fall. Tripp held onto my leg with his free hand, and once my body felt stable, I could no longer hold off the explosion as I screamed Tripp's name repeatedly.

My pelvis was practically grinding against his face as I moved his head by the hair, never wanting the feeling he was giving me to go away. Hunter's breathing started to get ragged from the side, making me snap my eyes back to him and shake my head.

"Don't come, Hunter. Don't you dare fucking come."

"What the fuck do you expect me to do?" He growled. "I need—"

"You get to come when she wants you to come," Tripp snapped as he rose to his feet. He scooped me into his arms and carried me around to the back of the couch, making me bend over it, facing Hunter.

Tripp took his hand to my ass and spanked me, making me squirm, and my pussy responded. Putting my arms down on the couch cushions, I held myself up as much as possible while Tripp took his shorts back down and lined himself up to me.

"If you think you're going to come," I told Hunter, "Then stop touching yourself."

Heeding my warning, he hissed and let go, then leaned forward, placing his elbows on his knees and interlocking his fingers together.

Tripp took his hand to my ass again, knowing I loved it when he made me red, and I moaned while Hunter realized how much I loved what Tripp was doing. When Tripp finally pushed inside me, I could no longer look at Hunter. All I could do was picture Tripp behind me, fucking me, his hips pistoning in and out of my body. He was so strong and perfect, but I knew he was weak when he was inside me, and the thought alone was enough to make me start coming again.

"So quick," Tripp growled. "You're squeezing me too tight."

His hand came back down, almost a punishment for coming

so quickly, and then he pulled out of me and turned me around. He started kissing my lips and rubbing my nipples, picking me up once again and wrapping my legs around his waist.

Instead of sitting down so I could ride him the way I loved doing, he put me back on my feet and spun me around. We were both looking toward Hunter as Tripp ran his hands up and down my body. Then he sat on the couch and pulled me back, positioning me so I straddled him while facing Hunter.

"Let him see your face," Tripp growled.

Lowering myself down onto his pierced cock, I let him hold my hips and keep control while I had my tits in my hands. In a way, I was still riding him, but in reverse, and the feeling was unlike anything I ever knew.

"This is the last time you come looking at another man. We no longer need that fantasy, Coconut."

The look of pain and regret was all over Hunter's face, but something inside made me want it to disappear. Maybe it was the love I knew I would always have for him. Or the fact that we had shared that moment that I knew I would never need again.

"Stroke yourself," I urged him again. "I want to watch you come."

Hunter leaned back, a frustrated snarl on his face, but did as he was told. His eyes were where Tripp and I were connected, his teeth biting his bottom lip.

"I bet you wish his cock were inside you," I taunted him, unable to help myself. "I bet he'd tear you open, make you hurt. But fuck, Hunt, it'd feel so good."

"Tay," Hunter warned, moving his hand faster.

"Enjoy it, Hunt. It's the last time you see Tripp come."

"This feels like a punishment."

"This is my fantasy," I reminded him. "Make it perfect."

"It may be your fantasy," Hunter snapped, "but you know damn well how much this hurts." His eyes rolled around in the back of his head. The closer he got to coming, the weaker his arm got, and he leaned back in the chair with his eyes closed.

"Tripp?"

"Yeah baby?" He wrapped his arms around me from behind the best he could, then pressed his fingers onto my clit.

"I'm..." I wasn't even sure what I was about to tell him. It certainly wasn't announcing that I was coming because I detonated without any preparation. "Oh my God..."

"That's it, Coconut. Ride it out. Soak it up."

Hunter's eyes were open, his hand had stopped moving, and he watched as I came on top of Tripp. That was three times, and Tripp was done letting Hunter watch. He lifted up, and I slid down his legs onto my knees. Turning around, he gripped my hair and jerked my head back as I opened my mouth.

"Did I come in your mouth?" Tripp asked Hunter as he pumped himself, touching the tip of his cock to my bottom lip. "Did you get a taste?"

"Fuck!" Hunter yelled as his hand urgently stroked. I could hear his grunts, familiar noises from when we were together. Peeking over, I saw ropes of cum spread over his chest and hand.

"Dammit, Coconut," Tripp hissed as his hips stilled. When I looked into his eyes, I realized he had never even seen Hunter; he had been watching me the whole time. I pursed my lips over his tip, making sure everything he gave me was on my tongue. Then I swallowed, and he jerked my hair one more time as he tapped his Prince Albert to my lips.

"So good."

As I stood up, I kissed Tripp and then made my way to Hunter, motioned for him to stand up, and did something I should have done long ago.

Chapter Thirty-Nine

Tripp

Completely naked and uneasy on her freshly fucked legs, Tatum approached Hunter, still covered in his own cum and looking a little dazed. Grabbing my shorts, I slid them on while I watched my girl.

I'm not sure what I thought she was going to do, but when Hunter stood in front of her and she swung her fist to his jaw, I was genuinely shocked. Hunter wasn't a small guy, and I was sure that punch hurt her more than it did him, but she didn't even wince.

Pulling her arm back, she started to punch him again, but I grabbed her arm, knowing her small hand couldn't handle two punches. At least not without me rubbing her knuckles and kissing her hand first.

"Okay, you're good. Do what you need to do."

She laughed, and Hunter watched us like we were lunatics, but then she reared back and punched him again, taking him off guard.

"Fuck, Tay!"

Leaning down, she picked up his shirt and threw it against

his chest, then stomped off toward my bedroom. "Go away, Hunter."

She slammed my door shut, leaving Hunter and me alone. Despite his mess, he pulled his shirt on and started marching toward the door without bothering to clean up.

"Hey," I hollered, making him stop and turn slowly around. "She deserved that. She deserved to feel like she had some power, because she's never done anything to deserve what you did to her."

"We can agree on that. I was out of my head," Hunter spoke solemnly. "I really thought you wanted me, Tripp. I had no idea you were drugged, no idea someone was taking pictures."

"Did I really agree to help you out that night? Did I come up with the grand plan to fill in for you on your date?"

"When I left here that next morning, I thanked you for agreeing to help me. But the only thing you agreed to do was bring me into the postseason camp. When I realized you didn't remember, and after you met Tatum, I changed my mind and tried using her to keep you close. I regret it, but I've stood by and watched everyone get what they want in their life but me. No soccer, no head coaching job, no love."

"Tatum loved you."

"Yeah," he winced. "But I knew, even before I left for League One, that I could never return that love the way she deserved."

I started to say, "Well I can." But I still wasn't sure if that was true. There was no doubt that she was mine, and I had no intention of letting her go, but how much of my heart could I risk when I was still so unsure of my future?

Hunter took my silence to mean the conversation was over, and he jerked my door open and left. I took a minute to collect myself, then made my way to my bedroom, needing to check on Tatum.

She was dressed in one of my t-shirts, lying on my bed, and curled into a ball. The curtains were pulled closed, so it was almost pitch black despite being midafternoon. Only the light from the doorway helped me see her, and once I closed it behind me, we were wrapped in blackness.

Carefully making my way to the bed, I climbed up and wrapped my body around hers. "Are you okay?"

"Is it bad that...that..."

"That you wanted him to watch us? Or that you liked it?"

"Both."

"No." Leaving it at that. Fuck, I would do it again if she wanted me to. I'd tie that bastard to a chair and make him swallow my dick if I thought it would make her happy.

"I hate what he did to you," she cried. "I hate him."

"He fucked up."

Turning around in my arms to face me, she reached up and ran her hand along my jaw. "How are you so calm?"

"Because I'm more worried about you than him, or me."

She sighed and leaned in closer to kiss me, gently touching her lips to mine. My heart started getting erratic again, body shaking as I tried to keep the same restraint she had. Just a kiss, just a connection.

"Who took the pic?" She whispered.

"I don't know. Could be a crazy fan."

"That happened before we met, but then I ended up with sliced tires and weird notes."

So they targeted me before I met Tatum and then brought her into it after we met. The only person who made sense or had anything to gain was Hunter, but from the look on his face when we told him, it didn't feel like it was him.

"I need to go back to work," Tatum said, then rolled to get out of bed. She walked into the living room and returned with all the clothes we had discarded earlier. Watching her get dressed, I started to worry about what else was in store. Because the fact of the matter was that it was easier to think our problems were with Hunter. Adding someone else to the mix and not knowing who or why made me want to hold her safely in my bed.

"What's your plan?" I asked, seeing the look on her face.

"First thing I'm doing is getting you back on the team, so that you can go to work. Then I'm going to talk to someone that may stand to gain from your scandal."

"Who?"

"My boss."

Everything in me wanted to pull Tatum back to bed, but I knew I couldn't tie her down. She had a job to do, whether it involved me or not, and I had to trust that she would take care of herself. Plus, I had my own things to deal with.

Picking up my phone, I called my mom first, hoping she was a voice of reason for me.

"Shouldn't you be at practice," she laughed, knowing my schedule as well as I did.

"Yeah." My voice was hesitant and made her stop laughing.

"What is it?"

Taking a deep breath, I told her everything, even about Hunter and me in the club. It made better sense why I didn't head to California for my break, but she was equally upset that I was in the middle of someone's corrupt agenda.

"And you're sure it's not Tatum?"

"Why would it be Tatum?"

"Look Tripp, I can tell you really like her, but she's the only other person that would gain anything. She could have followed Hunter to the club and spiked your drinks out of anger. Then once she saw the photo opportunity, she could have decided it was her best career opportunity as well. Create a conflict with you and Hunter, add herself into the mix when she realizes you're more into her. All I'm saying is, be careful baby. All of these problems started at the same time, and it wouldn't shock me if she and Hunter conspired together."

It was on the tip of my tongue to argue with her, but I would sound crazy because she had a point. The only thing was, she didn't know Tatum. She hadn't looked into her eyes and felt how much this affected her. She didn't know that Tatum had somehow gotten a position with the Inferno just so she could help me.

"You there?"

"Yeah," I spoke, my voice hoarse. "Mom, I gotta go."

Hanging up, I started pacing my room. Everything I just thought of was sinking in, and as much as it hurt to admit it, I realized my mom might have been right. Despite telling me it wasn't part of her job, Tatum seemed to find her way to the Inferno's realm. In fact, she made it happen quickly but never told me how.

Could she really be the one behind all this?

Chapter Forty

Tatum

Tripp didn't have to say anything for me to know how shitty the whole situation looked. He probably hadn't even considered me an option as someone who would be on the other end. I was good at what I did and had already analyzed how bad it looked. Even though I was innocent, I was the most likely person to be involved.

But I wasn't.

Meeting Tripp wasn't planned or part of any plan to assist Hunter with his twisted agenda. I had been just as shocked as Tripp when I saw that hole in Hunter's ear. We had spent so little time together, and with his hair longer than it used to be, I hadn't even noticed the small hole.

Until I did, and then everything clicked into place. Hunter had been struggling since he returned to Miami, and I thought it was me, soccer, or his job. But maybe he was always struggling with himself. With discovering who he really was.

More than trying to get to Tripp, I felt used much more personally. A way for Hunter to try denying his true self and be who he was before he ever left Miami. Something had always been off with us, though. Even when we were blissfully happy, Hunter's mind seemed to always be elsewhere.

Soccer. I had chalked it up to being nothing more than his love of the game.

If he had been honest with me from the beginning, though, I would have been a better friend to him. I wouldn't have had girlfriend expectations that he was never going to be able to meet. Instead of turning to me, he used me, hurt me, scared me.

Marching into work, I went straight to Sophia's office and slammed the door, making her jump and then stand up angrily.

"Excuse me?" She demanded.

"Is it you?" I didn't have any of the evidence with me, but if she was the one who had been terrorizing us, she would know what I was talking about.

"What?"

"This is a marketing and public relations firm, Sophia. You've been jonesing for dirt on the Inferno for a while. Did you create some? Did you use me as your little toy?"

"You better watch how you talk to me, and what you accuse me of," she yelled. "You will find yourself without a job."

"If you are the one responsible for the notes, the pictures and the tires, then I don't want to work here anyway!"

"Whoa," she held up both hands, clearly shocked by my accusations. "Sit down," she spoke softly. "Tell me what is happening."

Just like with Hunter, I believed her. Sitting down, I took a few deep breaths and then told her everything that I had been dealing with, including using that picture of Tripp to get close to the Inferno with no intention of distributing it. Sophia sat on the edge of her desk, listening quietly, with her eyes widening when I got to the most outrageous parts.

"Hey," she squatted down, her heels making it awkward and her pantsuit tightening on her thighs. "You should have told me this before. You should have trusted that I would have helped you."

"You are not above creating an issue, just so our firm can fix it."

She didn't deny my words but tilted her head and beaded her eyes. "Not at the expense of my employees."

"How was I supposed to know that? How am I supposed to believe that?"

"Fair enough," she stood up, walking behind her desk. "You didn't know that, but now you do. So what are we going to do about it?"

"I need to handle it. I'm going to arrange a meeting with the team for tomorrow morning and go over what I know. All I care about is getting Tripp back on that field."

"A picture is hard to deny."

"No one cares about that picture, Sophia. It's the drug test that got him kicked off the team, and now that we know he was drugged by someone, we should be able to explain the extenuating circumstances."

"Maybe you should start by calling the police and reporting the crime."

"It may come to that, but knowing Tripp, he wouldn't want that. I'm going to let any legal proceedings be his call."

"Then how are you going to prove he was drugged? Because if I was the team owner and coaches, I wouldn't believe the word of his girlfriend."

Girlfriend? Was I his girlfriend?

For the sake of keeping things simple, I guess I was, because there was no way I could deny how close we were. Especially since helping him meant telling the truth about everything.

"You have my full support," Sophia leaned up and started typing on her computer again. "Also, if you check the pictures you uploaded to the drive, it's clear that Hunter Ward was eyeing Tripp a little too hard. Those pictures may help you at least prove Hunter's role and give credit to Tripp's side of the story."

The pictures.

Yes.

Being so focused on looking for something menacing, I never stopped to look for something carnal.

"Thank you," I breathed, standing up, eager to get to my desk. "I'm sorry, I just..."

"Don't do it again," she bit at me, not even giving me a smile or accepting my apology.

Nodding, I excused myself and ran to my desk, spending the rest of the afternoon planning a meeting with the Inferno and getting copies of things I would need. Just after five, I looked up and realized I was once again the only one left in the building, and a shudder came over me.

Checking my phone, I thought I may have a missed call from Tripp or at least a text, but there was nothing other than a picture from Colton of him eating my food and a caption.

Thanks sis!

> You're welcome, you moocher.

You're never here to eat it. ;-)

> True, but I will be tonight. Make me something yummy.

Whoa. Are you coming home? Are things okay with lover boy?

> I don't know. But I want to run something by you. So stay there, I'm headed home.

You have stuff for spaghetti, so come hungry.

Smiling, I was glad he was there and waiting for me to get home. I needed to unload everything on him and see what he thought. See if he agreed that the craziness I was running through my head was actually possible. Because there was only one more person that I could think of who would do something like this. It was the one person so desperate for me to be someone I wasn't that they'd probably go to great lengths to make it happen.

"Yo!" Colton yelled when I opened the door to my apartment. It felt like it had been forever since I had been there because so much had happened since I was last home.

"Hey!" Setting my bag down, I walked toward my couch and fell face-first into the cushions. Colton laughed but kept stirring whatever he was tending to in the kitchen.

"Rough day?"

How did I tell my brother that my new boyfriend, who may not be my boyfriend, got kicked off the team because he was drugged, and my ex-boyfriend sucked his dick and someone took pictures? What was the proper way to tell your brother that instead of getting mad at the ex, you lost your mind and chose to make him watch you fuck your new boyfriend so he could fulfill your fantasy while also showing him he never stood a chance with Tripp? Colton would tell me I basically pissed on Tripp and claimed him, and probably wouldn't even talk to me once he realized how insane I had been.

No, maybe I should just stick to the basics.

"I think mom is fucking with me," I sighed as I turned over and looked into the kitchen at him.

"Mom? What the hell did she do this time?"

"I don't know," I groaned. "I mean, I know what she did, but it doesn't seem like something she could do alone. How are her and Dad right now?"

"Oh they are back together and more in love than ever." Colton rolled his eyes, then tapped the spoon on the side of the pan and set it down. Rounding the counter and coming to the couch, he motioned for me to sit up, and he sat beside me, crossing his hands in his lap. "Talk to me."

"Not real sure you want to hear about my love life, but…"

"If you tell me something gross, I swear I will tell you about the girl that jerked me off in the lecture hall while—"

"Stop!" I faked a gag and shook my head. "Deal. I will keep it clean, just never tell me that story."

He pulled my hand, and I fell into his hug as he settled back on my couch. "Tell me everything."

So I did… almost…

Chapter Forty-One

Tripp

"I knew something was off with him," Rhys told Ash as they sat in my living room later that night. He and Cruz had come by to check on me. Eventually, they invited Ash and Erin to chat and weigh in on Hunter—since he was technically still their assistant coach.

"But I didn't think it was the fact that he was gay," Ash added. "Who would care about that?"

"Maybe his parents? His team? Hell, I almost feel sorry for him," Erin sighed. "It's rough coming out for some people."

"He basically sexually assaulted Tripp, you Ding Dong, don't feel sorry for him." Cruz's accent while saying the word Ding Dong almost made me laugh.

"No," I waved Cruz off. "I'm not looking at it like that. Because whoever drugged my drink is the one that was responsible for the whole thing spiraling out of control. Not to excuse Hunter, but there's a chance, in his eyes, that he thought it was wanted, and reciprocated, at that moment. He was drunk as well."

"He had traces of drugs, but why can he remember and you can't?" Ash asked.

"Honestly, I think I drank more than he did," I admitted. "Once Cruz left I was kinda desperate for the company and ended up buying drinks."

"Dammit," Cruz yanked at his hair, angry at himself. "I shouldn't have left."

"Don't put it on you," I warned him. "I'm a grown man, I didn't need you to babysit me."

"Having each other's backs is what we do," Rhys reminded us. "You got Cruz home when he needed you."

"Exactly," Cruz stood up and started pacing. "No more leaving each other. Not for anything."

"I'll drink to that," I joked, raising my water. "Because I'm not sure there is anyone else I can trust."

"What about Tatum? Where is she?" Rhys asked.

Shrugging, I licked my lips and turned my head, hoping they let that subject drop for the moment. There were too many emotions, and it was all new to me. It was all I could do not to call her, trusting that she would do what she said she would do.

Before I was forced to answer, a knock sounded at my door, and I jumped up, hoping it was Tatum.

"I got it," Cruz stood up as well. "I asked Lily to grab us some food and head over after work."

Cruz let Lily in, and she smiled at me, handing Cruz the bags of food she was holding. After he had them all and headed to the kitchen, she walked toward me with her arms open for a hug. I started to shake my head at her and tell her I didn't want a hug, but she was so sweet and happy, and it felt good knowing that I really did have people who cared about me.

She tried wrapping her arms around me and twisting me side to side, but I was way too big, so it was more of a comic relief. Back when she first started staying with Cruz, he drank too much, and I had to carry him home. When I opened the door, Lily was standing there in the dark, scared out of her mind. I guess we bonded a little over our first meeting, and I was glad she had moved to Miami full-time.

"Are you done?" I teased her.

"Are you okay?"

"Of course," I snorted and waved her off. "Everything with me is fine."

Rhys started helping Cruz set my table, which had just enough seats for the six of us. We gathered around and let the drama for the day go as we talked about each of them and what they were up to.

Rhys and Ash were moving in together while Ash finished college. Erin was her best friend but had also become good friends with Cruz along the way. Cruz was helping her prepare for Women's League One, and hopefully, she would go pro in the National Women's Soccer League one day. Meanwhile, Cruz and Lily were no longer stepsiblings. Well, they were, but they would fight you to the death in denial. They were just happy that they were together and that there were no more secrets between them.

Then there was me.

Looking toward Erin, who sat next to me by default, I imagined Tatum joining the family we all had somehow formed. She'd fit right in, and from how good the food that Lily brought tasted, I knew she would be doing her happy dance after each bite.

Grabbing my phone from my pocket, I again considered calling her for a little bit. I knew I would end up asking her to come over, though. We'd end up having sex all night, and my head would never feel as clear as I needed it to be while I worked on everything.

"Did you hear me?" Rhys tapped my plate with his fork from across the table. "Luca is leaving the team."

"What?"

"Not sure what the story is there, but not long after you snatched that picture from him and stormed out, he got called into Coach's office. It's unknown whether he got cut or if it was something else."

"Holy shit!"

Luca was a good player; getting cut didn't seem likely. But what else could it be? Besides his wife being a gossip and him feeding her with information, I liked Luca. He may have loved dishing out news to his wife, but I'd like to think if I were married, I would tell her everything, too. Then again, I wasn't exactly attracted to how chatty his wife was. She was always causing trouble.

"I know what you're thinking," Rhys added, making me look back at him. "He wasn't involved."

"I wasn't thinking that. Now I am. What makes you so sure he wasn't on some crusade to make my life hell? Give his wife something to talk about? Maybe even replace his paycheck for mine?"

"Well when you put it like that..." Rhys laughed, never finishing his thought.

Erin took mercy on me and changed the subject again, but I was barely listening. There was laughter and noises in the background of my mind, but I wasn't sure who was doing what.

When we finished eating, everyone left except Erin, who offered to help me clean up. She and I hadn't spent much time together, but it was like having a sister when we were around each other. Erin had no issues telling my Alexa to play Cruel Summer by Taylor Swift while she danced around my kitchen, with no shoes, washing dishes by hand like I lived in Walnut Grove.

"The dishwasher does amazing things," I laughed, grabbing a clean dish and drying it alongside her.

"Oh," she shrugged. "My shift doesn't end for another hour, so we might as well do this the old fashioned way to kill time."

"Your shift?"

"We started another group chat but took you out, and added Cruz."

"Are you serious?" I laughed.

"We also took Cruz's mom out and replaced her with Lily. Let me tell you, Lily is taking this mission seriously, so when she shows up tomorrow, you better be nice."

"Why wouldn't I... wait... you really have me on a babysitting watch?"

"Don't act shocked, Maddux. We all care about you, just like we do Cruz. When he needed us, we were there. Now you need us, so we got this."

Backing out of the kitchen, I sat at the table and shook my head in disbelief as the song continued. The lyrics felt very on point because the summer had been way too cruel so far. But like she knew I would start wallowing in self-pity, Erin changed the song to Wake Me Up When September Ends by Green Day and started singing with purpose as she put everything away.

That was what I really wanted: to go to sleep and wake up when the story was over. But I couldn't deny how full my heart was. My teammates and friends cared about me. It amazed me how far they were willing to go for someone I considered a loner, a lost cause.

Me.

When Erin started to leave, she hugged me and pinched my cheeks, reminding me of my late grandma and how she would tell me how cute I was while smoke puffed out of her mouth. She would watch me when Mom had to work but would take me to the diner so everyone could see how red my cheeks were.

That was a good memory in the middle of my hard life in California before I found soccer. Losing my dad when I was young and being raised by a woman who worked her ass off and barely made enough to pay the bills always weighed on me. It was enough motivation to know that I still had to fight for my job, my career, my life.

There wasn't anything else I was qualified to do.

"See ya," Erin waved once more as she walked out the door, only to stop and pick something up. "This was on the floor in the hallway. Yours?"

"I think it's trash." I walked toward her and grabbed the paper that had been wadded in the corner of the landing from when I got home. When I saw Hunter and saw that ball of paper, I assumed it was something he had brought with him and then accidentally left behind.

Shutting the door and taking a deep breath, I started toward the trash can but stopped when I looked at the ball of paper again. If it was Hunter's, I was nosy enough to want to know what it said, so I opened it, expecting it to be a parking ticket or some other bullshit.

It wasn't that at all, though.

It was another picture. A better one.

Clearer than the first two.

No surprise, it was Hunter and me, him down on his knees in front of me in the corner of the dark club. Whoever took the picture had to get closer for that shot, and by making sure it was clear enough to see, I felt like it was telling me more than the four letters typed across the top.

MINE.

Chapter Forty-Two

Tatum

After I ate my spaghetti, Colton did the dishes while I worked on my computer for a little bit. My mother had been calling both of us, but after I told Colton my suspicions about her, he and I both decided not to answer.

Eventually, the phone stopped ringing, though, and we were left in peace and quiet.

"You staying over tonight?" I asked him, bringing a glass of wine to my lips.

"If you don't mind," he sighed as he sat back with me on the couch. "Kinda feeling a little big brother-ish."

"I'm older than you," I pointed out.

"I said big brother-ish. Because despite our age difference, I'm bigger."

"Touché," I smiled. "But I'll be okay. Head back to the dorms if you have early classes."

"I'm staying tonight." He spoke matter-of-factly and sliced his hand through the air.

Once again, my phone chimed, but I didn't look down. It was most likely my mother again, and until I knew how to approach her, I had to keep myself distant.

"You really think she sent those three pictures?" Colton asked as he got up, heading for a shower. "Seems weird, but I guess she is crazy."

I never answered; I just closed my eyes and tried to envision her figuring out a printer. When I heard the bathroom door click, my eyes shot open, and a light bulb went off inside my head.

"Three pictures?" I whispered to myself.

Picking up my phone to clear my mother's message, I paused when I saw it was from Tripp. It took him until almost nine in the evening, but he was finally reaching out, so I opened the message quickly.

Just got a third picture. It was wadded up outside my door.
Third?

"I never said there were three pictures," I mumbled again. "How would Colton know there were three if I only just found out?"

My entire body shook as I began to realize what was happening. It wasn't Hunter, or Sophia, or a random fan. It was Colton. Initially, he had urged me to stay with Hunter, just like my mom had. He never wanted me to see Tripp and made that very clear. Only once he backed off, I thought he was past the idea of Hunter and me together.

Then, another thought popped into my head. When Colton and I talked before, he said, *"I'm only a phone call away. But I bet that Inferno midfielder is on stand-by as well."* That was before I told him who I was seeing. It wasn't until a few hours ago that I confessed to him that I was seeing Tripp Maddux, and now that I thought about it even more, he didn't seem surprised either.

But why? What would he have to gain?
Send me the picture.
An incoming picture from Tripp came in just as I heard the

water turn off in the bathroom. It was taken on his counter, an image clear enough to see it was Hunter, with the words MINE typed across the top.

Who was his? Who was he talking about?

Before Colton made it out of the bathroom, I threw my shoes on and grabbed my bag. It wasn't that I was scared of Colton, but he had gone to great lengths to try and tear Tripp and me apart. Until I knew more, I had to leave so I didn't say anything I would regret.

After rounding the block a few times, I made some calls and headed to South Beach. It was getting late on a weeknight, and even though South Beach was the southern city that never slept, fewer people were out than on a typical party night.

In the dark, alone, I waited on the same bench I had been sitting on when I spoke with Hunter. The same day, Tripp saw us and thought we were getting back together.

"Tay?"

Hunter's voice was ten feet away, and I stood up to face him, realizing now that he was there, I wasn't sure if he was the right person to talk to.

"Tay, what's wrong?"

"Were you always gay? Are you bisexual? Did you ever love me?"

"Fuck," he ran a hand through his hair, looking down at his feet. When he looked back up, he glanced behind me, and his eyes widened, telling me I was no longer alone with him.

"Answer her," Tripp demanded from behind me, then slid his arm around my waist.

"I always knew," he spoke adamantly. "And no, I'm not bi."

"So what was I to you in college?"

"My friend," he shrugged. "Fuck Tay, I prayed every day that I could fall in love with you and give you what you deserved."

"What happened?" I asked, keeping my question vague and hoping he answered the questions I had yet to know I wanted to ask.

"I just thought I could have it all. And since you still loved me, I took advantage of that."

Tripp tensed beside me, but he held his restraint. There was a more significant reason that I had texted them both to meet me and now that Hunter was seeing how much I needed answers, it was time I got specific.

"How does Colton fit into all this?"

Hunter's face paled, and his hands started clenching and unclenching. His jaw was tight, and there was a second when I thought he would run. But he didn't. He got himself under control and finally sighed. "He and I had a thing."

"What?"

"He didn't want your parents knowing, so with me being your boyfriend, he and I were able to spend time together without anyone asking questions. But by the time I came home from League One, he still wasn't over it, and I had wanted to see where things would lead with Tripp. Colton never wanted you with Tripp because he knew there would be no reason for me to be around anymore."

"I think he's the one that sent the pictures," my voice was raspy.

"Colton wouldn't hurt you," Hunter bit at me in defense of my brother.

"He didn't hurt me," I scoffed. "But he tried to scare me into getting back with you."

The look on Hunter's face told me I was right, but Hunter was just now realizing the lengths Colton had gone to for him.

"You live close to my work. I bet Colton thought that when I realized my tire was flat that I would call you, run to you."

Tripp was cursing under his breath behind me, hearing this all for the first time as well. He didn't interject, but he was pissed, and I wasn't sure we could get past it all.

"He was pissed when I told him I was going to work out with the Inferno. He approached me at the school that day, the day I called and wanted you to come down and watch the work-out. He was there, and I knew if you came, he would leave, or have to tell you why he was there."

"You two were playing the same game," Tripp snapped at Hunter. "But for opposite teams. And Tatum was caught in the middle."

Not just of Hunter and Colton but of Hunter and Tripp. Tripp and Colton. Somehow, I ended up being everyone's fucking puppet while they all fought over who should be with whom. The only person who focused on me and my needs was Tripp. It was the reason I fell in love with him. The reason I could never walk away. The reason it hurt so much. Knowing that of all three of them, he was the only one I was scared to lose.

"I need to get out of here." Pulling away from Tripp, he started to follow me, but I held up a hand and stopped him. "I need to be alone. I need to think about myself. About what I want, who wants me, and what all of this cost me. Because right now, I feel alone and empty. Broken. You're a victim in all this, Tripp, but how could we ever get past this if all we were ever destined to be was casual? Not to mention the fact that my brother is involved. I can't take any more heartbreak, especially from you."

"I'm not—"

Waving at him, I turned and started running, not wanting to hear anything else for the night. Colton was still at my place, probably wondering where the hell I went, and I knew I needed to talk to him, but I couldn't. Not yet. So, it felt like I had nowhere to go.

Except I did. One place that I hated going to, but where the one person more fucked up than I was. We may not have seen eye to eye, and I may have thought she was capable of manipulating me to stay with Hunter. But when it came down to it, there was only one safe place for a girl that felt so fucked.

Home.

Chapter Forty-Three

Tripp

I let Tatum leave because she deserved to handle things however she needed to. She loved her brother, and I would end up saying something I would regret if I didn't give us both time to think things through.

"Do you love her?" Hunter asked like he had suddenly become her father and deserved an answer. It was none of his business, and I started to tell him that, but the truth felt better.

"Yeah, I think I do."

"Then can I give you some advice?"

"Fuck no," I laughed, turning around to walk away.

"Wait!"

Despite wanting to get as far away from him as I could, I turned back around to hear what he had to say. At the very least, it would give me something to laugh about with the guys later.

"I'm sorry."

He didn't have to keep saying it. As much as I hated him, I knew he was sorry for his role in everything. But using Tatum to get to me was about as low as it got, and I would never forgive him for treating her that way.

"Next time," I shrugged. "I'll make sure your hands are tied to the chair so you can't stroke your own dick."

Maybe I was hinting that one day, I'd let him watch me fuck Tatum again. Perhaps I was giving him one more slap to the face as I reminded him that she was mine. Or, I guess more importantly, that I was hers.

"If she wasn't the one you fell for, would we have stood a chance?"

"Are you asking if I'm gay?'

"I'm...yeah... or bi, since you clearly have feelings for Tatum."

"You seem to be extra nosy tonight."

"Well, I'm leaving Miami again tomorrow. The Inferno is not an option anymore. I quit the university today. So yeah, I'm being nosy because just like always, I have nothing to lose, and I'm not gonna be around to see how this all ends."

"Where are you headed?"

"As far from here as I can get."

That was fair because he probably had no clue. He was running, and I didn't blame him one bit. Even if he wasn't the villain we thought he was, he wouldn't be able to move past it.

"No," I answered his question. "We wouldn't have stood a chance." I didn't owe it to him to let him know my sexual preference. It wouldn't change my answer, anyway.

He nodded and slid his hands into his pockets. "Not sure why I thought there was something there."

"Because there was," I admitted. "In League One, we were a good duo. This past week at camp, we were volleying assists to one another like old times, and our connection showed. But it was only on the field."

"So what are you going to do? How is this going to end?"

"I don't know," I confessed, turning back around to walk

away. "But I know I'm not losing her." I added before getting too far away.

When Tatum texted me to meet her at Lummus Park, I didn't realize I would learn that her brother was the missing piece of the puzzle. It wasn't confirmed, but she suspected, and Hunter seemed to be able to verify that. It made everything more complicated because I wanted to kill Colton, and she would want to protect him.

What should I do?

Letting her go was my only option that night, but I meant what I said to Hunter, that I wasn't losing her. It just may take some time before we untie all the knots that were tangled up between us.

That night, I barely slept, which worked out well because my phone rang at seven with a call from the front offices of the Inferno. My agent had flown in from New York and was supposed to meet me there to discuss what had happened, but I didn't feel ready to discuss it.

Nonetheless, I hopped in Shelly and drove to the stadium, mentally preparing myself for a trade or release from contract. After the negativity that would come bearing down because of my actions, I expected nothing less.

"Sit," my agent, Max Higgins, motioned to an empty chair around a large table. "Let's talk this out before they get here."

I took the seat, but my mouth didn't move. If I had to tell the story twice in one day, I would lose it, so I just shook my head at Max. "I'll talk when they get here."

He wanted to argue; it was his job to know things and

protect me, but the doors opened again before he could lay into me for being irresponsible.

"Morning, Tripp," my coach mumbled alongside the owner of the team, Mr. Brent, and the lead medical doctor for the team. They all sat down around the table and dropped a folder into the middle, making Max reach out to grab it.

"What's this?" He asked, looking through everything.

"It seems as though the agency we hired for marketing the kids' camp had been doing a little homework on the side. Last night, we got this email from Ms. O'Neil."

Shit, she did it. Sent in everything that I wanted to hide. Those pictures would never go over well, and even though she probably assumed that it would explain things clearly, I was mortified that they had now seen me in such a compromising position.

"Look," I started to say, not even bothering to look at the file. "There was—"

"You were drugged?" My agent stood up, yelling at me for not having ever mentioned that to him in the first place. "Tripp! This is serious. Why didn't you tell me?"

"Mortification? Humiliation? Shame? Pretty sure they all mean the same thing here, and honestly—"

"Stop," Max cut me off again. Sliding the papers in front of me, he pointed at the drugs found on my piss test. "Look."

Glancing down, I saw the test and the pictures Tatum had taken of Hunter and me on the field. But the images of us in the club were nowhere to be found.

"Do you know who did this to you?" Coach asked, clearly concerned.

"Because we will be pressing charges," Mr. Brent added. "Without a statement from Ms. O'Neil, this could have cost not only our team, but you, and your well-being as well."

Glancing up, I looked into the eyes of everyone that was

there. Each one looked concerned for me, which was the opposite of what I had expected when they tossed that file down.

"I'm good. But only when I did the drug test did I know I had drugs in my system. It was weeks ago, and honestly, I thought I had drunk too much."

"Hunter Ward had the same drugs in his system, but at a much lower level. We called and asked him to come in for this meeting as well, but he declined. He did, however, agree to sign a statement that he was the one responsible for whatever happened that night."

What? Was Hunter taking the fall? For me, or for Colton?

Maybe for all of us since his obsession started the whole thing.

"Hunter didn't drug me," I was quick to defend.

"We know that much," Coach sighed. "But we need to know who did. Ms. O'Neil has documented every single thing in detail, except for whoever spiked your drinks and created this whole ordeal."

Shaking my head, I was already refusing to give them Colton's name. I hadn't even had a chance to speak to Tatum since she revealed her hunch, and since she didn't have his name in her report, I knew she wanted to protect him.

It wasn't a lie, either. Telling them I didn't know who did it was the truth. She protected my dignity by not adding the pictures to the file, and I was going to protect Colton for as long as possible.

"Well then," Mr. Brent sighed. "If you don't know who, then let's move on for now."

Shit, I was going to pay for my denial, and I had to think long and hard, as quickly as possible, before I let my career end. Not knowing what to do, I started to stand up and leave, but Max cut a glance at me and shook his head, silently telling me to stay put.

"I love her," I blurted, making them pause and look up at me.

"Who?" Coach asked.

When I didn't answer, he smirked and shook his head at the lunatic I had become. Mr. Brent cleared his throat and turned another file my way, pointing down at the fine print. Max grabbed it first and read over everything while I waited.

Then he closed the folder and put it in front of me as he looked back at Mr. Brent. "He'll do it."

Chapter Forty-Four

Tatum

My mom had so many flaws that she made the Ford Pinto look like a brilliant concept. And just like the Pinto, she burst into flames when no one even asked her to. She was complex and crazy, someone I didn't want to be and who I argued with most of my adult life.

But when I knocked on her door in tears at nearly midnight, and she opened the door and saw me, she pulled me into her arms, no questions asked. It made me regret even considering that she was behind everything. She'd never intentionally hurt or scare me.

I'd like to think Colton wouldn't either, but even without talking to him about it, I knew it was true. He had started calling my phone while I was talking to Hunter, and on the way to Mom's, I thought about calling him back, but I didn't.

Not yet.

"Your brother is worried about you. Should I tell him you're safe?"

Nodding, I let her text him instead, hoping that he would leave me alone for a bit.

While she did that, I grabbed my phone and forwarded the

file I had compiled to the Inferno's public relations lead. She would give it to the right people, and it spoke for itself, but there was no way I could face them and lie about who was responsible. Colton messed up, but he was still my little brother.

"Now tell me what's going on," my mom insisted. "Tell me everything."

Treading carefully, I told her as much as I could without telling her the secrets about Colton that he had the right to tell her when he was ready. In true fashion, Mom took the story as dramatically as possible but eventually apologized for pushing me so hard toward Hunter.

"I just don't want you to be lonely," she cried.

"I'm okay being lonely, Mom. Don't push your own fears on Colton and me."

She set the couch up for me to sleep on, and I finally succumbed to exhaustion. When I woke up, she and Dad were in the kitchen acting like they were the world's sweetest love birds, and it made my stomach turn. I was glad she was my mom last night, but by morning, she was his wife again, and now that I knew what real love looked like firsthand, my mom and dad kissing in the kitchen made me sick.

Assuming Colton had left my apartment for his classes and having already told Sophia I wasn't working, I decided to go home. It took everything in my power to not go straight to Tripp, but I hoped he was at work again, reinstated with his team, and being taken care of the way he should have been from the beginning.

When I opened my door, Colton was sitting on my couch with his head in his hands. It made me hesitate, but I had to remember that he was my brother, and I wasn't scared of him.

"Oh my God," he stood up when the door clicked shut. "Are you okay?"

"Are you?"

"No," he cried.

Tears were streaming down his face, and he started pacing in front of me. His body was shaking, and it looked as though his knees were ready to give out.

"Sit down," I demanded, realizing he knew I'd figured it out and we were about to talk about it.

"I'm sorry," he cried instead, falling to his knees in the middle of my living room.

"For what part?" I yelled, unable to hold back. "Fucking my boyfriend? Drugging Tripp Maddux? Slicing my tires and scaring the shit out of me?"

His tears got heavier, and his wails were louder. He grabbed his head and covered his eyes, curling into a ball on my floor.

"You're my brother," I cried in return. "I trust you with my life, to protect my heart, and to always have my back. But you've been behind everything, using me to get what you really wanted, even as I confided in you. You're no better than Mom. Actually, you're worse, because the only person Mom hurts for her own gain is herself."

"I'm so sorry," he cried again. His breathing had gotten intense, and I was afraid he would pass out, but I was too angry to care.

"You'd rather me be unhappy with Hunter, just so you could have access to him, than you would me be in a truly happy relationship. Now, I don't get either. Do you think Tripp will let this go? You think he will ever be able to look me in the eye and love me knowing my brother put him in a situation that completely fucked him up?"

"It was never supposed to be like that."

"So you admit it, huh?" He looked up as I sat down on the couch and buried my head into my own hands. "It was just a hunch, but you just admitted it."

"How do you know?"

"When you told me there were three pictures, and there were only two. While you were in the shower, Tripp texted me and said he found the third picture wadded up in his hallway, and it had been there for a while. That meant you knew there were three pictures before I did, and it didn't take me long to realize I had to get the hell out of here."

"I'd never hurt you," Colton explained, like I ran in fear from him.

"Not physically, but you've hurt me mentally. So hard that I'm not sure I will ever trust you again. We may never be the same after this."

"I was so scared that if Dad knew who I really was, he would leave for good. Every day of my life, I was scared that I would be the one thing Dad couldn't return to and it'd break Mom's heart forever. So I just never said anything, trying to be the person I said I was, while Hunter and I accidentally found something we had in common. He was struggling too, and when he came back to Miami, I thought maybe now that I was no longer living at home, he'd want to be open with me."

"But he didn't, did he?"

"He wanted Tripp Maddux. Then you wanted Tripp Maddux. It got so twisted I didn't even know what I was doing anymore, just trying to somehow bring Hunter back into my life, even if it meant he was with you, and not me."

"You need help, Colton."

"I know, and I will do anything to make this up to you."

"Just take care of yourself, and leave me alone."

He stood up, dejected and nodding, then grabbed the bag he always carried. Before he opened the door to leave, I approached him and put my hands on his shoulders to make him look at me.

"I love you. No matter who you love, I will always love you.

But this isn't about who you love, this is about who you are. You aren't the person I thought you were."

He nodded again, and I couldn't resist pulling him into a quick hug because I knew it might be the last one for a while. Then I let him go and walked toward my shower, shedding the clothes I had been wearing for far too long.

Once I was sure I was alone, I broke down and fell to my knees, letting the tears flow again. It felt like I would never be done crying, not just at what Colton had done, but the fact that I had most likely lost Tripp.

Chapter Forty-Five

Tripp

Not only was I reinstated, but I was offered a contract extension. The only condition was that I had to see a doctor twice a week until the drugs were entirely out of my system using hair folicles, and sign a report for the league explaining what happened to me. Per Tatum's marketing plan, it would serve as a teaching moment for the league to be careful and watch out for ourselves. We were targets, whether we knew it or not, and they made it my job to speak out so that others would not suffer the same fate.

No one ever knew about the pictures of Hunter and me, except those who saw them when it was posted to the bulletin board. Colton's name had been kept out of everything, and I ensured it stayed that way. He needed to pay for what he had done, but I couldn't bring myself to hurt Tatum any more than she had already been.

Especially when the outcome didn't bother me as much as it should have. In the end, I met her, and without all the drama, who's to say if I would have allowed myself to get close enough to her to fall in love. Maybe I was the one that was twisted, thinking of it that way, but I'd fall victim to anyone again if it meant I got to meet her.

The only thing she and I were terrible at was calling each other and connecting after the rough patches. I waited for her to call; she waited for me, and by the time we came back together, there was more trouble staring back at us.

Two days after I re-signed my contract, and with the head of IMG, Sophia Copeland, standing by my side, I announced in a press conference that I had been a victim of being drugged. It served as a warning and a movement, and IMG was heading up the initiative. More importantly, Tatum O'Neil was, but Sophia showed up in her place, letting us know Tatum was taking a few days off.

The buzz around the league was quick, and when I thought I would end up with a bunch of guys hating me for being weak, it turned out that there were more stories like mine. That being in the public eye made us targets, and even though my case was different because it was never really about me, there were a ton of guys who had gone through the stress of not remembering what happened to them the night they went out. Some were caught with the drugs in their systems, and some never even spoke up until I did, but I felt a little more validated, speaking out and knowing I wasn't alone.

My team was glad to see me back in the locker room and had secretly conducted their own investigation, learning that Luca had let a kid who claimed to be a super fan into the locker room that morning that he found the picture on the bulletin board. Luca was no longer around to confirm, but I was willing to bet that "kid" was Colton, so he could pin the picture to the board.

When things felt like they were starting to settle down, I pulled Sophia aside after one of our meetings. She was all business and exuded power and poise. You could tell she had been successful in her endeavors and never took shit from anyone.

But I needed her to let her guard down for a minute because I needed to know if Tatum was okay.

"Is she coming back at all?" I asked her, without even telling her who I was talking about.

"I honestly don't know," Sophia sighed. "I'm letting her work from home on some backend paperwork until she's ready to make a decision."

"Thank you," I nodded. "For giving her time to process everything."

"Oh," Sophia laughed, which came across as a little more annoyed. "She's doing grunt work. Trust me, this isn't a favor I'm providing, it's what she chose to do."

"Still..."

Sophia gave me a straight smile, then turned around and walked from the conference room. She wasn't the warm and fuzzy type, so I took her candor as a win.

Since there was no more camp or practices, I headed out to my Bronco, thinking of taking a drive around North Beach for a change of scenery. Climbing in, I cranked her up as something dangling from my rearview mirror caught my eye.

"What the—?" I mumbled, seeing the necklace made of driftwood beads and little S's carved into them. It was similar to the one I told Tatum about that my dad had around the mirror when I was young. She was the only one I had told, and I knew she had been the one to put it there.

Throwing my old Bronco into reverse, I left the field and drove straight to South Beach. North Beach was no longer an option. It was time to find my girl, to reassure her I was okay, and to make sure she was okay. Maybe I would never be able to look at her brother without disdain, but I knew I could spend forever looking at her with love.

If I was right, Tatum would be at Nikki's Beach Club. In fact, I didn't even try her apartment first. Grabbing the necklace from the mirror, I put it on and sprinted across the parking lot to head inside.

It was late in the afternoon but not quite dinner time, so the beach emptied out, but the dinner crowd had yet to make their way in. It was my favorite time of day to be at the beach, and it would make it easier to track Tatum down if she was there.

"Can I get you set up, Mr. Maddox?" The concierge asked as I sprinted by.

"No thanks," I yelled, knowing I wouldn't sit anywhere until I found her.

After looking around for a few minutes, I pulled out my phone and thought that I would break down and call her first. Maybe she wasn't even there, and thinking that our twisted tale turning into a fairy tale was stupid.

Then I glanced up toward the water and dropped my phone in the sand. She was there, strolling along the water's edge with her head down. She had on the same bathing suit cover that she'd worn the day we fucked in the cabana, and just the memory had my dick wanting to harden.

Moving my feet toward her, I remembered how she had run to me when her tires were sliced, scared and unsure where else to go or who to turn to. *Me,* I thought to myself, *always come to me.*

When I got near her, it was like she could sense that I was there because the waves made it too loud to hear my approach on the sand, yet she paused and turned around. My unbuttoned

Hawaiian shirt and bathing suit were what I usually wore, but her eyes went straight to the necklace I had around my neck.

"It was a peace offering," she mumbled without context. "I found it at the old thrift shop on 75th street, and it felt like it was meant to be yours."

"It's just like my dad's," I assured her.

"Whether you ever forgive me or not, I hope you keep it and think of him."

"I'm going to think of you. I'll always be thinking of you."

She gave me a weak smile, and even though she was wearing sunglasses, I could see how tired she looked. Colton and Hunter made a mess of her life, and it took me too long to find her. Now that I had, I wasn't leaving until she knew the entire truth about Tripp Maddux.

Right there, where we met when I first told her I wanted to fuck her and sincerely thought that would be all I ever wanted. Where I first heard her laugh and felt my heart twinge with the sound. Hunter didn't exist that day. She was celebrating being strong enough to let him go, but he wasn't an issue. We were just two people that met, connected, and were never the same again.

Taking her hand, she looked up, her tired expression only changing enough to show me how confused she was. "I'm glad I didn't meet you tomorrow."

Chapter Forty-Six

Tatum

I worked nonstop on menial paperwork from home for days following my confrontation with Colton. Sophia had been surprisingly understanding and told me to take all the time I needed. But after a few days of being cooped up inside, I decided to walk around the shops near my apartment.

That was where I found the necklace that reminded me of the one Tripp described. When I bought it, I walked home and hopped in my car, heading straight to the stadium. I knew Tripp was there because he was meeting with Sophia, and she was keeping me updated in case I decided to return to working with the Inferno.

All I really wanted to do was give it to him and let him know I was thinking about him. Then I headed to the Beach Cub to shake off the nerves that being in the Bronco had created. I didn't expect him to show up, but as I walked along the shore, I knew he was there.

He was wearing the necklace, and my hands started to shake with the need to touch him.

"Tomorrow?" I questioned, his statement confusing me.

"When I first met you, I told you I wished I'd met you tomorrow. That was so that you wouldn't have been celebrating your breakup, and I wouldn't have had anything holding me back from kissing you. But if I had met you any other day, maybe we wouldn't have had dinner together that night. Then when Hunter asked me to meet you at the restaurant, we would have been strangers. We wouldn't have already wanted each other on some level that we couldn't turn away from. So I'm glad I didn't meet you tomorrow, I'm glad I met you when I did, so everything that happened between us could happen the way it did."

"It was my brother," I reminded him. "He started this whole thing."

"He started it with me before we met. It was never your fault that you and I met when we did."

"But how can you look at me, knowing my brother hurt you?"

"What he did, and what I have with you, are not interconnected. They're separate. I'm not going to lose you because of something you couldn't control. I'm not going to hate him forever when you love him so much, either."

"I love him, but I can barely stand to think about him. I've been scared to call, scared you'd hate me because of him."

"When I saw this," he pointed to the necklace, "I knew it was time to find you. Time to let it go."

"I've seen your press conferences. Heard you got re-signed. I know you hate being the poster boy for scandals, but you're handling it well."

As he got closer to me, he shrugged and shook his head. "I don't hate it as much as I imagined, to be honest. I've heard from some guys who have gone through something similar. I'm just the current reminder."

"I'm proud of you."

"I'm proud of you, too. It was a genius idea to speak out."

The wind picked up as a late afternoon storm blew into the

area. It was only a matter of time before we were told we had to clear the beaches due to lightning, and I didn't want to move before things were okay between Tripp and me.

"Come home with me," Tripp moaned, closing in closer and grabbing my waist with his hand. "Don't let someone else's issues change what we have."

"But what we have is temporary, right?"

"No Coconut, it's not. Like I said, had I not met you when I did, maybe we would have been short term, but now I can't let you go. I'm staying in Miami, and I signed that contract knowing it would keep me closer to you."

Tripp touched his nose to mine, his arms encasing me. Even as the wind picked up, I could hear him breathing ragged gasps as he tried to take things slowly.

"I love you," he whispered over the wind. "I've been in love with you since you challenged me in the water the day we met. You didn't back down, called me out. Then over there in cabana number two," he smiled, "when you claimed my body with your own, thinking the server was encroaching."

"You were mean to lie to me about that," I whined playfully.

"You wanted her to know I was yours, and it did more than turn me on. It made me feel needed, taken."

"I do need you, Tripp. So bad. But I'm scared, and with all the hurdles we have—"

"Past tense," he interjected. "We had some hurdles, and that means everything else going forward is going to be a cake walk."

My laughter felt foreign because it had been so long since I had done it. "You make it sound so easy."

"It won't always be, but we will be together. And when we have those hard days, we know how to calm each other down."

Tilting my head up, I pressed my lips to his and nodded. There was no use arguing something I had no control over. Every part of me wanted him, and even though my heart was scared of being hurt again, I knew deep down that he wasn't the one who broke me, and he never would be.

"I love you," he muttered quietly against my forehead as he continued to place kisses on me. "I love you so much."

With those three little words finally sinking in, all the fears I had moments before were gone. Knowing he felt the way I did, that my love for him was reciprocated past our physical connection, and that he would have never said those words unless he meant them with all his heart.

"I love you, too."

"I was hoping you'd say that, because I need you to love me."

Scooping me into his arms, he spun me around and pressed his lips to mine again. Drops of rain started coming down on us, but we weren't moving. The waves had gotten more aggressive and crashed at our feet, soaking us and threatening to push us over in the sand.

"I got you," Tripp scooped me up into his arms. "I've always got you, baby."

"I wish I had met you tomorrow," I muttered in his ear as he carried me off the beach. He jerked back, looking at me like there was a punchline, so I giggled and finished my thought. "Because I'm having dinner with my mom tonight and if I had met you tomorrow, I wouldn't have to leave you right now."

"I'll wait up," he smiled, kissing me again.

"I'm glad we are making a point to do this more often," I told my mom as the waiter dropped our drinks off.

"Me too, dear," she smiled. "Your father sends his love."

She always spoke like a debutant, and I tried not to roll my eyes. If the last few weeks had taught me anything, though, it was people who coped and dealt with things in their own way. If acting like she had it all together helped her get through the days, then who was I to judge?

I'm sure if she knew I had Hunter watch Tripp fuck me just to be petty, then she would be trying not to roll her eyes as well. If she knew everything Colton had done to try to be with Hunter, she would probably need to be medicated. So, I was taking her quirks in stride and embracing them rather than avoiding her altogether.

"Hey," I said excitedly. "My boss was able to get two tickets to the football game so you can take Dad."

"Oh dear," she clapped. "That's wonderful. Thank you."

The rest of dinner was lovely, and by accepting her little quirks, I actually found her enjoyable to be around. I knew she kept waiting for me to tell her to drop my dad into the ocean or kick him out once and for all, but I didn't, and I never would again.

"Have you heard from your brother?" she asked as we pushed our plates away from us, stuffed full of the best Cuban food in Miami.

"Not in a few days," I admitted, still careful not to overshare. Just like my life was mine, and her life was hers, Colton's was his own, and his stories were his.

"He normally comes for dinner a few days a week and I haven't gotten anything more than a text."

"He's probably busy, Mom. A good looking college kid, living on campus," I laughed. "There will be times he's not worried about food."

"Well there will never be a time I'm not worried about him. He has a lot of secrets that he thinks we are blind to, and I keep waiting for him to talk to me. Every time he disappears for a few days, I worry that he's upset or hiding."

Holy shit. My adult self really didn't give my mom enough credit. She knew. She freaking knew, and she was smart enough to mention it to me with such subtlety that if I didn't know, I wouldn't be suspicious of anything.

She gave me a quick wink and leaned forward, changing the subject while we waited for our check. "Well, now that Hunter has left town again, are you going to continue seeing that new guy?"

"Even if Hunter stayed in town, I'd be seeing Tripp. He told me he loved me today and is waiting for me to come over after we finish here."

"What?" she nearly screamed, losing her poise. "What are you doing here? If a man tells you he loves you, that means—"

"I know, Mom," I laughed, even though I had no idea what she was going to say. "As soon as we leave, I'm going to—"

"Check please!"

Chapter Forty-Seven

Tripp

A small knock had my smile nearly reaching my ears. When I opened the door, Tatum was standing there shyly, clutching her bag to her side like I hadn't touched my cock piercing to the back of her throat before.

"Get in here," I pulled her arm, then tossed her bag onto the floor. "I've waited all night to kiss you, don't make me wait any longer."

She wrapped her arms around me, and I lifted her up so her legs could wrap around my waist. Our mouths molded to each other like there had never been any days between our kisses. Only that time, our hearts were involved, knowing that our kiss was between two people that loved one another. Somehow, it made it feel strong, more resolute.

"I love you," I mumbled, just wanting to tell her again.

"I love you so much," she cried back. "Please promise me you'll say that every day."

"You will get sick of me loving you so hard, Coconut."

"Yeah right," she laughed.

Falling onto the couch, we started ripping at each other's clothes. It had been a few days, and Hunter was in the room with us the last time we were together. I wanted to remind her that whether someone was watching her from the corner or not, I knew exactly how to worship her body. Never again would she have to think of anyone else but me when she wanted to come.

Although it was fucking hot. Whether it was because I wanted Hunter to see me fucking her, or it could have been anyone, being watched turned me on. I made a note to book a cabana at the Nikki's again, only I'd be sure the server really was watching.

"How come I feel like you're mentally creating a PR nightmare for me to handle?" she moaned as my lips ran down her neck.

Lifting my head, I smiled, loving how she knew where my thoughts were going. Maybe not exactly, but she knew.

"I'd never. No more scandals for Tripp Maddux."

"Somehow, I doubt that."

I bit her neck, making her squeal, and then finished shedding her clothes. Glancing quickly to the chair Hunter had been sitting in, I decided it needed us to save it, so I picked her up and sat down in the chair, her legs straddling me on each side.

"The first thing we need to do is give me a reason to not throw this chair off the balcony."

"You liked it," she teased. "You want to do it again."

"But maybe not here, and definitely not with Hunter."

Just talking about someone watching us was too much. My cock ached, the shaft settled between the folds of Tatum's wet pussy. She moved her slickness up and down on me, coating me with herself.

Marking me.

Then she lifted and lined me up, coming down hard on me and making herself scream.

"Easy baby," I assured her. "I'm not going anywhere."

As she began bouncing up and down on top of me, I

snatched her nipple into my mouth and sucked, soothing myself in a new and needed way. Any connection we had was dynamic, but being attached to her in every way possible was essential.

And with Tatum, I knew she would feed me with any twisted kink I had. Together, we would probably discover a lot more, never settling for images or stories of what could be.

Taking hold of her tits, she pushed them together, keeping her nipples closer to each other so I could taste them both. When her hands fell to my shoulders, though, I knew she was close and needed me to make sure her body didn't give out.

Holding her hips, I used her body to pump my cock, pushing inside of her as I pulled her down on top of me. Her screams were louder, and if I had thought about it, I would have opened the balcony door first so everyone around us could hear how much she loved fucking me.

"Louder," I hissed, even though I knew no one could hear her. "Scream my name."

She did, almost inaudibly, as she finally broke. Tears of pleasure streamed down her face, and I licked each one, savoring the salty taste. Then I pressed my forehead to her chest and let myself release, filling her body so full she would smell like me for days.

When we disconnected and cleaned up, we were ready for bed and settled into my cool sheets, wrapped in each other's arms. Her head was on my chest, and I methodically ran my fingers through her hair.

"You know," I sighed, thinking how crazy I was about to sound. "Hunter and Colton are no different than I am, really. Maybe it's sick and twisted, but I'd do way worse shit than they did to have you. If Colton cared that much about having Hunter in his life, then I understand him. If Hunter wanted me half as bad as I want you, then I get him. It wouldn't be my first choice to drug someone's drink, but if someone tries to take you away from me, Coconut, I can't promise I won't create the biggest PR nightmare you've ever seen."

"So to make my job easier, I need to make sure we are always together?" The humor in her voice made her statement sound like a joke, and we could pretend it was, but I had finally figured out that as long as we were together, everything would be easier.

"You're going to keep working with the Inferno, then?"

"Yeah, and Sophia is ready for me to get back too. Tina is already knee deep with a new rugby deal and Sophia is taking over the Formula One event. They need me to finish what I started and if I'm being honest, promoting a soccer camp for kids is what I need right now."

"Something easy?"

"Something positive. Wholesome. We're all so twisted that we can't see the good anymore. I need all the good moments I can get."

"I promise," I squeezed her, "from here on out, I will be the good for you. Rough days, shitty clientele, crazy brothers, whatever is making your day bad, I'll be the good."

"Want to help me with the project then? Be my assistant?"

"I'd love to assist. Just let me know what to do, boss."

"God, I love you so much," she looked into my eyes, then kissed me gently.

We made love again, only it was slow and gentle. Her fingers skimmed over my back, and I pushed between her legs, the sheet falling from my backside. My lips didn't stray from hers, choosing to taste her mouth and her moans as I built her up. Then when I was sure she was ready, I ground my pelvis down, rubbing her clit and making her shatter.

"I love you too, Coconut," I finally replied, my head against hers, breathing deep from the energy I had just exerted. "Always."

Epilogue

1 year later

Tatum

It was down to the last game of the season, and I was curled into a ball in the corner of the suite I was in with our friends and family. The previous season had been filled with so much drama for Rhys, Cruz, and Tripp that they considered that night's game their time for redemption.

If only they would score seventy-four points and be done. Instead, Atlanta FC kept it close, not allowing Rhys or Tripp into the goal all night. Thank God Cruz meant it when he said he would keep them scoreless.

"Honey?" My mom called from her seat. "Don't you want a better view?"

"No thanks," I mumbled, keeping my hands over my eyes just in case I accidentally saw something from the floor.

"Tripp is doing good. I think. It seems like it, anyway."

"He's kicking ass," Erin confirmed from her seat behind my mom, then turned to face me. "You're gonna miss his big moment."

"Fine," I snapped at her as she laughed and pulled me up

next to her.

She dragged me to the front row, where she had also lined up Ash and Lily. It was as if the guys had put her in charge of making sure we watched the whole game. She took her duties very seriously.

Ash, Lily, and I sat side by side, looking like the three monkey emojis on my phone. Ash covered her eyes, Lily covered her ears, and I covered my mouth. Surely, we all had a goal, but Ash was the only one that made sense because I couldn't watch.

"Rhys has it!" Marianna, Cruz's mom, shouted from the other side of the suite. Everyone behind us stood up, but we three girls stayed put. "He passed it to Tripp."

My eyes followed Tripp as he got down into the corner near the other team's goal. He faked left and then right before kicking it back to Rhys. The crowd roared when Rhys had the ball because they always knew he was the one most likely to score, but when he did a little twist and kicked it backward, Tripp was set up for the assist and kicked the ball past the Atlanta goalie.

We stood up, hugging each other and jumping around, screaming from the perfect twisted assist that Tripp and Rhys had worked on all year. Cruz was running in from the goal to celebrate with his team, but the game wasn't over, and after only a quick hug, he had to get back and defend for another few minutes.

Then the whistle blew, and it was official. The Miami Inferno were back in the playoffs and tabbed as the best team in the league. All their off-field struggles were long gone, and in their place were guys who learned to balance the game and their lives, finding a happy medium.

My mom came up to hug me, then held my face, looking at me with a proud expression. "You did it!"

"You mean Tripp did it?"

"I mean you did. Don't discount how much your marketing and PR work has done for this club."

"Mom," I blushed, loving her attention.

In the past year, she and I had grown closer. Instead of being focused on Tripp, she got inspired by my work with the kid's camp. Even volunteering and finding her own place with the team.

She said that passing out oranges to the kids was the highlight of her year, and I couldn't agree more. Seeing their faces and hard work made us feel like we had a bigger purpose in life. It was what we all needed from time to time, but no one more than my mom.

Dad was still around, but Mom wasn't begging him to stay. He just saw the same changes in her that I had and knew if he left, he may never get to come home. For me, I stayed out of their mess.

"Get over here!" Tripp's mom, Diane, joined us, also giving me a hug.

Tripp took me to California and introduced Diane and me after the kid's camp ended last year. She was exactly how I pictured her, being a waitress in a trucker's diner, with not too much fanfare. She and I became close, talking all the time in text messages. I had convinced her to get to Miami a few times already, but no trip was more important than that final game.

"Are you two still on for dinner?" I asked.

"Of course dear," my mom answered, looping her arm through Diane's. "We will meet you two there."

Ash and Lily had both been taken over the wall of our suite by Rhys and Cruz to celebrate, and I stood back, waiting for Tripp to finish his interviews. He was now the leading spokesman for the team, having spent so much time in the spotlight he was used to the pressure.

As he nodded to the interviewer as she asked a question, his eyes locked with mine, and he motioned for me to join him. Mom and Diane pushed my back, and I jumped over the railing, running as fast as I could toward Tripp.

Leaping into his arms, I cut whatever his words were to the interview off, and he spun me around laughing. The interviewer laughed and did her job, trying to let the viewers know that it was safe to assume Tripp's interview was over.

"I love you!"

"Love you more," he spun me again. When he set me down, he grabbed my neck and pulled my lips to his as the cameraman stayed close, panning around us.

"We are being watched," I teased him quietly against his lips.

"Mmm, your favorite," he laughed.

We stayed connected, not caring who watched as we kissed and celebrated together. But eventually, we had to leave, and Tripp scooped me into his arms and carried me straight to Shelly.

"Um," I laughed. "Aren't you going to shower? I thought we were having dinner with our moms?"

"We are. Can't I go dressed like this?"

"No," I laughed. "We are taking them to the Beach Cub. Not sure cleats are allowed."

"Grab my slides from the back for me," he laughed. "I can take the cleats off."

Rolling my eyes, I grabbed his slides. There was no use arguing with him because he was already pulling out of the parking lot and headed toward South Beach.

We listened to music and the wind blowing in as we drove. Our hands were locked, and he was kissing my knuckles every so often. When we passed our apartment, I thought he might pull in and shower, but he kept going, making me roll my eyes again.

A few months into our relationship, we decided that my apartment was useless. I stayed at his place every night, unable to separate my nights from him. Every so often, he would stay with me, but ultimately, we decided his place was bigger, right on the water, and safer from whatever craziness came our way.

Not that we anticipated any more twisted games. Hunter was back in League One, playing in Seattle. He was as far away from us as possible, and I truly hoped he was doing well. If there ever came a day he signed with a pro team, be it the Inferno or another team Miami had to play against, we would handle that when the time came.

As far as Colton, Tripp never mentioned him, but he paid attention when Mom gave me an update. Colton was still at The University of Miami and back on track to graduate next year. He had handwritten Tripp and me almost a hundred letters apologizing for everything he'd done, but Tripp always seemed uncomfortable reading them. He would wad them up and throw them away, never mentioning how he felt.

Until Tripp was ready, I wasn't speaking to Colton, but I made sure my mom and dad told him how much I loved him. Colton had confessed to them everything he did, and even though they were upset, I begged them to forgive him. Because I couldn't, not yet, and Colton needed someone to love him unconditionally. He was my brother, and I loved him, but I would never be able to move forward without Tripp being ready as well.

Tripp lowered the music as we pulled into Nikki's and looked at me, putting Shelly in park. He ran a hand over his necklace that hung permanently on the rearview mirror before whispering, "I love your shirt."

Looking down, I laughed at the "Tripp > Cheese Dip" shirt I had made with Ash and Lily, each doing one for Rhys and Cruz. "There was no better way to express my love for you."

"I believe it," he laughed. "But you don't have to choose. You can have me and cheese dip, baby."

Jumping from the Bronco with a laugh, he came around and pulled me out, holding me tight as we walked into the club.

I honestly expected the concierge to tell Tripp to change, that despite their laid-back beach vibes, they drew the line at sweaty soccer uniforms. But he didn't, just nodded and smiled as we walked in and out toward the back patio area.

"Did you reserve a cabana for after dinner?" I asked, hoping he did so we could be alone for a while. With Diane staying at our apartment, we weren't alone as much as I was used to.

"I didn't," he shrugged, then opened the door. "I reserved the whole fucking beach."

As I looked ahead, the first thing I saw were candles lit everywhere the eye could see. It must have taken hours to light them all, placed strategically on the walking paths, tables, and out into the sand. Then I realized there was no one else around, just us, and Tripp moved me forward as we navigated the candles toward the water.

When I turned around to face him in shock, I saw Diane and my mom with their arms looped and their heads pressed together with a smile. My dad was standing off to the side with his hands in his pockets and a smile on his face.

Behind him, I saw Colton, who looked unsure of himself and stood back farther than everyone else. He was there but wasn't sure he should be, which was fair since I had no idea what was happening.

"A little over a year ago," Tripp whispered, turning me to face him. "I saw you eating cheese dip and fell in love. The way your shoulders moved, and your body danced. Right here, in this spot."

Glancing around, I noticed the chairs had been moved, and we were standing exactly where I was sitting when we met.

When I looked back at Tripp, I realized what was happening, and tears started spilling from my eyes.

"I met you that day thinking I had it all figured out. That whatever it was about you that drew me in was nothing more than something I wanted to fulfill and move on from. Fuck I was such an idiot. Because from that moment, I would never get enough of you. I know we had some hard shit to get through, but honestly Coconut, I'd do all that hard shit over again to land here today."

"Oh my God," I whispered, bringing my hands to my mouth and making Tripp smirk.

Lowering himself to one knee, he pulled a ring from somewhere and looked up at me. "Will you marry me?"

"God, yes," I screamed, then launched into his arms. He fell back into the sand and held me tight as I kissed him. Even with our families watching, I couldn't stop, wanting to soak in the moment and his words.

"If you want someone to watch," Tripp whispered quietly, "please don't let it be my mom. Or your mom."

Busting out a laugh, I let him up just as our parents were crowding around us. Tripp slipped the ring onto my finger and lifted me for one more kiss.

When I looked back to where Colton was, he smiled and nodded before taking a few steps backward. I didn't make a move to stop him, but Tripp took a minute and nodded back at him before Colton turned and walked away.

"I asked him to come."

"You spoke to him?"

"Just in a text," Tripp shrugged. "I know we have a lot to work through, but I didn't want to start our forever without everyone we love being a part of it. It'll be okay, Coconut. Let him go. Let's celebrate tonight."

2 years later
Tripp

"Ash and Lily are both pregnant!"

"Calm down," I laughed, "you will be pregnant too one day."

"But I want to be pregnant with them," she pouted, jutting her lip out.

Leaning over, I took her lip between my teeth and pulled her toward me on the couch, making her straddle my lap. "Let me get you pregnant then."

"We've been trying!" Tatum threw her arms in the air, making me grab them and hold them at her sides.

"Let's try again," I moaned, pushing my cock up into her core, letting her feel me growing hard with just the idea.

"Maybe something is wrong with me."

"Nothing is wrong," I assured her, pressing my forehead to hers. "It's just not our turn."

"You guys did this to me!" She shook her arm loose from my hold and pointed at me, furrowing her brow. "You three all proposed to us on the same night. We all got married within the year, and now we all want babies."

"In my defense, we didn't exactly plan to propose on the same night. Great minds just think alike."

"I call bullshit," she pouted again. "You guys planned this."

Biting her lip again, I chuckled as I started unbuttoning her blouse. She had come in from work in a mood, threw herself down on the couch next to me, and crossed her arms.

We were in the playoffs again, and I had spent all day

studying my tablet to get ready, but now that she was home, I tossed it to the side, wanting to give her all my attention. No matter what games were ahead or what the outcomes were, I tried to make sure she knew she was always first.

As I opened her blouse and worked her bra off, I skimmed my lips over the top of her breasts, making her moan and push them toward me. Then she pulled back, hissing a little, as if I had taken fire to her skin.

"I'm so ready that it hurts," she moaned.

Taking her hard nipple into my mouth, I gently started sucking. She held my head to her, keeping me close, but almost as if she was ready to push me off if I hurt her.

"Why so sensitive?"

"Maybe I just want you so bad."

Latching back onto her, I moaned as my tongue swirled around, and she started grinding on top of me. I closed my eyes, enjoying having her in my arms and the peace I felt as my mouth was connected to her. Her fingers gently ran through my hair, and I moaned, ready to pick her up and take her to bed.

"I took that pregnancy test this morning," she sighed.

Taking my mouth off her, I tilted my head and looked up at her. "Did you buy one?"

"No, the one you put in my bag, remember?"

Snorting, I shook my head and squinted at her. "No?"

"Yes! You picked it up and waved it at me, then slid it into my bag."

"Baby that was an ovulation test, and you told me not to let you forget it."

She froze, her eyes focusing on something behind me as her brain rethought our entire morning. We had gotten ovulation tests, and I promised her that if she got a positive read, I would leave the field to fuck her and give her the baby she wanted so badly.

"Well that would explain why it was negative," she finally responded. "Shit, I feel so out of it. I can't even focus. It's like my brain is mush."

"You've been wanting a baby since the day we said I DO. Just relax and let it happen. Before you know it, we will have a little coconut on the way."

"What I really want is cheese dip," she sighed.

"Okay," I stood up, laughing. "Let's save baby making for later. You're still lost inside that head of yours. Let me feed you first, then I'll fuck you."

"No!" she laughed, wrapping her legs around me. "Fuck me first."

Backing her against the door to the balcony, I bunched her skirt up and slid her panties to the side. All I was wearing was my standard soccer shorts, so I pushed the elastic down to free my cock and slid inside her.

"Fuck you first," I moaned, pushing my hips hard into her with each word. Her tits were pressed against my chest, and her hands gripped my hair, pulling tightly as I moved.

"Tripp!" My name on her lips was somewhere between a scream and a warning. She came in from working with her body more ready for me than her head was. Like her body knew that I would calm her down and take all the worries away that seemed to be on her mind when she walked in.

"Let go of that stress, baby. Enjoy my cock being home, inside of you."

Her eyes squeezed shut, and her forehead fell to mine. "Tripp," she said again, only that time as a whisper.

"Do you need to picture someone in that chair? Someone watching us, someone so hard and desperate to come from how good you look riding me?"

She shook her head and opened her eyes as her pussy clenched and coated me. Even though it was no longer a need for her, I knew she still liked to think about people watching her being fucked. It was just a little kink of hers that I loved feeding into.

With her body becoming more pliable and spent, I pumped myself into her body a few more times and stilled as I released with my own pleasure. My grunts were loud, and just like almost every time I was with her, my heart beat out of my chest.

"There we go, baby," I whispered. "Take all of it. Take whatever your body needs to get what you want."

Her arms wrapped around my neck, and I sat back down, holding her as tears started to come down her cheeks. It wasn't unlike her to shed a few tears after an orgasm, but her body started shaking in what I could tell was an actual cry.

Pulling back, I brushed the tears from her face and kissed her cheeks. Letting her cry but also showing her I was there.

When she calmed down, she stood up, disconnected our bodies, and walked toward the shower. Before I followed her, I pulled my phone up and planned, tapping a few things on my screen as quickly as possible. Then I followed her and held her in a shower, cleaning her entire body and caressing her in my arms.

As we returned to the kitchen a little while later, there was a knock on the door. She answered and accepted the delivery, then smiled at me as she held up my gift.

"That," I pointed out, "is a pregnancy test."

"I can tell," she laughed. "But I took one, remember?"

"No Coconut. You took the ovulation test. Crazy girl. Go take that one."

She contemplated whether that was a good idea because it would stir emotions up all over again. But sensitive nipples, fuzzy brain, incredibly emotional...call it a hunch, but something told me we had already made the baby we so desperately wanted.

"Fine," she shook her head, walking toward the bathroom. I could tell she was readying herself for disappointment, and I prayed I wasn't wrong about my idea to have her take the test.

Waiting patiently in the living room, I stared at the floor and rested my elbows on my knees. She was taking a while, and I realized she was waiting for the result by herself before she came back out.

After what felt like an hour, she stood in the doorway to the bedroom with more tears running down her face. Leaping up, I instantly regretted suggesting she take the test. Especially when she was already so emotional.

"Fuck, I'm so sorry!" I wrapped her in my arms, then scooped her up and held her close.

"No, Tripp. It was positive," she cried again. "I'm crying because I'm a crazy pregnant woman."

"What?" I nearly dropped her and had to sit down on the floor where we stood to grasp what she was saying.

"We are having a baby!"

On our knees in front of one another, I let sink in what I kind of already knew. We were having a baby. A little coconut.

"I need to call my mom," I breathed, excited to start spreading the word.

"And I need to call Colton."

"Then call your mom and dad."

"Wait!" she laughed, "Let's tell our family first."

She meant our chosen family—Rhys, Ash, Cruz, and Lily. We had all become so close over the last couple of years that we were exactly that: family. We had Sunday dinners, shared family vacations, and now three babies were on the way to bond us in a way soccer never would.

"You scored!" I snorted, still in shock.

"Well I mean," she laughed and patted my cheek. "You did a good job with the assist."

Afterword

I always new Tripp and Tatum would have a wild side. I knew Tatum would have an ex and Tripp would want her more.

But when I wrote Hunter into Reckless Goals, I had no idea he would be Tatum's ex. His name was originally Will, and when I realized he would have a larger role in Twisted Assist, I renamed him to Hunter and the rest of his interference rooted itself.

As for Tripp and Tatum, I wanted to bring a different personality than Rhys or Cruz, while still giving you those book boyfriend moments. There were some things about Tripp I still don't know the answers to but I hope to revisit them one day and see how they're doing! You just never know with me!

A few fun tidbits:

-In Reckless Goals, the girl Hunter is with at Rosa Sky is Tatum.

-In Scoreless Nights, when Hunter shows up at the club that Cruz and Tripp are at, that is when Tripp's story began.

-All three books epilogues take place at the same game 1 year later. I pictured them all in that suite together, watching the game, each experiencing their own anxiety. Haha.

Acknowledgments

These acknowledgments always get me feeling extra weepy. It will never cease to amaze me how many people have my back and support me. This series was HARD to write through the summer, and with back to back to back releases, it sometimes felt overwhelming and I sincerely thought I may not be able to do it.

Along with these three books, I wrote So This is Love and Railbird at the same time... to say my mind was lost to these stories in an understatement.

So above everyone, I want to thank my kids. They have been the ones the most affected by the Miami Inferno FC. They've had to set aside their plans, spend less time with me, and do things on their own some days. They are the real QUEENS.

My husband, TJ, always always, always deserves the praise as well. He supports me in ways that he doesn't even realize. But no babe, I haven't hit it big enough for you to quit your job. Hahaha. Maybe one day.

To my friends that get me through those tough days, I love you all so much!!!!

To my cover designer KB Barrett. You've become such a good friend and someone I totally just to read my mind when it comes to these covers. We have more surprises ahead, don't we. ;-)

Brenda, my editor. Not sure I deserve you in my corner.

Michelle and Meg, my beta readers who keep it REAL. As

always, your honesty and feedback, along with your support is irreplaceable.

Kandace, again, I could not have done this without you. When it comes to keeping my content up, you take so much stress off my shoulders, you have no idea!

To my admins, Jenn, Elizabeth, Caitlin, and Ashley. Always more than admins, you ladies are some of my favorite people in this industry and my friends!! LOVE YOU!

My street team and ARC team: Thank you all for your trust in me! Every share and review means so much! Sincerely SO MUCH!

Also a special thank you to The Author Agency, Shauna and Becca, for so much more than just PR. Y'all have become friends, lifelines, and encouragement. Love y'all so much and cannot wait to work together again.

TO MY READERS! I aways save y'all for last because this is where I really get the most emotional. Every. Kind. Word. is soaked into my pores and gives me life. Every page flip, every purchase, every hype video, every review. You all are just amazing and make this rollercoaster of a career sooooo worth it. I LOVE Y'ALL SO MUCH!

About the Author

Katie Rae is a wife and mother, first and foremost. She and her husband, TJ, have been married twenty years and have two girls who she homeschools. They live in South Florida and enjoy boat days, sunshine, and family time.

Visit www.katieraebooks.com for signed paperbacks, merch, events, and extras.

Join Katie Rae Reader Group to chat all things books.

Also by Katie Rae

Miami Inferno FC Series (Interconnected Standalones)

Reckless Goals (soccer)

Scoreless Nights (soccer)

Twisted Assist (soccer)

The GAMES Series (Interconnected Standalones)

The Games We Play (baseball/football)

The Lies We Tell (baseball)

The Love We Make (baseball)

The Way We Dance (football)

The Way We Fight (football)

Men of the Military (Complete Standalones)

Ranger (Army)

Raptor (Air Force)

RECON (Marines)

Rogue (Navy)

The Boys of Summer Novella

Pretty Boy

Man of the Month Club Novella

Love Bites

Another One Bites the Dust

Silverbell Shores

Now and Then (brother's best friend)

Co-Write with Zoey Drake

Dirty Monsters (Check trigger warnings)

Christmas Freebie

Manny Christmas